A Home for Christmas

KATIE EAGAN SCHENCK

CHAMPAGNE BOOK GROUP

A Home for Christmas

Published by Champagne Book Group
2373 NE Evergreen Avenue, Albany OR 97321 U.S.A.

First Edition 2022

pISBN: 978-1-957228-74-7

Cover Art by Robyn Hart

www.champagnebooks.com

Version_1

In loving memory of my mother,
Kathy Eagan. I kept my promise.

Dear Reader:

I am very grateful that you have chosen my book out of the many options out there. I hope you enjoy it.

The holiday season is often a time filled with joy, but it can also cause feelings of loneliness. I hope Shelly's story of reopening her heart resonates with you, and Brad's journey of discovering the true meaning of "home" brings you comfort. This book serves as a reminder that love can come from the most unexpected places if we are open to receiving it.

I invite you to grab a warm beverage, snuggle up under a cozy blanket, and allow yourself to be transported to the sweet, small town of Eagle Harbor.

Katie

Chapter One

The terminal shops glittered with colored lights, their reflection dancing and dazzling off dainty orbs hanging from the crisp evergreens displayed in the center of the walkway. Windows and doors were likewise covered with festive stickers and wreaths, encroaching on the various sale signs that served as brash reminders of how many shopping days remained.

Shelly Evans maneuvered through the crowded airport, ready for the last leg of her journey, which would take her home. She adjusted her uniform blazer as she walked, paying little heed to the glitz and glamour of the fast-approaching holiday. The last thing she wanted to worry about was *gifts*. Her purse had been feeling lighter and lighter over the last few months, and if she didn't find a new tenant soon… well, she didn't want to think about it. Instead, she focused on the mental checklist that always occupied her before each flight. It helped to keep her centered and focused when she was upset or worried.

First, she'd sign into the computer. ID badge? Check. Then she'd make the boarding announcement. She cleared her throat. No hoarseness. Good. Check. Third, she'd… no. This wasn't working. Even now, Shelly's thoughts were veering elsewhere—particularly toward her daughter, Lilly, who she was at odds with more often these days.

Shelly struggled to remember what had caused the argument this time. The usual suspects of grades, boys, and technology were potential culprits, but none of those explained Lilly's change in attitude. Normally a reserved teen, she had been extra snappy, which was out of character for her. Shelly couldn't put her finger on what had changed, but she knew the problem would not be resolved easily. It never was.

She sighed as she reached the check-in desk, where she was expected to assist the gate agents because of the anticipated increase in travel. Her best friend, Kylie, was already there with two harried gate agents, answering customer questions and checking seat availability for last-minute changes. The murmuring sea of weary passengers crowding the seating area confirmed the holiday travel season was in full swing, and a packed flight seemed inevitable.

Pushing thoughts of Lilly from her mind, Shelly adopted the cheerful demeanor she had developed over the years as a flight attendant. She pasted a broad smile on her face, pulled her shoulders back, and worked to relieve the tension in her hands. It was not her dream job, by any means, but it helped pay the bills and gave her a chance to travel, even if her enjoyment of her destinations was limited to hotels and restaurants within a few miles of the airport.

As she signed into the computer, she noticed a man standing near the counter with a bookbag slung casually over one shoulder. He gave off a calm and disciplined disposition, which was unusual for any passenger, but particularly rare this time of year.

Despite what Shelly assumed had been a long wait, he wasn't staring at a smartphone or reading a book to while away the time. Instead, he stood almost at attention, with squared shoulders and a wide stance, looking straight ahead. In contrast, most of the customers were frazzled holiday travelers who often took their aggravation at any delays, perceived or actual, out on the gate agents, or Shelly and her fellow flight attendants.

Beyond his unusually peaceful persona, there was something familiar in the man's appearance and posture. He was tall and broad-shouldered with short black hair and neatly pressed attire. She was about to ask him if she could assist him with something when Kylie tapped her on the shoulder.

"Wow, Shelly, cutting it a little close, aren't you?" Kylie placed her hands on her hips. "It's go time." Waving a hand at the microphone, she reached up to fix her disheveled brown hair back into a bun. Taking in Kylie's appearance, Shelly smoothed her own auburn hair, confirming her French twist was still intact.

"Connecting flight delays," Shelly said. "The sooner we can get everyone on the plane, the sooner I can get home to Lilly."

Kylie's brows furrowed. "Everything okay with you two?

Shelly gave what she hoped was a nonchalant shrug. "Yeah, we're fine. Have to be." She turned away from Kylie to hide her face as she made the boarding announcement.

"Attention passengers of Flight 539, traveling directly from Atlanta to Baltimore; we are ready to begin boarding. Anyone needing additional assistance may approach the check-in counter now. First and business class passengers may line up behind the white line. Thank you."

Immediately, the once murmuring sea of people changed into a hurricane of activity as passengers collected their things. A few families with young children and an elderly couple approached the counter for priority boarding.

Shelly immersed herself in her duties, going through the motions until everyone had passed through the gate. She and Kylie logged out of the computers and closed off the jetway ramp before heading to the plane.

"Welcome aboard, Shelly!" Eric, the pilot, called out.

He winked at her, and she forced a small smile she hoped didn't resemble a grimace. His open and friendly behavior had taken on a different tone as of late. There was no denying he was a handsome man, tall and lanky, with blond hair and blue eyes. However, he had a reputation for being a womanizer, particularly with the other flight attendants, and that was the last thing she needed. She boarded the plane and put as much distance between them as she could muster.

Shelly followed Kylie to the back where they would begin getting the galley carts ready. Two other flight attendants were handling the safety lecture, and she wanted to stock up the carts before they got underway. She passed the same man she had seen by the counter earlier. Their eyes met, and an unexpected jolt of recognition ran through her, though she was certain she had never seen him before.

As she reached the galley, she pulled out her compact mirror to check her hair and make-up. Her brows furrowed as she scrutinized her reflection. Her critical green eyes swept over her deep auburn hair and the smattering of freckles on her nose. Satisfied the brisk walk through the airport had caused no unruliness in her appearance, she put the compact away and prepared the refreshment carts for the flight.

Eric's voice came over the loudspeaker, announcing they would taxi to the runway in a few moments, and Shelly joined the other flight attendants in the last safety check. She made her way down the aisle, checking everyone had their seat belts fastened and loose items stowed. The routine was a comfort. She was so absorbed in her role, she didn't watch where she was going and crashed into something warm and solid.

"Whoa!" said a deep voice, and a pair of firm hands grasped Shelly's shoulders, steadying her as she started to topple.

"Oh! I'm so-sorry!" she stammered.

She stared at a broad chest and had to tilt her head back until she met a set of deep blue eyes. It was the man, the one from the counter, but her assessment of his height and stature seemed woefully out-of-place now that she was standing close to him. He was at least a foot taller than she was, and after their collision, she was even more aware of his muscular build.

"No, it was my fault. I should have been in my seat." His smile was kind and open. "Are you all right?"

Looking into his eyes, Shelly was surprised by how familiar he was, which made her more unsteady. She shifted her weight, and the man released her shoulders.

"I'm f-fine," she said.

"Well, I'm sorry to have interrupted your work." He stepped out of the aisle and sat in his seat. "Let me buckle myself in so I don't get into any more trouble." His smile grew wider, and she couldn't help smiling in return, her unease fading.

"I appreciate that, sir." She checked to make sure he was fastened in then continued her walk down the aisle. Every seat was full, and many other customers gave her tight smiles in what she perceived as an attempt to hide weariness or flight jitters.

Safety check finished, she sat in her flight seat and buckled in for takeoff, happy to have a moment to herself to gather her thoughts. At her core, she preferred quiet solitude; however, her job required an outgoing, friendly persona, and she often assumed this pretense as part of her professional demeanor. Sometimes the strain of working in customer service necessitated quiet time to recharge her batteries, and this was definitely one of those moments.

As the plane lifted into the air, her mind drifted to when she ran into the man in the aisle. She couldn't remember the last time she had been drawn to a passenger, or if it had ever occurred before. The sense of familiarity he caused haunted her, and the memory of his intense blue eyes floated around in her head.

The plane soon reached cruising altitude, and the captain announced it was safe to move about the cabin. Shelly and the other flight attendants headed to their respective locations to pass out refreshments. Her heartbeat quickened as she anticipated another interaction with the man. It took additional effort to maintain her calm and friendly attitude as she made her way down the aisle of passengers. The closer she got to him, the more her palms sweated, and her stomach tightened into knots.

Finally, she arrived at the man's seat. Once she had taken the orders of the others in his row, she gestured toward him.

"What can I get you?" she asked, shifting her weight from foot to foot.

"I'll have a coke, with a little extra ice if you don't mind," he said, with a twinkle in his eye. "I'm a bit tender after our encounter earlier."

She laughed. "We have a first aid kit, if it's that bad."

"No, no, it's not quite to that level." He chuckled and then gave her a quick once over. "Although I'm surprised you aren't bruised from the collision. I'm a pretty sturdy guy."

"No harm, no foul," she said. "I'm stronger than I look." She grinned at him and handed him his coke with extra ice. His fingers were warm when they brushed hers, and his kind blue eyes held a hint of mischief in them. "Tell me if that's not enough ice for you."

He winked at her, his eyes crinkling as his grin broadened. "I'm sure this will do fine."

She began to move on to the next row when he cleared his throat.

"Before you go, what's your name?" the man asked, then hesitated. "You know, in case I need to contact you for insurance purposes."

Shelly laughed again and introduced herself. "And you are?"

"Master Sergeant Brad Collins." He bowed his head slightly. "At your service."

"O-oh, um, t-thank you for your service," she stammered, as she realized why he had seemed familiar to her before. The way he carried himself, his posture and mannerisms all reminded her of her father, who had also been a Marine.

He put out his hand, and she took it, anticipating the firm handshake she was accustomed to from members of the armed forces. Instead, he held her hand for a moment and gave it a gentle squeeze.

"It's nice to meet you, officially," Brad said. He released her hand and waved toward the remaining aisles. "But I don't want to keep you from your work."

"Right, I should get on with this." She maneuvered the cart to the next row, a smile pasted on her face, but her mind whirled. The man's stance, haircut, and overall disposition were large enough clues on their own, but it hadn't sunk in until he introduced himself by rank.

Her father was killed in action, right before Christmas, when she was eight years old. Since the uniform brought painful memories, she had made it a point to avoid military personnel most of her life. She continued down the aisle, shaken, her heart hammering in her throat, the beat slowing only after she put some distance between them. When she was far enough away, she could no longer sense his eyes on her back, her shoulders loosened.

After drink service was over, she returned to her flight seat to rest for a moment and gather her thoughts. She couldn't pinpoint the exact reason for why she was so unsettled. There were thousands of Marines flying home for the holidays, but there was something about Brad that caused her anxiety.

Was it the way he appeared calm and collected despite the chaotic holiday travel occurring around him? Or perhaps it was the way he seemed to see her as an actual person instead of only through her position with the airline. He was attractive, to be sure, and she often found herself a little tongue-tied by attractive men. However, she had sworn off men after her marriage ended the year before. She had enough on her plate raising her daughter on her own.

Shelly was so distracted she didn't realize Kylie was talking to her until a hand waved in front of her face.

"Hello?" Kylie called. "Earth to Shelly! Are you still with us?"

"Oh!" Shelly did her best to hide how unsettled she was after her conversation with Brad. "I'm sorry. I was in my own world."

"Your thoughts wouldn't happen to be on that handsome man you were talking with earlier, would they?" Kylie teased.

"N-no." Shelly protested, wincing as she stammered. Kylie smirked, and Shelly rushed on to hide her embarrassment. "I mean, obviously, he's attractive, but I'm not interested in starting anything with anyone, particularly a passenger I doubt I'll ever see again."

Kylie snorted. "Who's talking about starting anything? What's wrong with a little harmless flirting?"

"I wasn't flirting with him!"

"Really? Well, whatever you were doing, I'm just happy you genuinely smiled for a change."

Embarrassed, Shelly stared at her hands. She hadn't considered anyone at work, even someone she was close to, would see through her pretense.

"Let's go do our favorite pastime." Kylie stood and headed toward the back of the plane.

Shelly followed, wiping her clammy hands on her uniform. Her nerves heightened in anticipation of interacting with Brad again, but she took a deep breath and headed down the aisle to collect trash. It wasn't her favorite part of the job, but it often meant the flight was nearing its end. As she approached his row, he was not in his seat.

The warring feelings of relief and disappointment were overwhelming and caught her by surprise. She shook her head at her ridiculousness. After all, he was just a passenger, and there was no reason she should treat him any differently.

She sensed a presence behind her, and a throat cleared. Startled, she glanced back. Brad stood in the aisle, waiting patiently to return to his seat.

Shifting, she made a move to step out of his way. "Oh, I'm sorry."

He laughed. "I don't think the aisle is quite large enough for me to move by you. Please, take your time. I'm in no rush."

Her nerves rattled once more as she went clumsily down the aisle, dropping the trash multiple times and becoming more agitated as she went. She thrust the bag at the other people in Brad's aisle before she scurried away.

"Excuse me, Shelly?" he called.

Her body stiff, she turned. He lifted an empty cup and gestured toward her trash bag.

"I'm sorry, I missed you." She opened the bag, and he dropped in the cup. Her eyes met his, and his brows furrowed.

"Are you okay? You seem..." He bit his lip. "Distracted."

"Oh yes, I'm fine." She gave what she hoped was a reassuring smile and moved on.

The rest of the flight passed without further incident, and Shelly exhaled at the announcement they would land soon. She and the other flight attendants began landing prep, including a final trash service. Thankfully, Brad didn't have any additional trash, so she avoided looking like a fool again, though he gave her a cheerful grin. She responded with a hesitant smile then returned to her work area to secure the carts before heading to her seat for landing.

Once the plane was safely on the ground, she was too busy with disembarking procedures to give much more thought to Brad and the way his presence had unsettled her for the entire flight. She finished cleaning and checking the cabin for any forgotten items.

As she wandered back down the aisle during her final check, a black wallet peaked from between the seats. She pulled it out and opened it to check for identification. Brad's blue eyes stared back at her from the Maryland license. Curious, she checked his address, and her heart swelled in surprise when she discovered they were from the same area.

Wow, small world! She put the wallet into her purse to take to the lost and found. *I wonder if he still has family there.*

Eric was waiting for her at the front of the plane. "Welcome home, Shelly!"

"Thanks Eric." She reluctantly fell into step beside him as they walked up the jetway into the airport. "Are you sticking around for the holidays, or are you flying out again?"

"I'm not scheduled to fly again until the new year, but I am hoping to find a jump seat for a flight home to Maine before Christmas," he said.

"I'm sure your family would love to see you for the holidays," Shelly said. She took a small step to the side as they walked as he kept bumping into her.

"Though, I was hoping, while I'm in Maryland, maybe we

could—"

Shelly stopped short. Brad stood by the check-in counter, frowning and running a hand through his dark hair. But when he turned and saw her, the anxious crease between his eyebrows evaporated, and he broke into a broad smile that made her breath catch in her throat. Eric gawked at her, but she was too focused on Brad to care.

"Hello again," he said, moving toward them. "I seem to have misplaced my wallet, and I was wondering if anyone had found it."

"Of course!" she exclaimed. "It was wedged between the seats." After digging through her purse, she pulled it out and maneuvered around Eric. His smile had faded during their interaction. "Here you are."

Brad took the wallet. "Thank you. I would have been in quite the bind if my wallet was still in Atlanta."

"You're welcome." Shelly shifted her weight to her other foot, debating her next words. "I hope you don't mind, but I opened the wallet to determine who it belonged to and…" Her mouth went dry, and she swallowed.

"Yes?" he pressed.

"I-I saw y-your address is in Hallowed Point in southern Maryland, which is close to where I grew up." Her stomach fluttered with both nerves and excitement at finding someone from near her hometown. It was rare to meet anyone from that area she didn't already know.

"Where did you grow up?" he asked.

"Hidden River City."

"Wow, you were just across the river from me. I grew up down there as well, but I haven't been back in years." He gestured toward the corridor. "May I walk you out? I'd love to find out if we know any of the same people."

"Well, actually, we were just—" Eric straightened.

"That would be lovely." Shelly relished the chance to escape from Eric. "Merry Christmas, Eric. I'll see you in the new year." She spun on her heel then walked away before he could respond.

"Do you still live down there?" Brad asked.

"Definitely not," she said. "It would be a nightmare commuting to the airport from far away. I moved further north when I was old enough to live on my own. I live in a little town called Eagle Harbor, right on the northern Patuxent River."

"There seem to be two types of people from that area: those who can't imagine living anywhere else and those who can't wait to leave," Brad joked. "The military was sort of my ticket out of there. I'm with you, though, I find myself missing it now and then."

"Where is your family now?"

He was silent for a moment. "My parents passed away when I was barely eighteen and my sister moved to Texas with her husband a few years ago."

"I'm sorry for your loss," she murmured. "My father passed away when I was young as well, but my mother still lives in the area." She frowned, then glanced up at him. "Are you staying here for the holidays with friends, then?"

He shook his head. "Actually, I don't have plans for the holidays. I recently retired from the Marines, and I haven't figured out what my next step is going to be. I mean, I have a job lined up in DC that starts in the new year, but my living situation is still up in the air. My plan is to rent a room for a few days and spend the holidays searching for a place to live." He shrugged. "Christmas hasn't been the same for me since my folks died."

"I can imagine." Stopping, she stared at him, confused. "Wait, you're retired? When you introduced yourself, I thought you were still on active duty."

He slapped his forehead and chuckled. "I'm sorry, I'm still adjusting to civilian life." With his right hand, he performed a mock salute. "Besides, you know what they say, once a Marine, always a Marine."

She smiled. "I believe I've heard that saying once or twice." They continued to walk in silence as she digested his situation.

"I secured my new job before I retired, but I'm not the type of person to rent or buy something sight unseen," he said. "So, if you have any hotel recommendations for the area, I'd appreciate it."

"You shouldn't stay in a hotel for the holidays! I-I mean, no one should have to stay in a hotel at Christmas. I have a spare room over my garage I rent out. It has a separate entrance and everything." She blinked in surprise at her offer.

What are you thinking? You don't even know this man!

Brad stopped, and his mouth fell open. "Are you sure? I would hate to be an inconvenience or intrude on your holiday."

"Of course, I'm sure. It's the least I could do after trying to run you over on the plane." A nervous laugh bubbled up in her throat as she silently screamed at herself.

Part of her was questioning her sanity, but another part of her was hoping he would say yes. Beyond the sense of familiarity, there was something about knowing they had grown up near each other that had touched her heart. And if she was being completely honest, she needed the extra income.

She took a deep breath then said, "Honestly, you'd be doing me a favor. I haven't had a tenant in a while."

Besides, if Dad were alive, he'd do the same for a fellow Marine.

A thoughtful look crossed Brad's face as he mulled over her offer, and her stomach churned. Would he think she was crazy?

"That would be wonderful," he said. The tension in her shoulders eased. "I'm often rather lonely at Christmas and I haven't had many Christmases where I wasn't deployed." He hesitated with a sideways glance. "Your, uh, your husband won't mind?"

Her hand balled into a fist at her side. "I'm, uh, I'm divorced." She bit her lip. "I have a teenage daughter, but she's used to people renting the room."

Normally, she had an extensive vetting process before agreeing to rent to them. While the room was an in-law apartment and separate from the house, she liked to know more about a person before allowing them to live in such proximity to her and her daughter. But she found a kindred spirit in Brad, and her gut instinct told her he was safe.

"Besides," she said. "I'm thrilled to meet someone from southern Maryland. I don't meet many people who have even heard of it, much less grew up there."

"Isn't that the truth!" he exclaimed. "It was weird for me as a Marine because you had people who would say 'oh I'm from the Midwest,' or 'I'm a southerner, born and bred,' but Maryland is hard to explain as it is somewhat in the middle. Few people call themselves 'mid-Atlanticers.'" He cleared his throat. "If you're sure your daughter won't mind, I think I'll take you up on your offer. I was honestly a little concerned I wouldn't find a hotel with vacancies this late in the holiday season."

"I'm sure you could find one," Shelly said. "However, it may not be the nicest of places."

"Yeah, well, I'm a Marine, not an airman." He winked. "I'm used to less than ideal accommodations."

"Touché," she said. "Let's grab your luggage and we can head to my car." Together they went to baggage claim. While they waited, she texted Lilly.

Hey sweetie, I'm off the plane and heading home. We are going to have a guest staying with us for the holidays. Please put the sheets on the bed in the guest room and make sure everything is ready for when I arrive, okay? Love you!

"How old is your daughter?" he asked.

Shelly sighed. "She's thirteen."

Brad laughed. "Fun age, huh?"

"I knew the teenage years would be difficult. I just wasn't expecting to handle it alone."

"Her dad doesn't help you at all?"

"No," she said quietly, fighting with the wave of emotions which threatened to take over.

While she was still struggling with the divorce, she didn't want to burden Brad with her baggage. There was a small comfort in knowing her mother and sister were there to help with Lilly when Shelly was away for overnight flights, but it wasn't the same.

"I'm sorry," he said.

The luggage carousel started up, and they stood together waiting for his bags as the other people around them gathered their belongings. There were elderly couples whom she assumed were visiting grandchildren for the holidays. A few families, the moms and dads harried and tired after wrangling their energetic children on the flight. Her heart squeezed a bit as she gazed around, missing what she once had.

Several times, he offered to assist his fellow passengers with their luggage. He lifted a heavy bag for an older man, helped a little girl find her lost doll, which had fallen from her suitcase, and sorted through identical luggage to ensure it went to the right family. His kindness and conscientious actions only reinforced her impulsive decision to offer him the room for the holidays.

After a few more minutes, he grasped a blue suitcase and what appeared to be a guitar case. He looked at Shelly and shrugged. "That's everything."

"That's not much to start over with."

"I didn't keep many personal things while a Marine. It makes it easier to pick up and go at a moment's notice, which is often required in the military."

She gestured to the case. "Do you play?"

"Not as well as I'd like." He grinned. "I was the lead guitarist in a band at one of the bases I was stationed, but it's been years. Still, I can hold my own."

They left the airport and headed to the employee garage. Shelly led the way to her car, a bright orange hatchback.

Brad chuckled behind her. "I never would have pictured this as your car."

Her hand fumbled for her keys, and she frowned. "Why do you say that?"

"You just seem more… subdued than the car would suggest."

She grinned. "It's easier to find in a parking garage!"

"It certainly stands out." He put his luggage into the trunk and walked to the passenger side. "I guess I'm going to need to buy a car as well."

"Perhaps, although I suppose that depends on where you want to live." She climbed into the driver's seat. "If you move closer to the city, you could probably get away with riding the metro and using a car service to get around."

"I know it would be a better commute to move close to DC, but it's not really me. I doubt I'd go back to southern Maryland, but I don't think I'm interested in living in an urban location either."

"I can understand that," she said. "People ask why I don't just live in Baltimore since I'd be much closer to the airport. But I like where I live. Eagle Harbor isn't as congested as the city or some of the surrounding areas. It's a small town, and everything I need is conveniently located. My commute is a little longer than if I lived closer to the airport, but I don't mind it." She put the car into gear and backed out of the parking spot. "People also commute to DC from where I live, but it makes for a long day."

They rode in silence for a few moments as she navigated their way out of the airport loop and onto the highway.

"Have you been back much since you joined the military?" she asked.

"I visited when my sister still lived here, but not often."

"Why didn't you go to Texas to spend Christmas with her?"

Brad ran a hand through his dark hair. "I thought about it and, to be honest, she wanted me to, but it made more sense for me to get settled. If I had gone, I was afraid I'd be overly anxious the whole time about what I should be doing before I started work, and I worried I'd ruin their Christmas." After shooting a quick glance at Shelly, he turned his face toward the window. "Honestly, we're not that close. She was still in high school when I joined the military, and she resented me for not sticking around after our parents died."

Having a close relationship with her own sister and their mother, a bond which had only strengthened after losing their father, she didn't know what to say. She struggled to imagine a strained relationship with them. Her heart went out to Brad and what he had gone through at such a young age, without a support system to fall back on. While she was still shocked she had offered to host him for the holidays, she was glad someone who must have faced so much loneliness in his past wouldn't be dealing with it this Christmas.

Chapter Two

The silence stretched until they arrived at her home. Brad appraised the house in the gathering dusk as Shelly parked the car. It was a small two-story colonial house with an in-law apartment over the attached one-car garage. It was reminiscent of a dollhouse, with white siding and blue shudders. There was a bay window that overlooked a flowerbed filled with the remnants of summer rose bushes, their thorny stems stretching toward the soft light pouring from within. A feline silhouette perched on the windowsill, watching them.

"I meant to ask," Shelly said. "You're not allergic to cats, are you?"

"No, ma'am. I'm a lover of all animals and have no allergies to speak of."

"Great. The cat isn't allowed outside, let alone in the guest room, but if you had allergies, I would have suggested not coming into the main house." She shut off the engine and gestured toward the side of the house. "Your room has its own entrance on the side of the garage. It has a private bathroom and a kitchenette with a microwave and a mini fridge. I normally offer guests breakfast as part of the room, but since you're coming so late, you're welcome to join us for dinner."

"I'd like to put my stuff away first, if you don't mind." And he could use a few minutes to himself to process the day as well as freshen up a bit. He rubbed his chin and winced at how scruffy it was.

"No problem. I'll help you with your luggage." Shelly opened her car door, and Brad followed her to the trunk.

Together, they grabbed his things and headed up the wooden staircase. The landing was dark, and his eyes struggled to adjust. A moment later, a light blinded him when she flicked an unseen switch.

She stepped inside and set his suitcase by the bed. "So, as you can see, here's the bedroom. There's a dresser there and a closet in the corner for your clothes. The bathroom has some toiletries, like soap, shampoo, and the like, and the shower is pretty self-explanatory." Her heels clicked on the hardwood floor of the room as she flipped on the thermostat beside the door. "We keep the heat on low or off when the room isn't rented. Uh, let's see what else. The television is in the cabinet over there, and the Wi-Fi password is posted on the inside of the cabinet door."

"This works perfectly, thank you. I appreciate you taking me in like this, especially during the holidays." Her offer to stay had caught him off guard, but her generosity warmed his insides. "It's much nicer than any hotel room I could hope to find."

Setting his luggage down, he took in the room. It was a simple setup, with a blue comforter on the bed and matching drapes. The floor was a dark wood find, and the white walls were bare. He assumed long-term tenants were permitted to apply their own personal touch, but he wasn't sure how long he'd be staying, and he'd never been one for decorating.

"How much is it per night?" Numbers flashed before his eyes as he considered how much he had in his bank account. While he'd planned to put room charges on a credit card, he was willing to dip into his savings.

She waved her hand. "Why don't you just get settled for now, and we can discuss all that later? Whenever you're ready, you can come over to the main house, and I can fix you something to eat." With a brief nod, she turned toward the door, then spun back around. "I almost forgot. Here's the key to the room."

As Brad reached for the key, his fingers brushed hers. Her touch sent electricity shooting through him, and his heartbeat quickened. He lifted his gaze from the key to her emerald eyes and found them guarded and filled with emotions he couldn't quite place.

"Th-Thank you," he choked out, breaking the silence and the spell that seemed to hold them both in abeyance.

She flashed an enigmatic smile before she left.

The moment he was alone, he sank onto the bed and groaned. It had been a long day of traveling, and he was emotionally and physically drained. He chuckled as he acknowledged how much easier today would have been in his youth. As a young Marine, he likely would have jumped at the chance to tour the rest of her home, but now that he was older, he lacked the energy.

Despite his exhaustion, an unfamiliar elation filled him at having met Shelly. While she was attractive, something deeper had piqued his interest in talking to her. He had sensed a certain sadness around her and was drawn to her from the moment she had appeared at the check-in counter. When she spoke to him, she immediately put him at ease, despite the stress he was under from facing a new chapter in his life.

Starting over would be the more accurate statement. He honestly was not sure what to do with himself. After twenty years of discipline and order, he was lost in the chaos of freedom. No one was there to tell him what to do, where to live, who to follow. Civilian life was foreign to him, and he worried about how he would adjust after everything he had seen and done while in the military. Even time was different; to someone like Shelly, it was nearing five o'clock, but to him, it was almost seventeen hundred hours.

At least he had a job squared away, and he clung to that knowledge. He appreciated his military experience working in Information Technology would transfer well to his new position as an IT manager at the Department of Defense. It would be nice to get back to work in the new year and have a schedule again. He had taken little leave while in the Marines, and he wasn't used to having a lot of free time.

Overwhelmed, he gazed around the room, trying to locate an anchor in a sea of uncertainty. It had taken him completely by surprise when she suggested he stay with her. The invitation was welcome, as the thought of spending another Christmas alone was a depressing prospect. Even if he didn't spend Christmas with Shelly and her daughter, he was comforted just knowing someone was nearby and that the someone was not a complete stranger.

The memory of how excited she'd been to discover they were from the same area brought a smile to his face. Most of the people he had grown up with had opted not to leave his hometown, but Brad struggled to return because it held many painful memories.

Hoisting himself off the bed, he started unpacking, as maybe the simple act of putting some sense of order into his life would reduce his internal panic at facing his newfound liberty. He put his clothes away, set up his things in the bathroom, and placed the family photo he carried with him on the nightstand. The simplicity of the room had a calming effect as it reminded him of the barracks before he had moved to off base housing.

A quick glance in the mirror over the sink confirmed he was a bit rough around the edges. His button-down green shirt and jeans were wrinkled from sitting on planes all day, and his dark facial hair had far surpassed the five o'clock shadow due to not having time to shave that morning.

He set a fresh pair of jeans and a blue sweater on the bed. Then he headed to the bathroom sink to shave. As he lathered up his face and drew the razor through the cream, he wondered just who he was trying to impress. After all, Shelly had already seen him looking scruffy and travel-weary. He chocked it up to the pride and discipline the military had instilled in him, contemplating the many hours he had spent shining his boots.

It was as good of an excuse as any, even if deep down he knew seeing her again was a strong contributing factor. Shaking his head, he finished his work and rinsed the remaining residue from his chin. Then he changed into fresh clothes and headed over to the main house.

The neighboring homes sparkled to life with shimmering strings of lights that encircled their doors and windows or dangled from the eaves. He had not noticed when they first arrived, but now her house stood out in stark contrast to her festive neighbors. The only lights shining from her house were the porch lamps which bathed the sidewalk in a soft glow. Has she not been home long enough to decorate or had the recent family turmoil left the inhabitants of the house without the holiday spirit?

He knocked softly on the door, and it swung open moments later, revealing a petite, gawky girl with brown hair and dark brown eyes that widened at the sight of him. Her appearance took him by surprise as he expected a smaller version of Shelly, but he guessed the girl had inherited quite a few of her features from her father. Still, her mother's imprint in the girl was clear in her high cheekbones, the delicate sprinkling of freckles over her nose, and the deep set of her eyes.

"Hello there," he said. "I'm Brad, and I'm a guest of your mother's."

The girl started at the sound of his voice then nodded, stepping aside to let him in. The inside of the home was as devoid of holiday decoration as the outside. The living room was sparsely furnished with a worn red couch, a cluttered coffee table, and a television stand.

Despite its simple furnishings, the room had a homey feel to it, as there were collages of photos on the walls, mostly of the girl in her younger years. A shadowy figure slinking behind the couch appeared to be the cat he had spotted earlier in the window.

The scent of roasting onions and garlic wafted through the air, and his stomach growled with anticipation. It had been years since he had a home cooked meal. He'd never learned to cook himself, and none of his military friends or their wives bothered with it much either, unless microwavable meals counted.

Footsteps sounded behind him, and he turned as Shelly entered the room. By the disheveled state of her hair and the wrinkles in her blue blazer, it was clear she had not changed before starting dinner. She seemed shorter than when he first met her, and he realized her high heels had been discarded. Her face broke into a smile as she stepped up beside her daughter, putting an arm around her shoulders.

"Brad, this is Lilly. Lilly, this is Sergeant Major Brad Collins of the U.S. Marine Corps. Recently retired," she added, shooting Brad a mischievous grin.

He held out his hand. "It's nice to meet you, Lilly."

Lilly bit her lip as she accepted it. "Nice to meet you too." She let go quickly and shrank back into her mother.

"I'm making chicken parmesan for dinner. I hope you like Italian," Shelly said. "Please make yourself at home. Lilly can show you how the television works or you're welcome to sit at the table. Whatever you prefer."

Lilly flinched at the suggestion she assist him, and Brad sensed she would be more comfortable if he did not impose.

"Do you need any help in the kitchen?" he asked.

Shelly raised an eyebrow as she scrutinized him. "Do you cook?"

He laughed. "No, but I'm amazing at following orders, after all."

"I bet, but I've got it from here."

"In that case, if you don't mind, I'd like to just sit at the table and answer a few emails." Brad gestured toward the dining room.

Lilly's shoulders relaxed, and when Shelly wasn't paying attention, she disappeared up the stairs.

Shelly led the way and indicated a seat at the table before walking back to the kitchen. The table was round, with four chairs and had been set for three. A chandelier hung from the ceiling. There was a buffet table against the wall by the kitchen, decorated with more photos of Shelly and Lilly. A sliding glass door, accented by green curtains, opened to the backyard at the rear of the room. A doorway and a half wall separated the dining room and kitchen, giving him a clear view of Shelly. The kitchen was small and dark with rich mahogany cabinets and marble countertops.

He sat at the table and scrolled through his phone, but he struggled to concentrate with Shelly close by. His gaze strayed to watch her as she seemed to dance around her kitchen, stirring a sauce here, dredging chicken there. Whatever she was making struck him as complicated, but she moved with an ease, suggesting she belonged there. It was the happiest he had seen her since they met. She was clearly in her element cooking and, based on the tantalizing scents alone, she was also very good at what she did. His stomach growled again as he returned his attention to his phone in hopes of distraction.

"Thirsty?" She appeared in front of him with a glass of water. He jumped then nodded sheepishly. "I don't have much else to drink at the moment. I'd planned to go grocery shopping tomorrow."

"Water is fine." He sipped deeply, realizing he had nothing to drink since the soda with extra ice on the plane. "Would you mind a tagalong at the store? I need to pick up a few things myself."

"That would be great." Shelly moved away from the table but smiled back at him over her shoulder. "You can push the cart."

Without thinking about it, he put his phone aside and watched her, giving up the pretense of emails. She prepared a salad, chopping the vegetables with a gusto and softly humming a tune he did not recognize. Her hair was breaking free of its confining clip and cascading down her back in waves of a tumultuous red sea. For a moment, he wondered what it would be like to run his fingers through the waterfall. Would her hair feel as soft as it looked?

The oven timer interrupted his thoughts, and he shook his head. Shelly removed the chicken from the oven and walked into the dining room to set the pan on the table, then went back to get the salad.

"Help yourself," she said, before heading up the stairs.

He served himself then sank back into his seat. Both his military training and good manners would not allow him to eat until everyone was at the table. Although the delicious scent of roasted onion and garlic made his stomach growl again, and he was impatient for Shelly and her daughter to join him. When they did, Lilly demurely took her seat and passed her mother her plate to be served.

After handing Lilly her dinner, Shelly slid a chicken filet onto her plate and took a small bite before popping a pill into her mouth. When Brad looked at her questioningly, she smiled and held up the now empty package.

"I'm lactose intolerant."

He glanced at Lilly with a raised eyebrow then stared at Shelly. "If you're lactose intolerant, why are you serving a meal that's covered with cheese?"

"There are certain dairy products I give up without hesitation, like ice cream and milk, but I'm hopelessly devoted to cheese."

Lilly giggled. "I could never give up ice cream."

"I'm with you," he said with a nod. "Ice cream is a mainstay. What's your favorite flavor?"

"Chocolate chip cookie dough." Lilly's face broke into a broad grin, her enthusiasm causing her to forget her shyness.

"That's a good one. I'm partial to rocky road, myself." He leaned toward Shelly with mock sincerity. "Have you always had this abominable affliction?"

"No. I started to have issues with certain dairy when I was in my twenties, and it's just gotten worse from there."

"My condolences," he said, his voice theatrically grave. Lilly rolled her eyes at his antics, but he was unphased.

He took a bite of the chicken, which tasted even better than it smelled. The tomato sauce held a subtle sweetness, which complimented the savory oregano spice in the breading. Without further hesitation, he dug into his meal, helping himself to seconds with Shelly's encouragement. Lilly gawked at him with wide-eyed fascination, often holding a forkful of chicken suspended before her open mouth. Shelly shook her head, admonishing her daughter for being rude, but Brad found her unabashed wonder endearing. What did she make of her mother's decision to rent the spare room? Did she interact often with the guests, or did she keep to herself?

"How are the rehearsals going for the Christmas pageant, Lilly?" Shelly asked, breaking the silence.

"They're cancelled," Lilly said with a groan.

"What?" The shock in Shelly's voice caught Brad's attention, and he looked back and forth between mother and daughter.

Lilly heaved a sigh. "Mrs. Whittaker has the flu, and there's no one else available to play for us." With a shrug, she stabbed a piece of chicken with her fork. "So, they're cancelling the pageant."

"I'm sorry," Shelly said, shaking her head in dismay. "I know you were excited about it."

"What's the pageant?" he asked.

"It's one of the town's biggest Christmas events." Lilly rested her chin on her hand, her big brown eyes filled with disappointment. "Mrs. Whittaker is the music teacher at my school and was going to play piano for us. I was going to be the lead this year."

"Could you perform a cappella or without music?" Brad asked, as an idea formed in his head.

"I mean, I guess," Lilly said, her tone suggesting this wasn't an option she would prefer. "But it wouldn't be the same."

"The pageant isn't just a local performance; it's also one of our biggest fundraisers." Shelly gave Lilly's arm a squeeze. "People from all over the state come to see it, and it helps to provide recreational programs to less fortunate children."

Brad chewed his chicken as he mulled over their dilemma. His nickname in the Marines was "Mr. Fix-it" because he was always trying to fix everything, from mechanical breakdowns to other people's personal problems. This might be a situation where his former reputation could come in handy. While his guitar skills were more than a little rusty, perhaps, with enough time, he could stand in for the sick accompanist.

"Just to make sure I understand," he said. "The pageant was only cancelled because there's no one to play music?"

"Uh, yeah." The unspoken "duh" was clear in Lilly's tone.

He bit his lip to hide a smile. "Well, I might be able to help. I play the guitar."

Lilly's eyes widened, and she beamed at him. "Really?"

"Now don't get too excited," he said, holding up a hand. "I'm more than a little rusty. When is the pageant?"

"In four days." Shelly's lips set in a thin line.

"That's not a lot of time," he admitted. "But I think I can work with it." He gestured at Lilly. "Do you have a copy of the music? At the very least, I could look at it and see what I can do."

She nodded, her dark eyes growing brighter with each word he said. After asking to be excused, she ran up the stairs, leaving him to hope he hadn't bitten off more than he could chew.

"That was kind of you," Shelly said. "But don't feel obligated."

"I'm happy to help if I can." He pushed back from the table and overdramatically patted his stomach. "That was the best meal I've had in a long time."

"I'm glad you enjoyed it," she said, her face lighting up. "I take it you haven't had a home cooked meal in a while?"

"You would be correct. The mess hall wasn't that bad, and once in a while a friend might have a cookout, but there's nothing quite like home-cooking."

"I'm happy to cook for you during your stay." After taking a sip of water, she cleared her throat. "As I'm sure you can guess, I don't get the opportunity often. When I'm home, I try to make dinner every night, but it's depressing to make the effort for just the two of us, especially since Lilly can be a picky eater."

"Do you normally cook for your guests?"

"Hm." Her chin rested on her hand as she appeared to ponder his question. "As I told you earlier, I provide breakfast for them, sometimes dinner if requested, but most guests go out to eat." She crossed her arms and narrowed her eyes. "But what you're really asking is whether food is included in the price of the room."

Brad laughed. "You saw right through that."

"The usual rate is fifty dollars a night. I have a weekly charge of two hundred dollars for the room." Her green eyes appraised him. "While I've never had a monthly guest, that's something we can discuss if you think you'll need a place for that long."

"Well, why don't I pay you the weekly rate for now and maybe in the next few days, I'll have a better sense of how long it will take me to find a place. Does that sound fair?"

"Works for me," she said as she exhaled heavily in what he assumed was a sigh of relief.

"I also insist on helping with the dishes. You said usually only breakfast is included, and I'd like to earn my dinner." With his most charming grin, he began clearing the table.

She opened her mouth to protest, but then closed it and nodded. "I suppose I can accept those terms." After carrying dishes to the kitchen for him to wash, she wandered back to the table as if uncertain of what to do with her unexpected free time.

He began stacking the dishes by the sink, but he did not know what was dishwasher-safe and what wasn't, let alone where anything went. With a shake of his head, he spun on his heel and went back to the doorway. "I, uh, might need some help putting everything away."

"Of course." Shelly surveyed his stacks. "The plates, silverware, and glasses can go into the dishwasher. The rest needs to be washed by hand." She grabbed a towel. "How about you wash and I dry?"

"Sounds like a plan." As he began loading the dishwasher, he gestured toward the living room. "I noticed you haven't decorated for Christmas."

"Not yet. Lilly was waiting for me to have a break in flights so we could do it together." Her face softened. "We were planning to get a Christmas tree when Lilly gets off school tomorrow."

"Wow, I can't remember the last time I had a Christmas tree." While the sink filled with soapy water, he picked up a pan and washed it. "Is tomorrow her last day of school before break?"

She nodded as she took the pan from him. "It'll be nice to spend some time with her."

"It must get lonely when you're gone," he said as he scrubbed a spatula.

"My mom and my sister come stay with her for overnights, and our next-door neighbor, Mr. Simmons, is retired, and he checks in on her as well." She hung the pan on the rack. "My ex-husband worked a normal nine-to-five job, and she wasn't home by herself for very long. We've been struggling to adjust since he left."

"I can imagine." Unsure of what else to say, he rinsed a bowl and handed it to her.

"But we make do," she said. "I'd love to have a job with a normal schedule. I've considered going back to school, but I don't have the money, and it'd be hard to keep up with classes with my schedule as erratic as it is." She shook her head. "This is definitely not my dream job."

"What is your dream job?"

Her chin dipped, and she fidgeted with her blazer. "You'll probably think it's stupid."

"I doubt that." He gestured with the spatula he was washing for her to continue.

"When I was little, I always wanted to be a journalist. I've always enjoyed writing, but there was something about reporting on actual events that fascinated me. I worked on the newspaper in high school." Her hand brushed an auburn lock out of her eyes. "Actually, I was working on a degree in journalism when I met Lilly's father. After a whirlwind romance, I found myself married with a baby on the way. I quit school and spent the first year of Lilly's life at home. Then when money got tight, I contacted a friend of mine who worked for the airline. She helped me to get an interview, I went through the necessary training, then I started as a flight attendant."

"Huh, I thought you might say you wanted to be a chef," Brad said. "Your cooking is certainly good enough."

Shelly laughed. "Thank you. I enjoy it, and I love baking, too, but I couldn't do that full time. I'm on my feet enough as it is in my current job."

They were quiet as he finished washing the last of the dishes. After drying his hands, he leaned back against the counter.

She sounded a little miserable in her job. How difficult would it be for her to change careers? "I think you should follow your dream."

"I don't know," she said, a wistful quality pulling at her words. "I'm afraid I'm too old to go back to school. All those young people would intimidate me. Besides, one attraction of being a journalist was traveling the world and writing about exciting events. At least I still get to do the traveling part. Besides, I haven't written anything of substance in years." Her laugh this time was dry. "My writing these days consists of logs for the airline and grocery lists."

He crossed his arms. "I understand if you've moved on, and I imagine being a single mom complicates things, but if journalism is still your dream, I bet you'll find a way to come back to it."

As she wiped down the counter, she pursed her lips. "Hm. Maybe. It's a busy time of year, though. And I want to spend as much time as I can with Lilly while I'm home."

"That's true." He stretched and yawned. "Anyway, I'm not sure about you, but I'm pretty beat. I know it's early, but I'm going to turn in."

Her teeth worried her lower lip, and he could swear there was disappointment in her eyes, but she quickly recovered with a smile. "Let me know if you need anything."

"I will." Without thinking, he closed the distance between them and grasped her hand. "Thank you, again, for inviting me to stay."

Her eyes widened in surprise at his touch, but she didn't let go. "Y-you're welcome."

He gave her hand a light squeeze before releasing it and smiled. "Well, goodnight."

"Goodnight, Brad." Her voice was barely above a whisper.

He headed to the front door, his head swimming. Once outside, he stopped and breathed deeply, lifting his gaze toward the twinkling night sky. The cool air provided a stark contrast to the heady warmth of the kitchen.

This is not at all how I expected to spend my first night back in Maryland. But I'm thanking my lucky stars it happened.

The cool air was becoming brisk as winter made itself known. He suspected this part of the state got more snow than his hometown. The chill bit through the soft cotton of his sweater, and he rubbed his hands over his arms to keep warm. With one last look at the stars, he headed up the stairs to his room.

After changing into his pajamas, he laid on the bed. He debated watching TV or checking his social media, but the stimulation would not help him sleep. Instead, his mind replayed the events of the day, starting with the early flight on the small plane from Jacksonville, North Carolina, to Charlotte, and then a connecting flight to Atlanta. He would never understand why airlines made such strange choices, such as sending someone further south when their destination was north of their starting point. Perhaps that was something he could ask Shelly.

The first leg of his journey had been rather uneventful, especially compared to his connecting flight to Maryland. Recalling his initial meeting with Shelly brought a smile to his face, and a warmth flowed through his hands as he remembered how it had felt to hold her after she tried to knock him over.

It had been a long time since a woman had last been in his arms. There had been a few women he had dated while he was a Marine, though only one of them blossomed into an actual relationship. He had been disappointed to learn a lot of women were more attracted to the fantasy of the uniform than they were to the actual man wearing it, and even fewer were up for the challenges presented by military life. The constant deployments and regular duty station changes would put a strain on any relationship. He had grown accustomed to being alone, but it wasn't until Shelly literally fell into his arms he realized just how lonely he was.

When he'd made plans to come back to Maryland, his focus had been on getting a job and figuring out how to transition to civilian life. He never really considered finding someone and settling down. Most of his brothers in arms who had married had done so at a young age and went on to have children, but Brad was approaching forty and believed he was too old to start a family. Even marriage itself seemed a long shot, as most women his age had already settled down. While he was content, deep down, he regretted the lack of love in his life.

He replayed his last conversation with Shelly in his head. Despite the stress of his own circumstances, his heart went out to her and Lilly. Shelly's ex-husband had left them in an awful situation, and Brad could not imagine someone being so cruel as to turn their back on their own child.

Shelly was strong though, that much was clear. Despite the significant upheaval the end of her marriage had caused, she had continued to provide a home and as much stability as she could muster. He was surprised that, while she was clearly upset with her ex-husband for abandoning their daughter, she did not appear to harbor any ill will toward him. She had told the story of his betrayal in a matter-of-fact tone, with little emotion. It was clear she had come to terms with the lot life had dealt her and was trying to make the best of it, and he admired her for her resilience.

As he pondered the day's events, his eyes drooped, and he yawned again. It was time for bed. He rolled over to shut off the light and slipped under the covers. The last thought he had before succumbing to sleep was of the unfathomable emotion he had seen in her emerald eyes when he held her hand.

Chapter Three

Shelly stood by the bay window, watching Brad. What was he thinking? His head tilted back as he gazed at the stars. She hoped she'd hidden her disappointment at his decision to go to bed, as she didn't fully understand it herself. It had been a long day of traveling, so it was no surprise that he was exhausted. Still, she had wanted to spend more time getting to know him without the distraction of dinner or driving getting in the way.

When he disappeared from view, she left the window and made her way to Lilly's room. They had a lot to discuss after how they had left things the last time she had been home. She knocked softly at the door and Lilly cracked it open, peering from within.

"I think we should talk," Shelly said, her tone low, but firm.

Lilly nodded and opened the door wider to allow her mother to come in. The room was purple, which was Lilly's favorite color. There were posters on the walls, one of three little kittens and another from a video game she enjoyed. In one corner, there was a fuzzy purple chair next to a bookcase overflowing with books. A net filled with stuffed animals was hanging from the ceiling. They sat down next to each other on the white comforter on Lilly's bed and, after a moment of silence, she leaned her head on her mother's shoulder.

"I'm sorry, Mom." Lilly mumbled. "I didn't mean any of the things I said. I was just angry."

"Can you tell me why you were angry?"

Lilly shrugged. "It's stupid."

"If it upset you, it can't be stupid," Shelly insisted before stopping herself and taking a breath. "I don't want you to tell me if you're not comfortable, but I want you to know I'm always here for you."

Lilly nodded as she stared at her hands, then stood and walked over to her closet, opening the door. For a moment, she disappeared and when she reappeared, she was wearing a black hoodie with the hood up to hide her face. Instead of returning, she began rearranging the stuffed animals on her closet shelves, as if organizing them would somehow bring order to her chaotic life.

"It's just... my friends were talking about the plans they have with their families for Christmas. They shared how they went tree shopping and their—" She shot a sideways glance at Shelly.

"Go on."

Lilly sighed, turning back to the closet. "How their *fathers* helped them carry the biggest trees off the lot. Then the whole family decorates the tree and sings Christmas carols. They bake cookies together..." Lilly sniffled. "We used to do those things, and now we can't. It makes me hate this time of year."

Shelly's heart sank. It had been hard on Lilly since Carl had left them, but Shelly hadn't considered how much more difficult it must be not to have him around at Christmas. While her marriage had been a rollercoaster ride, somehow, she and Carl had always made the holidays a special time for Lilly.

In years past, they would go to a Christmas tree farm, and Carl would hoist Lilly on his shoulders and insist they had to find a tree that was taller than the two of them combined. Shelly would bake cookies to share with their neighbors, and he would joke she should open a bakery. For those precious years, Christmas had become a joyous time for her again. Now, she felt much like she did after she lost her father.

She took in a deep breath. "Lilly, would it be easier on you if we didn't celebrate Christmas this year? I don't want you to miss out. Or maybe—would you like to make some new traditions for just us two?"

Lilly lifted her shoulders in an exaggerated shrug before letting them drop. "Part of me wants to pretend Christmas doesn't exist, but then another part of me doesn't want to miss out on things I used to enjoy. I don't know we could recreate it without Daddy though."

Without warning, she slammed the closet door and stomped back to the bed. "I don't even know why I care that he's gone. He doesn't care about me!"

Shelly started to argue but stopped herself again. As much as she wanted to reassure her daughter Carl loved her, she wasn't sure what to say. The old adage of actions speaking louder than words popped into her mind, and she understood Lilly's mixed emotions.

Carl's actions in leaving and essentially abandoning them both spoke volumes. Shelly had forgiven him for everything he had done to her, more so to give herself some peace than because he had apologized. But she struggled to forgive him for what he did to Lilly. It was something Shelly just could not comprehend, no matter how much time had passed.

She put her arm around Lilly's shoulder. "It's normal to have mixed emotions, given the circumstances." Her head rested on top of her daughter's. "I don't want to force Christmas on you or try to fake holiday cheer. I don't think either of us is up for that this year." With her other hand, she rubbed Lilly's arm. "But I do think it might be nice to celebrate. Maybe we try some new traditions. We could just spend our weekend in our jammies watching Christmas movies. We don't even have to decorate if you don't want to, but we should try to find something that will help us move forward together."

Sniffling again, Lilly leaned against Shelly. "I like that idea." Her fingers fiddled with a loose string on her hoodie. "I still want to decorate, though. It wouldn't feel like Christmas without a tree, but how would we get one?" With an arched eyebrow, she surveyed her mother. "No offense, Mom, but you're no lumberjack."

Shocked, Shelly threw back her head and laughed. "Gee, thanks! I guess I take that as a compliment." She tickled Lilly, who squirmed away, fighting back a laugh.

"Maybe we could invite Brad to come with us," Shelly said.

Lilly's eyes widened. "Oh no! I forgot to give him the music for the pageant."

"I'm sure you can give it to him tomorrow," Shelly said. "I doubt he would have been up to practicing tonight, anyway. He seemed pretty beat."

"That's true. I'll try to remember to give him the music before school tomorrow." Lilly tilted her head thoughtfully. "D'ya think he'd want to go tree shopping with us, though? Isn't he just here to rent the room?"

Shelly bit her lip. How should she handle this? It had been rather hectic when they arrived home and there hadn't been time for Shelly to go into the full story. Now, she wasn't sure how to approach the subject of Brad's connection to her hometown with Lilly, or if it even mattered. Did Shelly even understand the significance of Brad's entrance into their lives? Perhaps not, but his presence was having a profound effect on her.

"He's not exactly a typical tenant," she began. "I met him on my flight from Atlanta. He used to live in Maryland before joining the Marines, and he's moving back now he's retired. We got to talking, and I learned we grew up close to each other. When he told me he planned to stay at a hotel until he found a place to live, I invited him to rent the room from us."

Lilly's eyebrows pulled together. "So, do you, like, know him from your childhood?"

"No, that was just an interesting coincidence. I've never met him before, but I thought it might be easier for him to rent the room here than to stay in a hotel for the foreseeable future. I didn't have any guests lined up for the holidays, and the extra income can't hurt." Shelly tucked a lock of brown hair behind Lilly's ear. "He asked about our Christmas decorations, and I told him we were going to get a tree tomorrow. I wanted to check with you before I asked him, but would you mind if he joined us? I think he has a hard time with Christmas too."

Lilly gave a noncommittal shrug. "I mean, I'm okay with it." She grinned. "At least then we can get an enormous tree and not something Charlie Brown sized."

Biting back a smile at the reference to the cartoon they watched every year, Shelly slyly reached behind Lilly's back then grabbed a pillow from the head of the bed. When Lilly wasn't paying attention, Shelly swatted her in the head with it.

"Hey!" Lilly cried, then snatched a pillow of her own to defend herself. They shrieked and giggled, striking soft blows wherever they could. Once they had both gotten a few good hits in, they fell onto the bed, breathless with laughter.

"We should go to bed," Shelly said. "It's getting late, and you have school tomorrow."

"At least it's the last day before Christmas vacation," Lilly said. "I'm ready for a break."

Shelly leaned forward and kissed her daughter on the forehead. "It'll be nice to be home and spend some time with you." Lilly reached up for a hug, and Shelly pulled her into her arms, giving her a tight squeeze. "I love you, sweetie. Goodnight."

With a yawn, Lilly settled back on the pillow. "'Night, Mom."

Shelly closed the door and dragged her feet to her room. The day was catching up with her, and her body was heavy with weariness. She glanced out her window. Was Brad still up? The lights were off in his room. Yawning, she prepared to take a shower before bed to wash off the grime of the day and to loosen up her aching muscles from pushing the heavy drink cart.

After her shower, she towel-dried her hair and put on her pajamas. As she climbed into bed, she was glad to have cleared the air with Lilly, though Shelly's heart still ached. Parents always wanted to shield their children from heartbreak, but sometimes it wasn't possible.

Her mother couldn't hide from her children the reality of their father's death and, likewise, Shelly couldn't protect her daughter from the repercussions of divorce. All she could do was be there for Lilly, listening to her and loving her every step of the way.

Her mind drifted from the talk with Lilly to the conversations she had shared with Brad. Shelly had surprised herself with her general openness. Since Carl had left, she had been a lot more guarded around people, protecting herself. She couldn't remember the last time she had shared her childhood dream of being a journalist with someone. It was a dream she had given up on long ago, and she was a little astonished the yearning was still there.

What would the next few days bring? Christmas was just around the corner, and she didn't know how long Brad would be with them. It would be an interesting holiday season, to say the least.

~ * ~

The alarm went off at 6. Shelly groaned and rolled over to shut it off. As she lay back on the pillow, she stared at the ceiling. It felt like she had just gone to sleep a moment ago; morning had come too soon. As she rubbed her eyes, her mind went over everything she needed to do today. Make breakfast for Lilly, go to the store, locate the Christmas decorations in the garage, and get a tree.

I need to make breakfast for Brad too. Shelly bolted upright in bed. *Brad.* His name brought forth all the memories of the day before. With renewed energy, she swung her legs over the side of the bed and hurriedly dressed for the day. Her heart was full of anticipation at seeing him again, and she shook her head at her ridiculousness. *He's just a guest,* she chastised herself. *Stop overreacting.*

Was he still sleeping? She descended the stairs and stepped into the dining room. To her surprise, Lilly was already eating breakfast, and the delicious smell of bacon wafted from the kitchen.

"W-what? How?" Shelly stammered.

Lilly looked up at the sound of her voice and smiled. "Morning, Mom! Brad made bacon and pancakes for breakfast."

Shelly scratched her head, then continued into the kitchen. There was Brad, standing over the griddle with a spatula in one hand and tongs in the other. He was engrossed in what he was doing; he hadn't heard her come in.

She cleared her throat. "Uh, good morning."

He turned. "Good morning!" His face broke into a grin. "I thought I would try my hand at cooking the one thing I know how to make."

"B-but I told you breakfast was included!" she blurted out.

His grin grew wider as he raised an eyebrow at her. "I mean, I'm using your ingredients. I'm just providing the labor."

"How did you find everything?" she asked, bemused.

"I remembered where you put the mixing and serving bowls from watching you put away the dishes last night." He inclined his head toward the dining room. "And Lilly was kind enough to help me locate the rest if I made her pancakes extra special."

"Oh." Her eyes refocused on his appearance. His dark hair was damp from a recent shower, and he was dressed for the day in a black sweater and khakis. "What time did you wake up?"

"Around 4 or so? I'm still on military time, I guess." He nodded to the floor. "I also made breakfast for your cat. He's really friendly when he's getting fed."

Shelly glanced down to where Newton was licking his bowl clean. "I-I, uh, thank you."

"You're welcome. Why don't you go sit at the table, and I'll bring in your plate when it's ready. Are two pancakes enough, or would you like more?"

"Two is fine." Still struggling to process this turn of events, Shelly went into the dining room and sat at the table. "I can't remember the last time someone cooked for me."

"Daddy only cooked when you weren't home. I'd say the last time someone cooked for you was Grandma," Lilly said before enjoying the last bite of her breakfast. She stood and took her plate to the sink, thanking Brad while she was in the kitchen. On her way toward the stairs, she stopped and gave Shelly a quick hug.

"I hope he rents the room for a long time," she whispered in Shelly's ear. "He makes amazing pancakes. He even added chocolate chips to mine, which you almost never do."

Shelly laughed and patted her daughter on the arm. "That's because the last thing you need before school is more sugar."

Lilly rolled her eyes and trudged up the stairs. A moment later, Brad appeared with two plates of pancakes and bacon, one for each of them. "Bon appétit!"

"Thank you," she said. "Lilly seems to have come out of her shell this morning."

"I give all credit to the chocolate." He winked.

"Mmm, you have found her weakness. She is a fiend for sweets."

"Aren't we all?" He slathered butter onto his pancakes. "What time did you want to head to the store?"

"I need to make up a list first, but it shouldn't take me long." After cutting into her pancake, she took a tentative bite. It was fluffy and sweet. "Did you need to run any other errands while we're out?"

"I guess I should pick up a paper to check out local rentals. But no, I don't need to visit any other stores right now. I'd just like to stock up the little fridge in the guest room and pick up some snacks."

"You realize you can search rentals on the internet, right?"

"That's true," Brad admitted. "I'm used to the housing office handling a lot of this. I'm out of my element."

"I can help you. If you like, there are quite a few apartment complexes near the city. Once Lilly is on the bus, I'll make my list and then we can go."

"That sounds like a plan."

"Oh," she said as she cut another piece of pancake. "I—uh—spoke to Lilly last night. You're welcome to come with us to find a tree tonight if you'd like." She pressed her lips together to hide a smile. "I hope you will because she's afraid we'll have to resort to a Charlie Brown tree otherwise. Apparently, I'm not strong enough for a full-size one."

Brad laughed. "Thank you. I'd love to join you." While wriggling his eyebrows, he lifted his arm, flexing his bicep, and she almost choked on her pancake. "I'm happy to bring some much-needed muscle to the situation."

They finished their breakfast in silence, which was only broken when Lilly returned with her backpack on and her brown hair in a ponytail. Shelly walked with her daughter to the door.

"Have a good day at school," she said as she hugged Lilly goodbye.

Lilly grimaced. "No promises."

After Lilly left, Shelly wandered back to the kitchen and was surprised that Brad had already cleared the table. "I'm happy to do the dishes since you cooked."

He glanced over his shoulder. "No worries, I got it. Go make your list."

Shelly decided not to argue so they could leave sooner and grabbed a pad of paper and a pen on her way back to the table. However, as she noted the usual items she bought for herself and Lilly, Shelly realized she did not know what sort of food Brad would prefer. He had enjoyed the dinner she'd made the previous evening, which meant it was a safe bet he was a fan of Italian.

As she pondered her recipes, it dawned on her she was assuming he would have dinner with them again. A tingling sensation swept up the back of her neck. *There I go again, thinking of him as more than a guest.*

She had told him breakfast was included, so, it was safe to at least start there with meal planning. Perhaps it would be prudent to plan for slightly larger dinners than she would normally cook for just herself and Lilly. That way, if he wanted to join them, there would be plenty to share and if he didn't, she and Lilly could enjoy leftovers. Satisfied this seemed the path of the least awkwardness, Shelly finished her list and lifted her head.

He was leaning against the doorjamb, drying the last of the dishes and watching her. The way his gaze moved over her made her self-conscious, and she smoothed her hair.

Her movement broke the spell he seemed to be under, and he smiled sheepishly. "Sorry, I guess I was lost in thought."

She held up the paper, hoping her hand wouldn't shake. "I've finished my list."

"Dishes are done. Are you ready to go?"

With a nod, she headed into the living room. She slid her feet into her shoes and reached for her coat, but Brad had already lifted it from its hook. He held it so she could slip her arms in; his chivalry surprised and pleased her.

As he settled the coat on her shoulders, his fingers brushed her neck, causing a spark of heat that sent goosebumps down her arms. She turned to thank him, and their eyes met. The air around them hummed with electricity as they gazed at each other, his fingers lingering on her skin. Her pulse quickened, and her breath hitched as the moment intensified.

Meow, Newton wailed. His furry face pressed between their shins, physically pushing them apart.

Brad laughed as he released her coat and bent down to pat Newton's head. "Do you need some attention, sir?"

Grateful for the distraction, Shelly worked to catch her breath. *What was that?* She shook her head to clear it.

Brad raised his head, his deep blue eyes twinkling. "Shall we?"

"Yes," she said, desperate to put some distance between them. "Let's go!" Keys in hand, she rushed out the door.

Once they were in the car, separated by the console, she relaxed. Whatever had taken over her in the house seemed to have dissipated. He didn't act like anything was amiss. Maybe she had imagined the intensity of the moment because she was lonely. She hadn't been attracted to anyone since Carl. She hadn't even been on a date!

Dismissing it as a weak moment, Shelly chocked it up to Brad being the first man she had spent any time with since the divorce.

On the short drive to the store, they talked more about their childhood, comparing notes on places they both frequented and people they knew. It amazed her that she had never met him before, as they had quite a few shared friends and experiences. She filled him in on the lives of many of the people with whom he had lost touch.

Eagle Harbor had gone all out for Christmas, as they did every year. The streetlights were wrapped with garland topped with little red bows. As they drove through the town square, she noted there were wreaths hanging on the doors of the local stores. She pointed to the Christmas tree being set up and decorated in the center of the square.

"The tree lighting is this Saturday," she said.

"It's a bit late in the season, isn't it? I thought most towns had their Christmas tree lightings right after Thanksgiving."

"The neighboring towns have already done theirs. We had a bit of a delay in getting our tree," she said. "But I figure, better late than never!"

She drove into the parking lot for Tidewater Grocery, which was rather busy for a Friday morning. The store had even wrapped red and white ribbon around the poles of the cart returns. Twinkling white lights bordered the windows and wreaths adorned every door.

"This is a much smaller town than I expected," he said, as they grabbed a cart before entering the store. "I expected this part of the state to be more congested and urban, but I guess you can find small towns anywhere."

"At least this one is closer to civilization than the ones we grew up in."

The inside of the store was decorated as well, with bows on the meat and deli cases, and jingle bells hanging off the freezer doors. Holiday carols wafted over the radio, and Shelly resisted the urge to hum along.

She and Brad shopped together, carefully separating their items in the shared cart. He remarked often on the things she placed on her side, asking what meals she made with the different ingredients and sharing some of his favorites.

Her concern about including him in meals with herself and her daughter dissipated. It was becoming more apparent he was thinking of his stay at her home as less of a paying guest and more of a friend. This pleased her, and she shared her dinner plans with enthusiasm, making mental adjustments based on his commentary and feedback.

"Good morning, Shelly!" the cashier, a plump elderly lady with braided gray cornrows, called as they approached the check-out line.

"Oh, hello, Donna. How's business?"

"Going well," Donna said as she began scanning their items. "But we're struggling to staff the store so close to the holidays, so I'm filling in." She gave Shelly a warm smile. "I'm glad to see you back in here. Home for Christmas, I hope?"

Shelly nodded. "Just got back in last night, but I'll be home until the new year."

"That's good to hear. And it's good to see you've moved on."

Donna inclined her head toward Brad, who paused in his work of placing items on the conveyor belt and looked up, an amused smile pulling on his lips.

Shelly's chest tightened and her throat went dry. "N-No! It's not— I mean—" Her stammering wasn't helping anything, and she stopped to take a breath. "Donna, this is Brad Collins. He just recently retired from the military and is renting a room from me for the holidays. Brad, this is Donna Sampson. She and her husband own the store."

Donna raised a skeptical eyebrow but took the explanation in stride. "Nice to meet you, Mr. Collins, and thank you for your service."

"Thanks, Donna. Nice to meet you as well." He gave a brief smile then turned back to the cart, but not before Shelly heard him chuckling softly.

"It's a shame about the pageant, isn't it?" Donna asked Shelly as she scanned another item.

"Lilly is disappointed." Shelly cast a sideways glance at Brad, but he didn't share his offer to fill in as the accompanist. Had he changed his mind?

Much to her relief, the rest of the transaction went forward with no further comments on her personal life. Maybe it was time to find a new place to shop. This was one detriment of living in a small town. Who knew what Donna would say if Brad joined Shelly every time she went shopping, or worse, what she would say when he got his own place and moved on? The last thought brought Shelly up short, like someone had punched her in the stomach.

Of course, he won't be here forever. She tried to shake off the morose feeling that had taken over her. *He's just staying with me until he secures a more permanent place.*

Yet even with the silent rebuke, she was overwhelmed by a sense of loss. She followed him back to her car, her steps slowing by the weight of her confusing emotions. Her feelings made little sense to her, as they'd just met, but perhaps they hinted at a deep-seated issue she had not wanted to acknowledge or address.

Carl's leaving had caused her to fear abandonment, and she had often needed to check herself to not become overly attached to the people in her life. Between her father's sudden death and the abrupt end of her marriage, she struggled with being deserted or rejected. Her relationships with her family were healthy, and she loved living in Eagle Harbor because she belonged and had found community there. Nevertheless, she attempted to maintain boundaries, both physical and emotional, to protect herself and her daughter from further heartbreak.

While she had only known Brad a short time, she had to admit his presence was touching her heart in ways she hadn't expected. It concerned her how quickly she was becoming attached to him. She tried to keep most new people, or at least, most men, at arm's length to protect herself from being hurt again, but Brad, whether he knew it, was overcoming a lot of her barriers. It was both scary and exhilarating, but the strength of her despair at the thought of him leaving rattled her.

She was quiet as they filled the trunk of her car with the groceries. They stopped at a few apartment complexes nearby, so he could inquire about vacancies, but Shelly tried to maintain a bit of distance from him. It wouldn't do her, or Lilly for that matter, any good for Shelly to become involved with someone new right now.

On the drive home, she worked to shake off the lingering sadness. Even once he left her home, that didn't necessarily mean he would leave her life. There was no reason they couldn't stay in contact and remain friends once he found a place of his own. Of course, it wouldn't be the same as having him living in her guest room, especially if he moved closer to the city, but it was better than nothing.

By the time they arrived back at the house, her mood had lightened, and she smiled at him as they unloaded the groceries. "I really appreciate all of your help."

His head shot up. "My help?"

"Shopping at the store, helping to unload the car, breakfast and the dishes this morning, offering to help with the pageant." Shelly ticked off the considerate things he had done for her in his short time at her home. A laugh bubbled up in her throat. "And not pressing charges for colliding with you!"

"Well, the statute of limitations hasn't run out on that last one yet. But in all seriousness, I'm happy to help. I like to be useful. Lilly gave me the sheet music for the pageant, and I plan to spend some time today going over it." He followed her into the house and set the bags down in the kitchen. "I hope I didn't make things awkward for you, though."

"Awkward?" Shelly asked, puzzled. "How would you have made things awkward?"

"At the store, with Donna?"

Heat rose in her face, and Shelly pivoted toward the counter to hide it. "Oh. That." Her fingers fumbled with the bags as she sorted through them. "I used to be more of a regular at the store when I was married, and I guess I got to know Donna pretty well. Her husband is also the mayor, so we see each other a lot at town events. She noticed when my visits became more sporadic and my groceries lighter, even though I never actually said anything. It didn't take long for word to spread about the divorce." She focused on unpacking the groceries and putting them away. "But you did nothing wrong. I honestly hadn't even considered how it might look to bring you until she started talking."

"I take it you haven't brought many other men grocery shopping with you?"

Her hand froze midway to a shelf. Was this his way of asking if she was dating anyone? Wary, she glanced at him. "I, uh, I don't normally have company when I go shopping, except Lilly."

"Then I'm honored." His blue eyes were sincere.

She resumed her work of restocking her kitchen, though her heartbeat irregularly in her chest. It was such a strange question to be asked, and yet, she couldn't shake the feeling there was a deeper meaning behind it and his response. Her head was spinning as she put the rest of the groceries away.

"I think I'll head back to my room and try to make heads or tails of the pageant music. Come and get me when Lilly gets home, and I'll be happy to play lumberjack." With a charming smile, Brad took his share of the groceries and headed back to his room, leaving Shelly to overthink their entire conversation.

Chapter Four

Brad climbed the stairs to his room, an amused smile still playing on his lips. The incident at the grocery store had caught him off guard as well, but Shelly's reaction was endearing. It didn't hurt to know she wasn't seeing anyone. Although they had known each other less than a day, he couldn't deny the connection he had with her, or the attraction growing inside of him.

She was a kind, thoughtful person. A little shy, perhaps, definitely guarded, but he understood her reasoning. From what he had gathered, the sudden end of her marriage had been quite a shock to both her and Lilly.

He set his groceries on the floor and began putting them away. There wasn't a lot of storage space, but he hadn't bought much. Just a few snacks and drinks to keep in the fridge. When he had stored everything, he walked over to his closet and pulled down his guitar.

The familiar weight in his hand brought back memories from his days in the service. He missed playing in a band. While he and his bandmates weren't very good as they'd struggled to find time to practice with their varying shifts, let alone perform gigs, he had spent some of the best nights of his life rocking out with his friends.

Setting the case on the bed, he opened it and removed the guitar. It was in good condition despite how long it had been since he last played. He sat on the edge of the bed and strummed the strings, wincing at how out of tune they were. While he didn't have a tuner in the case, he had previously found a decent app on his smart phone. Pulling it from his pocket, he flipped through his apps then clicked on the right one and began following the prompts.

Once he was finished, he picked up Lilly's music and set it on the bed beside him. Many of the songs were familiar carols. He messed up the fingering a few times, but as he continued to play, the rust seemed to fall off both his fingers and the guitar. It was like riding a bike.

In his mind, his old friend Howie crooned into the mic at some seedy bar in the town surrounding their base. His short blond hair and deep blue eyes had always been a hit with the ladies. Seth was behind them, banging away on the drums, his usually pale face red from the heat of the lights and the exertion. John stood beside Brad on the bass, his wide grin stretching across his face.

Brad missed them all. They followed each other on social media, but it had been years since they had jammed together. The others had left the service after their second tours, and everyone had gotten married except for Brad.

He snapped a picture of himself with the guitar. Not one for selfies, he wasn't sure if it was a good picture, but it got the point across. He shared it on social media and tagged the guys with a message remembering the good old days.

Pushing his memories from his mind, he set his phone down, picked up the sheet music again, and flipped back to the beginning. He played through the whole pageant once more and was pleased with his improved performance now that he'd shaken the dust off. It still wasn't quite to the standard he would have preferred, but it was a start. He'd give Lilly and Shelly a preview this evening to get their input, then maybe, with his help, the pageant could go on as planned.

~ * ~

Hours later, an engine roared beneath his window, followed by the distinct squeal of brakes. A peek outside confirmed Lilly's bus had arrived. She rushed across the street and up toward her house, a noticeable spring in her step. It was the start of her winter break, and he vaguely recalled his own joy at having time off from school.

He hadn't spent the whole day playing the guitar, as the calluses that had long since healed began to take shape on his fingertips again. Instead, he had reviewed his options for housing. There weren't many complexes nearby, but Shelly had been gracious enough to take him around to some earlier. The prices were decent, and some of them were within walking distance of a metro station. All of them had indicated they would have openings in the new year, which meant Brad wouldn't have to impose on Shelly's hospitality for too long.

Moments after Lilly arrived home, footsteps sounded on the stairs outside his apartment, then a soft knock came. He opened the door and greeted Shelly and Lilly with a wide grin.

"Are we ready to find a tree?"

Lilly nodded. "Grab your coat and let's go." She took off back down the stairs and stood waiting at the car, tapping her foot in impatience.

Brad glanced at Shelly. "Where did the shy, quiet girl of last night disappear to?"

"You won her over with your willingness to play lumberjack, or perhaps it was your pancakes," Shelly joked. They made their way to the car and climbed in.

"So, do you go to a tree lot or a farm?" he asked as he buckled his seatbelt.

Shelly stole a quick glance in the rearview mirror. "We usually go to a farm, but I want to leave that decision up to Lilly."

"Friendship Pine farm works for me," Lilly said. "You brought the handsaw, right, Mom?"

"It's in the trunk." They backed down the driveway and headed in the direction of the tree farm.

"Are we going to the tree lighting with Grandma and Aunt Susan?" Lilly asked as they drove through the heart of town.

"I haven't discussed it with them," Shelly said. "They're coming up this weekend to bake cookies, but they might stay a bit later than usual to go." Brad caught her glancing at him from the corner of his eye. "You're welcome to join us, if you'd like."

"I wouldn't want to impose." He twisted his hands together.

She shrugged. "It's no imposition. Besides, it would be a good way for you to see more of the town."

"Then I'd love to," he said with a smile.

As they drove away from the downtown area, the houses and stores grew sparse and were replaced by vast rolling hills. Plowed fields stretched as far as the eye could see, and fences housed grazing cattle. It was surprisingly rural, although they had just left the town square.

"I didn't realize you lived so close to farms," he said.

"It's wonderful, isn't it?" Shelly's green eyes lit up as she spoke. "We have all the conveniences in town, but wide-open spaces are a short drive away." As they drove, she pointed out the different farms. "The Henderson's have an apple orchard, and they put on a full fall festival in October. Over there, the Garretts have various berry picking throughout the spring and summer." They slowed as she made a right turn into a gravel driveway under a sign that said, "Friendship Pines." "And here we have the Montgomerys and their Christmas trees."

Brad swiveled his head back and forth, trying to take everything in, unconcerned with how childlike he appeared. Urban, suburban, and rural areas were usually well separated. How had he forgotten how much of Maryland held small towns in the middle of nowhere?

Once they parked, Lilly bolted from the car with enthusiasm, leaving Brad and Shelly to exchange an amused look in her absence before they climbed out after her. Shelly went to the trunk to retrieve the handsaw. They walked past an old barn as they headed into the forest of pines.

"Lilly, tell me how this works," Brad called, as Lilly had rushed ahead of them in her excitement. "Do you just pick whatever tree you want or are there rules?"

"The trees for sale are tagged," she said as she gestured to a yellow tag on a nearby tree. "You can only pick a tagged tree, and you cut it yourself. Then you go to the barn we passed on the way to pay."

"Do you have a specific type of tree you like?"

"Big ones! At least six feet tall!" Lilly held her arms high above her head in demonstration.

"We prefer Fraser or Douglas firs," Shelly clarified. "Which are over there." She gestured to a field down a sloping hill.

They headed in the direction she indicated; their footsteps quieted by fallen pine needles blanketing the ground. Brad breathed deeply, inhaling the fresh, woodsy scent of the evergreens. His warm breath puffed against the chill as the sun set on the horizon, turning the sky above a dizzying array of purple, pink, and red.

When they reached the field with their choice of trees, Lilly charged ahead again without them. Her eyebrows drew together as she scrutinized the options, and he hid a smile. He'd never seen someone stare intently at an evergreen before.

"Is she always so intense about trees?" he stage-whispered to Shelly.

Her responding laugh warmed his insides. "She can be picky, that's for sure. I think some of that is genetic. We have a few perfectionists in my family."

"What exactly is she looking for?" Brad asked. "Does she have certain criteria the tree must meet?"

"Hm" Shelly tapped her chin. "She likes tall ones, as I'm sure you've gathered, but we have a lot of ornaments, and we'll need one with plenty of branches to hold them all."

"Do you have any say?" He raised his eyebrow.

Shelly shook her head; her pained expression caught him off-guard. "No, she and her father used to pick the tree together." Her voice had taken on a wistful quality. "Most of the time, they were in sync, but there were a few years where they couldn't agree, and I had to be the tiebreaker."

"That doesn't sound like a fun role to play."

"It wasn't all bad." She shrugged one shoulder. "Honestly, their choices were practically identical. I tried to be fair."

Ahead of them, Lilly had stopped short in front of a tree. She stepped back, and the narrowing of her eyes told him she was assessing it as an option. As she circled it, Brad noticed a little frown on her face, and he bit back a laugh at her concentration.

"Have you found something, Lilly?" he called.

"I think so." Lilly dashed back to meet them. Her hands grasped each of their wrists and she yanked them forward. "Come see."

"Wow!" Shelly's exclamation was filled with awe. "Did you find the biggest one they have?"

"Not the biggest, but probably pretty close." Lilly's chest lifted with obvious pride. "There's a few scraggly branches on the bottom, but otherwise, this one is perfect."

Brad took in the tree. It was well over the six-foot height requirement and full of thick, sturdy branches. With one hand he shook the trunk a bit, assessing the needles. Few fell to the forest floor.

"I hope you maintain these standards as you age," he muttered under his breath, low enough so Lilly wouldn't hear, but Shelly clapped a hand over her mouth and choked back a laugh.

She walked to the trunk, and he followed her, taking one end of the handsaw. Together they cut down the tree, aiming it to the wide row between the trees to avoid knocking over any others. They also took off the branches Lilly didn't like, and soon they were hauling it across the farm.

Despite her assessment of her mother, Shelly could hold her own in carrying the tree. She took the top while he hefted the trunk, but he didn't feel like he was carrying more than his share. When they arrived back at the barn, an employee helped Brad wrap the tree in netting for easier transport.

"Can we buy some ornaments while we're here?" Lilly asked.

"New ornaments?" Shelly's eyebrows pulled together. "What's wrong with the ones we have?"

Lilly shuffled her feet and stared down at the ground. Sensing this was going to be an uncomfortable conversation, he hoisted the netted tree on his own. "Here's the tag for the tree. I'll load it onto the car."

~ * ~

Once Brad was gone, Shelly put a hand on Lilly's arm. "Which ornaments don't you want to use?"

"The ones I made for Dad," she said, her shoulders dropping. "Your anniversary ones. Stuff like that."

Shelly's heart fractured anew for her daughter. Maybe picking a tree had been a bad idea. The last thing she wanted to do was bring Lilly more pain.

Lilly raised her head and met Shelly's gaze briefly before

scowling. "Let's just see what they have." Before Shelly could respond, she rushed off into the barn.

Shelly trailed after her, her stomach fluttering. Sometimes Lilly's mood swings gave Shelly whiplash. One moment, Lilly seemed close to tears, and the next, she was annoyed or angry. It was difficult to make heads or tails of her emotions most days.

When they arrived at the barn, Lilly began digging through the lovely handmade ornaments for sale. Shelly had to admit Lilly had a point. The idea of decorating the tree with sore reminders of her failed marriage left a bad taste in her mouth. Besides, she had told Lilly they would make new memories this year, and what better way to do that than to start fresh with some new decorations?

They chose a dozen different ones before they went to pay for them and the tree. By the time they were walking to the car, Lilly was smiling again, and the bounce had returned to her step. Brad had expertly mounted their Douglas fir on the top of Shelly's SUV, and Lilly's eyes lit up at the sight. Shelly decided in that moment to let go of her preconceived notions of what was right for Lilly and instead to follow her daughter's lead, allowing Lilly to heal in her own way.

As they drove home, dusk took over and the twinkling lights on the storefront and homes of their friends and neighbors accented their drive back. Shelly loved the way the town lit up for Christmas. It was like a bright star on a dreary winter's night, enveloping everyone who saw it in a warm, loving embrace. She hadn't realized how much she needed that warmth until now, but as she maneuvered through the darkening streets, a welcome peace settled into her bones. While the decorations at the airport had only served as a harsh reminder of what she had lost, somehow the lights of Eagle Harbor provided a sense of hope.

The feeling of hope dissipated as they parked in the driveway of the only dark house on the street. Shelly suppressed a sigh as she surveyed her home. If only she had found some time earlier in the month to decorate.

Brad climbed out of the car, and together they carefully extracted the tree from the roof, placing it in the garage until they were ready to bring it inside. Lilly brought in their new ornaments and grabbed a few boxes of other decorations as she entered the house. They set up the tree stand in front of the bay window, moving the coffee table back a few feet to allow plenty of room for the tree to expand.

Shelly brought the tree in with Brad and there was a lot of laughing and bumping as they struggled to fit the monstrosity through the door of the house. Under Lilly's direction, they set it in the stand and rotated it until she was satisfied with its placement. Shelly held the tree steady while Brad secured it. They all stepped back to survey their handiwork. Full, deep green branches almost completely obscured the windows, and the scent of fresh pine filled the room.

"We should let it settle before we decorate," Shelly said.

Brad nodded. "We need to water it too."

"I'll show you where the watering can is, then I'll get started on dinner." She led him into the garage.

"I see Lilly convinced you to buy some new ornaments," he said, as she rummaged through the shelves.

"She had a point," she said simply. She pulled the watering can from behind a box of Halloween decorations and handed it to him. "There's a box of décor, including the lights, in the living room. Feel free to go through it with Lilly."

They went back into the house, and he headed to the sink to fill the watering can while Shelly removed a package of beef from the fridge and set the oven to preheat. Her mind wandered as she stabbed two potatoes with a fork.

The trip to the tree farm had brought back painful memories and served as a bitter reminder it had been almost a year since Carl left. Despite the passage of time, she remembered the events of the day clearly.

It was the day after Christmas. She and Carl were fighting in the kitchen, trying to keep their voices down so Lilly wouldn't hear. Shelly had spent Christmas day alone, as he had taken Lilly to his mother's. Her mother-in-law, Cindy, had never been Shelly's biggest fan, and last year, she had just been too tired to deal with the covert insults and mind games. So, she had claimed a migraine and told them to go on without her. The next day, she discovered his secretary, Deborah, was there. Shelly had suspected Carl was having an affair, but this was the unwelcome confirmation she'd been avoiding.

As she roasted the onions and garlic in a skillet on the stove, she replayed the argument in her head. Their marriage had been falling apart for years, but this was the final straw. Shelly had confronted him, and he hadn't even bothered to deny it. However, the thing that upset her the most was, not only did he bring his mistress to a family Christmas, he involved their daughter in the affair by asking Lilly not to tell Shelly Deborah had joined them.

Shelly shook her head as she slid the skillet off the burner and set it aside to cool. After placing the ground beef in a large bowl, she dumped breadcrumbs, cheese, and the rest of the ingredients on top before plunging her hands in to mix them together, using more force than necessary.

Lilly let it slip during an otherwise benign conversation. It was kind of funny, in a weird way. Cindy usually had Christmas dinner catered, but this year, someone had brought a homemade apple pie.

When Shelly had jokingly asked who had committed such a faux pas, Lilly blurted out Deborah's name. It was only when Lilly's cheeks flushed, and her teeth gnawed on her bottom lip Shelly realized this was meant to be a secret. Carl had come into the room, and she struggled to keep her composure as she asked Lilly to go upstairs. She'd intended for Lilly to go to her room, but later learned Lilly sat on the stairs and heard the whole thing.

The worst part? Had Carl not kept it a secret Deborah was there; Shelly might have remained in the dark about the affair. He owned a small law firm with a few other partners, and he was always bringing someone from the office to holiday gatherings.

Shelly huffed in frustration as she scraped the roasted onions and garlic from the skillet into the bowl and kneaded them into the meat mixture. When it was well combined, she pressed the meatloaf into a ball and placed it into the pan. She slid the pan into the oven and slammed the door. As she washed her hands, she tried to push the awful memory from her mind. This was no time to let the ghosts of Christmas past darken her holiday present.

As she came back into the family room, she stopped short. Lilly knelt on the floor and stared at two stockings with a frown.

"What's wrong?" she asked.

Lilly held up the stockings, one in each hand. "There's only two. Did Daddy take his?"

Brad had started to walk over to them but stopped at the boxes of decorations. Instead, he busied himself by removing the ornaments and organizing them into separate piles.

Shelly shifted uncomfortably. "No. I put it in another box of his things this afternoon. I didn't think you'd want to see it, and after your request to buy new ornaments, I thought I made the right decision."

"You're right, I don't want to see it. I was just surprised." Lilly stood and went to the railing of the stairs where they always hung their stockings. "But it's uneven with just two."

"Maybe we can find something to fill the space when we go Christmas shopping later this weekend," Shelly said. "Dinner is in the oven and should be ready soon." Her gaze swept over the piles Brad had made of their ornaments. "Is there any rhyme or reason to your organizing?"

"Not really, but I separated everything that I thought was

homemade. I figure you two can determine what goes on the tree and what doesn't." He opened a different box. "Ah, and I assume these are the lights for the tree. Do you have a separate box for outdoor decorations?"

"That one." Lilly pointed at an unopened box closest to the door. "But we can wait until tomorrow to put those up. As long as they're up before Grandma gets here."

"Why do they need to be up before she arrives?" he asked.

"Because she likes to fix them." Lilly shook her head.

"Fix them?"

Shelly nodded and sighed. "My mother is a bit of a perfectionist."

"Is that where you get your Christmas tree scrutiny from?" He raised an eyebrow.

"Maybe. But it paid off in the end." Lilly gestured triumphantly to the tree.

Brad plugged in the lights to test them, then began wrapping them around the tree with Lilly's help. Shelly perched on the red couch as they passed the lights back and forth until they neared the top where Lilly couldn't reach. Under her direction, Brad finished placing the lights, and they both stepped back to admire his work.

"That looks really beautiful," Shelly said before going back to the kitchen to set the table.

A few minutes later, the oven timer beeped, and she removed the meatloaf and baked potatoes from the oven, setting them on the counter. As she let the meat rest, she threw a bag of green beans into the microwave to steam.

Once everything was ready, she brought it into the dining room. "Dinner's ready."

Lilly entered the dining room and sniffed the air. "Smells great, Mom."

As they sat to eat, Brad's eyebrows pulled down over his eyes as he surveyed the table. Lilly had a serving of meatloaf and green beans on her plate, but only he and Shelly had foil wrapped baked potatoes.

"Did you not have enough potatoes to go around? I'm happy to forego mine or split it with you so Lilly can have one."

"Lilly doesn't like potatoes," Shelly said.

"Doesn't like potatoes?" He gasped, putting a hand to his heart. "My Irish ancestors would be greatly offended to hear such a thing."

Warning bells began sounding in Shelly's head as a quick glance at Lilly told her this conversation was sounding all too familiar. There had been many arguments over dinners when Carl was still there. He was raised with multiple siblings and while food wasn't exactly scarce, it was never wasted.

Sometimes, his family would have leftovers for days until they consumed every morsel, or so he insisted to Shelly and Lilly. As a result, he often made sarcastic remarks about Lilly's picky eating or would yell at her if she didn't finish her dinner. She had confided in Shelly after he left how much worse those dinner time battles were when she was on a flight. Lilly went to bed many nights in tears because of his angry tirades about food.

"I've learned over the years not to serve certain things to avoid creating waste as Lilly will not eat them, and I don't believe in forcing her." Shelly worked to keep herself calm and shared a meaningful glance with Lilly.

"Potatoes are good for you," Brad continued, oblivious to the growing tension in the room. "They have fiber and potassium, which are both essential nutrients for a healthy body."

The tone was different, and he certainly wasn't threatening, but the words were like Carl's, and the flush that crept over Lilly's cheeks confirmed her daughter had a thin grasp on her self-control.

"She gets those nutrients through other foods she doesn't have such strong aversions to." Shelly wracked her brain for a way to diffuse the situation. "Everyone has foods they don't like despite their health benefits. I'm not a fan of oranges, even though I know they're an excellent source of vitamin C."

"Maybe if you made them in different ways," Brad said, almost as if Shelly hadn't spoken. "Mash them up with some cheese or roast them with garlic and onions." He winked at Lilly. "We might get you to like them yet."

"You don't know anything!" she lashed out. "What I eat and what I don't eat is none of your business." The chair fell back as she shoved away from the table and stormed up the stairs, slamming her door.

He turned wide eyes to Shelly. "What did I say?"

With a few deep breaths, she managed to keep a firm grasp on her own temper. He meant well, but he failed to see the minefield he'd set off.

"It's a sore subject," she said, hoping he wouldn't press.

"I'm sorry," he murmured. "I didn't know."

"There's no reason you would." She set her napkin on the table and pushed her chair back. "I'll go talk to her."

"Maybe I should." He stood as well. "I want to apologize."

She held up her hand. "Just… stay here. Her room is her

sanctuary, and if you go in there uninvited, it'll only make things worse." His face crumpled, and a stab of sympathy hit her chest. "I'll see if I can convince her to rejoin us. It'll probably go over better if we give her a moment to calm down."

He nodded and sank back into his chair. She went up the stairs and tapped on Lilly's door. A muffled reply, which didn't sound like "go away," came from within, and Shelly opened the door.

Lilly was sitting on her bed with her head bowed and her hands clasped in front of her, looking every bit like the cowed child Shelly recalled after Carl's tirades. Shelly's heart broke for the second time that night. Without a moment of hesitation, she went and sat on the bed, sliding an arm around Lilly's shoulders.

"I'm sorry that happened," Shelly said. "I should have told Brad to butt out before it went that far."

Lilly's head shot up. "You mean you're not mad?"

"Of course not," she said. "Your food choices are nobody's business but yours. So you don't like potatoes. Big deal. You love bananas, and those have a lot of the same nutrients."

"But I yelled at a guest."

"Who was being kind of a jerk about something he had no right to comment on." Shelly placed her hand under Lilly's chin and lifted it. "I believe he meant well, and obviously he's not aware of the history, but it's still not okay for him to comment on your diet. He realizes that and wants to apologize to you whenever you're ready to come back downstairs."

With a sniffle, Lilly wiped her eyes. Shelly handed her a tissue from the box by the bed. They sat together in silence for a moment, broken occasionally by Lilly sniffling and hiccupping as her tears subsided. Shelly gave her shoulders one last squeeze before she stood and stepped toward the door to give Lilly some space.

"Let me wash my face, then I'll come back down," Lilly said as she crumpled the tissue in her hand.

"Take all the time you need," Shelly told her with a gentle smile. "We're not going anywhere."

When she came back into the dining room, Shelly was surprised Brad had covered their plates with aluminum foil. He was sitting with his elbows on the table and his forehead resting on his clasped hands. Bracing herself, she sank into her chair.

"She'll be back down in a minute," she said.

He gave a solemn nod. "I tried to keep the food warm."

"I appreciate that." Her eyes narrowed as she debated her next words. "Listen, I know you meant well, but in the future, please don't comment on how I parent my daughter."

"I was just trying to help," he protested with a frown. "I crossed a line, and I didn't mean to upset either of you."

"I understand, and I should have said something sooner to stop the conversation. But I need you to recognize there are some deep-seated issues here that can't be fixed with simple suggestions." She raised an eyebrow. "I suspect you're used to fixing things."

Brad ducked his head. "Is it that obvious?"

A laugh bubbled up in her throat. "A little."

Footsteps on the stairs interrupted their conversation, and she held her breath as Lilly entered the dining room. Brad straightened in his chair and waited until she had sat back down before he spoke.

"I'm sorry, Lilly. I had no right to comment on your food preferences," he said. "You know, I was a bit of a picky eater myself when I was a kid. I had to get over it when I joined the military. They don't have many options for food in the mess hall on base. But I understand where you're coming from." He gave her a lopsided grin. "Personally, I'm not a fan of Brussel sprouts."

"Have you tried smothering them in cheese?" she retorted, throwing his own words back at him.

"Fair question," he admitted. "But I doubt it would help."

"I'm sorry too," she said as she removed the foil from her plate. "It's not the first time someone has commented on my pickiness, and I guess it just touched a nerve."

"I can understand that." He looked at Shelly and Lilly in turn. "I want you to know, I appreciate how welcoming you both have been to me. But if I do something wrong or overstep, please tell me so I can make it right."

Shelly nodded and glanced at Lilly, who gave him a tentative smile. They ate in silence for a moment as the tension in the room dissipated.

"I meant to tell you earlier, but I spent some time this afternoon playing your pageant music on my guitar." Brad cut into his potato.

"Really?" Lilly's dark brown eyes lit up as her earlier outburst was forgotten. "Do you think you can do it?"

"I'm happy to try," he said.

"I'll call Mr. Ryan, the director, and ask if he thinks it's plausible," Shelly offered, passing Brad the butter. "I can't promise he'll be amenable to it, since you only have a couple of days to rehearse."

"It's worth a shot." Lilly shrugged. She glanced at Shelly. "Can we still decorate the tree tonight?"

"Of course we can if you're up for it."

"Will you still help us?" Lilly directed this question to Brad, and the tension in Shelly's shoulders relaxed.

"If you want me to." He smiled.

Lilly nodded, and they quickly finished eating. Brad and Shelly cleared the table while Lilly headed toward the family room. She had only walked a few steps when she stopped short in front of the stairs.

Shelly was coming behind her and almost ran into her. "Lilly, what—"

"Newton, no!"

Chapter Five

Brad was filling the sink with water when Lilly cried out. His military instincts kicked in as he rushed to the doorway of the kitchen just as a blur of gray fur launched off the couch into the Christmas tree. The tree swayed erratically with the momentum. Newton's howls ripped through the air as he dug his claws into a branch, his lower body dangling beneath him.

Shelly and Lilly stood, frozen with shock, at the bottom of the stairs. Brad shoved past the transfixed mother and daughter and rushed forward. One hand grasped the trunk, but it wasn't enough to stop the violent shaking of the tree caused by the suspended cat. He gripped the tree with both hands and worked to steady it. Shelly and Lilly shook off their trance and raced over. While Lilly grabbed Newton's swinging body, Shelly worked to coax his claws free from the bark. Newton hissed and growled in fear as they lifted him from the branch. Shelly and Lilly narrowly avoided being mauled by his flailing hind legs.

"Are you okay, little Newton?" Once he was free of the tree, Lilly pulled him against her chest, tucking his frantic, grasping paws into the thick fabric of her sweater and cuddled him. He made a few feeble attempts to escape as he appeared worn out from his adventure. After several additional whines, he relaxed into her, purring in surrender.

"At least we hadn't decorated it yet," Brad said as he checked to make sure no lights were broken. "But we should cat proof it before we put any ornaments on. Do you have something I can use to anchor it?"

Shelly went to grab fishing line and metal hooks. Together, she and Brad tied the line around the trunk and installed the metal hooks into the walls in the two back corners of the room, then tied the ends of the fishing line to the hooks. Once he was confident the tree wasn't going anywhere, he turned as Lilly leaned over, studying the separated ornaments, the cat nowhere to be seen. She seemed to avoid the handmade pile, and he imagined her emotions were still pretty raw from the confrontation earlier.

"We can sort through those later," Shelly said, placing a hand on Lilly's shoulder. "Want to help me call Mr. Ryan?"

She nodded, and they sat on the worn-out red couch while Shelly dialed the director's number on speakerphone. Brad went back to the kitchen to finish the dishes but could overhear bits and pieces of the conversation. The director sounded enthusiastic, which Brad took as a good sign. It wasn't a long conversation, and he made quick work of the dishes so he could learn the verdict on his offer.

"The director told me to thank you profusely for saving the town's pageant," Shelly said when he joined them. "He was wondering if you would be at the Christmas tree lighting tomorrow as the children are supposed to perform a song, and he thought it would be a good chance to hear how you sound together."

"That sounds like a plan, and I'm happy to help," he said with a smile. "Are we ready to trim this tree?"

Shelly and Lilly nodded and stepped over to the piles of ornaments he had set up. He walked over to the back of the tree and bent down.

"What are you doing?" Shelly's voice startled him as he reached to unplug the lights.

He glanced up at her, drawing his brows together. "I thought we'd decorate the tree with the lights off, then flip them on for a big reveal when we're done."

"My mom is very particular about her decorating," Lilly scoffed. "She has a thing about not putting ornaments and lights of the same color next to each other. It gives the wrong *aesthetic*." Her fingers curled as she put air quotes around the last word, and Shelly playfully swatted at her.

"Really?" he asked, surveying Shelly. "Grandma is not the only perfectionist, I see."

"I'm not a perfectionist!" she protested. "I just prefer to decorate the tree with the lights on." She picked up a box of blue ornaments and hung them on the tree, avoiding the blue lights. With a mischievous grin at Lilly, Brad stealthily unplugged the cord, plunging the tree into darkness. Shelly cocked her head in bewilderment before she saw the cord in his hand.

Lilly burst into giggles. "That was priceless!"

"Ha, ha," Shelly said, her voice edged with sarcasm. "Everyone has their quirks."

He laughed and plugged the lights back in before turning to her and patting her shoulder. "I'm glad I know one of yours now."

"We need music!" Lilly raced off.

Shelly frowned after her, but he shrugged. "It seems appropriate to have holiday music playing while decorating the tree."

A moment later, the beginning notes of "The First Noel" played. He and Shelly each picked a new box of ornaments and began hanging them together, stepping around each other in a delicate dance. When he noticed Lilly wasn't with them, he searched the room behind them. She was standing by the stairs, watching their progress with her face partially hidden by her long brown hair.

Shelly glanced over her shoulder. "Lilly? Aren't you going to help decorate?"

Her mother's voice seemed to break her from her trance, and she came over, picking up another box of four ornaments, shaped like various pieces of fruit.

"Are you sure you want to put that there?" Shelly asked Brad.

He paused and pulled his arm back. "Is there something wrong with this spot?"

As Lilly came around the tree, she laughed. "Oh, Brad. Did you miss the red light?"

"But the red light is below the branch where I'm going to hang my ornament!"

"True, but the bauble is long enough it will hang over the light," Shelly pointed out.

"Forget perfectionist," he muttered. "You're obsessed."

Lilly bit her lips to suppress a giggle and gestured to an empty spot on the tree. "If you hang it there, you'll save her the necessity of moving it later."

He shook his head. "Is she like this about anything else, or just Christmas trees?"

With a thoughtful expression, she tapped her finger on her chin. "Hm, her spice cabinet is pretty organized."

Shelly was glaring at both. "There's nothing wrong with wanting things a certain way."

"There is when you go back and redecorate the tree after we leave," Lilly said.

Brad chuckled as he stepped back and surveyed their handiwork. They had hung all the ornaments, and the twinkling of the décor momentarily dazzled him. "All we need now is a tree topper."

"It's here." Shelly removed a small gift box containing a lighted silver star.

"Who does the honors?" He gazed back and forth between Lilly and Shelly.

Lilly clasped her hands to her chest. "When I was little, my dad would hoist me up on his shoulders, and I would place the star." With a wistful sigh, she glanced down at herself. "I'm afraid I'm a bit too big for that now."

"We have a step stool in the garage," Shelly said, then turned a critical eye to the towering evergreen. "Although, even with it, you might not be tall enough to reach the top of *this* tree."

"Then Brad should do the honors." Lilly waved her hand toward the tree.

"I suspect even I will need a bit of height," he said. "It's got to be at least a foot taller than me!"

Shelly retrieved the stool and set it up for him, then stepped back to put her arm around her daughter. With careful movements, he placed the star on the sturdy top branch and plugged it in. He climbed back down and came to stand beside them. The room was quiet as they took in the tree in its full splendor.

"Well, team," he said, breaking the silence. "We did a great job!"

"It's perfect." Lilly covered her mouth to stifle a yawn.

"We finished just in time for you to get ready for bed," Shelly said, giving Lilly's shoulders a squeeze. She nodded and hugged her mom before heading up the stairs.

Brad began putting the empty ornament boxes back into the container. For once, Shelly didn't protest his help and instead sank into the couch, rubbing her temples. When he had finished packing everything up, he sat next to her. "Long day, huh?"

"Longer than expected, that's for sure." She sighed. "Thank you for cleaning up the debris."

"My pleasure." Lilly's phone was still connected to the speaker and "I'll be Home for Christmas" played. "I love this song, though it's bittersweet."

"Because you haven't had a home for Christmas?"

"Well, yes," he said, staring at the tree. "However, the lyrics aren't really promising the singer will be home for Christmas. He mentions at the end how he'll only be home in his dreams. For me, home isn't about a specific place, but more about the people who make it a home." He turned toward her. "My parents are gone and, as I told you before, my sister and I aren't close. So my home for Christmas is truly in my dreams, because it doesn't exist anymore."

Shelly's eyes softened, and she took his hand. "I hadn't thought of it that way."

"It's not your fault, and I'm not surprised." He gave her a half smile and patted her hand before letting go. "Leave it to me to turn a lovely Christmas song into something depressing."

"But you're right, it is kind of a sad song."

"Perhaps we can make it happier." He stood, then performed a slight bow and offered her his hand. "Would you like to dance?"

She raised her eyebrows dubiously, but she accepted his hand, and he pulled her to her feet. They faced each other, both unmoving, until Brad brought her closer to him and placed his free hand on her waist. Her hand rested on his shoulder as they swayed together to the beat.

She was soft and warm in his arms, and he detected the faint scent of cinnamon and something floral. As they turned in the limited space of the room, he was reminded of earlier that morning when he helped her into her coat. The way his fingers tingled when they touched her skin. He recalled how the look in her eyes made his heart stop. Now, his heart was pounding, and the air seemed to hum with electricity, just like that morning.

He directed her to twirl, then caught her at the waist. This time, she was close enough to rest her head on his chest as they continued to sway. He tightened his arm around her and wished this could last forever. For reasons he couldn't quite explain, it felt like they had known each other for years, instead of only one day.

The song's last notes played, and they stopped swaying in the sudden silence. When she gazed up at him, her emerald eyes were sparkling. She was absolutely radiant, the happiest he had seen her since they met. He released her waist, but he held onto her hand.

With a smile, he brought her hand to his lips and kissed it in what he hoped was a gentleman-like way. "Thank you for the dance."

Shelly averted her gaze. "You're a wonderful dancer."

"My mother loved to dance, and my father had two left feet, so I was often her partner."

The bathroom door opened upstairs, and Brad discreetly stepped away from Shelly as Lilly came down to say good night. The last thing he wanted to do was upset Lilly when it was clear she was still coming to terms with her parents' divorce. Shelly and Lilly shared a warm embrace and then, to his surprise, Lilly came over to him.

"Goodnight," she said. She shifted her weight from foot to foot as she stared up at him, like she was unsure if they should hug.

"'Night, Lilly." He held his fist out, and she bumped it with her own, an amused grin on her face. "See you in the morning."

After she left, Shelly glanced at him. "Are you heading back to your room?" There was something in her voice that made him wonder if she was hoping he would say no.

"That depends."

"On?"

"I know you've had a pretty eventful day. If you're tired, I can take a hint." He gauged her reaction and was rewarded with a sweet smile. "But if you don't mind, I'd be happy to hang out here a bit longer. Maybe we could share childhood memories over a glass of wine?"

She nodded. "I'd like that. Are you a red or white kind of guy?"

"I enjoy both. Whatever you have works for me."

"Okay, why don't you have a seat, and I'll bring us each a glass?"

He went back to sit on the couch. Though he stared at the tree, his thoughts were on Shelly. It seemed the more time he spent with her, the more he wanted to know her. Aside from his misstep at dinner, he hadn't regretted a moment of the day with this mother-daughter duo. He also couldn't deny the growing affection he had for Shelly, especially after their dance.

When he made plans to come back to Maryland for Christmas to prepare for his job, he had expected a very lonely holiday of takeout dinners and apartment hunting. Instead, he found himself warmly welcomed into their home, lives, and traditions.

Shelly reappeared with two glasses of red wine and handed one to him before taking a seat on the couch. They were both silent and he enjoyed how companionable it was, despite how short a time they'd known each other.

"What do you remember of your time in Southern Maryland, before your parents passed away?" she asked.

"It took a really long time to get anywhere a teenager would want to go."

She laughed. "That's true, but that's not what I meant."

"I know," he said, then contemplated his next words. "Despite the limitations on activities, I remember enjoying growing up in that area. There was plenty of room to run around, and we lived close to the river." He took a sip of wine before continuing. "My parents were very active, and they liked to take us to historical sites. I remember going to visit a lot of places on your side of the river: St. Mary's City, Sotterley Plantation. On my side of the river, we'd go to Solomon's Island and Chesapeake Beach. I loved being near the water."

"I only went to historical sites on field trips through school." Her lips twisted.

"You're not alone there," he said. "But I enjoyed going. My father was a big history buff, and I loved learning from him."

"What did your parents do?"

"My dad worked for the federal government, and my mom was a teacher." He lowered his eyes. "They were coming home from an event where my mother was recognized as a finalist for the teacher of the year award when they were in a head-on collision." His voice cracked and he took a deep breath. "The driver of the other car had fallen asleep at the wheel and crossed into their lane."

"That's awful," she murmured. "It must have been hard to lose them both suddenly and unexpectedly."

"It was. I had already flirted with the idea of joining the military, though my mother had tried to encourage me to attend college instead. Their deaths solidified my decision."

"Where were you stationed?"

"Oh, all over." He raised his head and smiled. "The last station was at Camp Lejeune, in Jacksonville, North Carolina. I was in IT, and I worked at various bases throughout the U.S. as well as internationally. I was deployed several times."

"That sounds exciting and adventurous, though I'm sure at times it was dangerous." Shelly sipped her wine. "Do you think you'll miss the marines?"

"I'm sure I will. The Corps was my life for many years." Brad set down his glass on the coffee table. "But I was ready to move on. I loved my time in the Marines and the bonds I formed. However, sometimes it was incredibly lonely and isolating. Right after my parents died, it was a needed and welcome distraction, and it helped me to grow up quickly. As the years went on, I suspect I kept re-enlisting because I was afraid I couldn't hack civilian life. I heard stories from my friends about people who had families while serving and struggled in the civilian world after being discharged. They ended up re-enlisting, either to the Marines or another branch. I didn't have a family, and I probably would have been all right, but the military gives its members and their families a lot of financial benefits they would not receive as a civilian, like housing assistance. It's hard, and it's not a life for everyone, but the transition out can be brutal."

He picked up his glass swirling the wine. "Making it to retirement was a good move for me as I have that to fall back on in case I struggle with civilian life. But I have a great job lined up, still in IT, and—" he leaned toward her. "I have at least one friend."

She smiled, clinking her glass with his. "That you do."

"What was lifelike for you, growing up? You said you lost your father."

"He was a Marine himself," Shelly said. "He was stationed at the Patuxent Naval Air Station, or PAX, as it is more commonly known, in the Marine Aviation Detachment and was killed on deployment." She took a shaky breath, and he imagined it was hard for her to talk about.

"I didn't realize he served as well," he murmured.

"It's not something I discuss often. Of course, we knew the risks of deployment, but I never imagined he would die so suddenly. Somehow, children always think of their parents as invincible. I was only eight, and to me, he was a superhero with fatigues instead of a cape." She paused and cleared her throat. Her eyelids fluttered, and Brad worried she was on the verge of tears. Before he could change the subject, she continued, "It was hard for the first few years. My mom had stayed home with us, but she went back to work within a year after his death. She ended up commuting to DC, and we remained in the area. I suppose we could have moved closer to the city, but my mom didn't want to cause any more upheaval in our lives."

He was quiet as this information sunk in, surprised to learn they shared a deeper connection than just growing up in the same area. She understood military life in a way few other civilians could.

While the military had never stationed him at PAX, Brad was familiar with the base and recognized her father probably believed it would be a relatively safe and secure location to finish out his last few years. Yet, every Marine knew the possibilities and remained mission ready regardless of their current duty station or circumstances. She hadn't said how long he had served before his death, but based on her age at the time, Brad assumed her father had been in for a long time.

"I'm glad I had my dad for as long as I did, and I appreciate my family so much more because of that loss," she said, interrupting his thoughts. She shook her head. "It's why I struggle with my ex-husband's complete abandonment of Lilly. I understand why he left me, and I honestly don't hold it against him he fell in love with someone else. But Lilly…" Her eyes filled with unshed tears. "I just couldn't imagine not maintaining a relationship with my own flesh and blood, let alone my child."

"Is he close to the rest of his family?"

She frowned. "You know, now that you mention it, no. He had a weird relationship with his siblings and his mother. His father wasn't around while he was growing up." Her eyes closed for a moment, and Brad wondered if she was fighting against some emotion. But they were clear when she reopened them. "I guess he learned how to be an absentee father from him."

"As I told you, I'm not close with my sister, but I regret that distance, and I am hoping to change it, especially now I'll have a more predictable work schedule." He swallowed the last of his wine. "But I would hope, if I had children, I wouldn't have a strained relationship with them."

"Did you, uh, did you ever want to have children of your own?" Shelly lowered her gaze as she asked the question.

"I considered it when I was younger, but the longer I stayed in the military, the more unlikely it became." He searched her face. "But I suspect that's not really what you're asking."

Her cheeks warmed to a pink hue. "It is part of what I was asking."

"And the other part?"

She started fiddling with a string on the couch and refused to meet his eyes. Her shyness was endearing, and he debated whether to prolong her obvious discomfort or put her out of her misery. He bit back a laugh and opened his mouth to respond when she raised her gaze to meet his.

"What I-I mean is, was there ever anyone special you maybe wanted to have children with?"

Brad smiled at the hesitant way she phrased the question. "Not really. I dated a few women, only one seriously, but it never went anywhere."

He didn't want to put her on the spot, but at the same time, he ached to learn the reason she asked. Something was growing between them, but he was treading a fine line because of Shelly's situation. She was not simply a single, attractive woman; she was a single mother, which made her part of a package. The last thing he wanted to do was upset the delicate balance she and Lilly had created since her ex left.

"But that's not to say I wouldn't be open to something serious in the future," he said when she didn't respond.

Shelly shifted away from him. Worried he'd overstepped again, he hurried to explain. "I know we just met, and I'm not trying to take advantage of you or your hospitality." He took a breath, trying to find the words to say how he was feeling. "I just want you to know that, besides appreciating everything you've done for me, I also enjoy spending time with you. I'm happy I met you."

"I'm glad I met you as well. It's strange. I've been cut off from people since my ex-husband left. I've kept my distance and struggled to connect with anyone. But with you, it comes easily."

"It feels." He cleared his throat before continuing. "I feel like maybe something is building between us. Something, perhaps, more than just friendship."

Her eyebrows shot up, but he couldn't tell if her reaction was positive or negative. He waited as she processed what he said, trying to be patient, but worried he had been too forward or spoken too soon.

"I appreciate your honesty," she said, finally breaking the

silence. "And you're right, there is something between us."

"But?" he asked, hearing the hesitation in her words.

"But I'm not sure I'm ready to pursue anything with anyone." She released his hand and set her wineglass on the coffee table. "It's only been a year since Carl left, and I'm just getting into a groove with Lilly, but as you saw, everything is pretty raw for us, and we're still processing it all. Besides, as you said, we hardly know each other."

"I understand," he said, trying to hide his disappointment.

It wasn't like he hadn't expected her response. Between Lilly's reaction at dinner and Shelly's hesitant mannerisms, he had assumed she wasn't ready. Still, he couldn't help wishing things were different. Maybe if her marriage had ended more amicably, or if more time had passed since the divorce, she would be less tentative toward him.

"I just wanted to be open and honest about how I'm feeling. You've been very kind to me," he went on, desperate to fill the heavy silence that followed her words. "Above all else, I appreciate your friendship and, to be clear, I'm not asking you for anything. Lord knows, I'm facing upheaval in my own life right now. I don't want to start something until I'm more settled myself." He ran his hands through his dark hair, not sure if anything he was saying was making sense to her. "But I guess what I'm saying is, I'm open to whatever the future may bring, and I'm hoping you may be as well."

"I would like to get to know you better," Shelly said, putting her hand back over his. "I can't deny you have touched a part of me I believed was closed off for good." She took a deep breath. "If you're willing to be patient with me, then perhaps, in time, we can explore our feelings together."

A sense of relief flowed through him, and his disappointment dissipated. It felt good to give a voice to the growing feelings inside of him, but he was also buoyed by the knowledge the attraction he had wasn't one-sided. He understood her hesitation. After all she had been through with her ex, her reluctance to pursue a relationship was unsurprising.

She yawned, then covered her mouth in embarrassment. "I'm sorry."

He laughed. "Am I boring you?"

"Of course not! I'm just overwhelmed, and when I get overwhelmed, I get tired."

"In that case, we should say goodnight."

With a nod, she stood to walk him out. When they reached the front door, Brad turned back to her. "Thank you for a lovely evening."

"Thank you for helping to decorate the tree. You made Lilly's night, and mine," she added shyly.

"I'm excited for some more Christmas fun tomorrow. Cookie baking, right?"

"It's a family tradition!"

"Until then," he said, stepping into the chilly night.

As he strode back to his room, he barely felt the brisk winter chill because the conversation with Shelly had filled him with warmth. He was sure he had made the right decision in not going to spend Christmas with his sister because if he had, he might never have met Shelly.

While he got ready for bed, his insides vibrated with excitement about what the next day would bring. This was the happiest he had been at Christmas in a long time.

Chapter Six

Shelly woke up earlier than normal on Saturday morning. While she wished she could say it was to get chores done, or to make an elaborate breakfast, the truth was, she wanted to spend more time with Brad. His admission last night of his attraction to her had changed their relationship.

Deep down, she knew she felt the same way toward him, no matter what her logical, analytical side said. But she must tread carefully to protect Lilly, not to mention Shelly's own heart. Her daughter had already been through a lot. How might she react to the possibility of her mother dating again?

To be fair, the subject had never come up because Shelly had sworn off men entirely. She needed to confront her feelings head on before broaching the subject with Lilly.

Shelly spent more time than usual choosing her outfit for the day, her desire to see Brad warring with wanting to spend extra time on her appearance for him. Then she headed downstairs to unlock the front door and start breakfast. His light had been on, but she beat him to the kitchen this time. She decided to make cinnamon rolls and scrambled eggs, and she began putting it together.

Lilly would likely sleep in this morning, since it was a Saturday and her first official day of Christmas vacation, but the warm scent of cinnamon wafting through the house would help to wake her. The sooner she got up, though, the better, as Shelly's mother would arrive soon to get started on cookie baking.

A light tap on the wall behind her startled her, and she spun around. Brad stood in the doorway.

"Morning," he said with a grin. His hair was damp from a recent shower and was darker than usual. "I knocked, but nobody answered."

"I'm sorry. I was in my own little world." She fiddled with her necklace, his sudden appearance unnerving her. "D-did you sleep well?"

"I did. The bed up there is comfortable. And you?"

"Yes, it's good to be in my own bed, though I'm not used to spending so many consecutive nights at home. Would you like some coffee?"

"I would, but I can get it." He entered the kitchen.

She smiled and went back to the stove to tend to the eggs. His presence made her elated and unsettled all at the same time. Her hands trembled as she flipped the eggs, and she dropped the spatula. Brad picked it up without hesitation, bringing it to the sink to wash and dry for her.

When he handed it back, his fingers brushed hers, her skin tingled with that now familiar spark. Their eyes met, and their conversation from the night before flooded her brain. Her pulse quickened at the memory, and she spun back to the stove. Thankfully, he took the hint and carried his coffee into the dining room.

Moments later, a bleary-eyed Lilly appeared in the kitchen, her disheveled brown hair cascading down her back. She approached Shelly for a quick hug, then sniffed the air. "What smells so good?"

"Scrambled eggs," Shelly teased, knowing full well what her daughter meant.

Lilly frowned in sleepy confusion. "I mean, what's in the oven?"

Shelly shook her head in amusement. "Cinnamon rolls."

Lilly's dark brown eyes brightened, and she went to the cabinet to grab plates. Setting the table without being asked? What had gotten into her daughter? Perhaps it was Brad's influence or the excitement of baking cookies, but whatever caused the change in her daughter, she welcomed it.

Just as the oven timer went off, the doorbell rang. Lilly answered it and squealed in delight. After removing the pan from the oven, Shelly came around to discover who it was. She was startled to find her mother, Beatrice, had already arrived, with Shelly's sister, Susan, in tow. Her mother's fading auburn hair was pulled back in a no-nonsense bun, and her big green scarf obscured her face.

"Mom! I wasn't expecting you until later."

"Later? We're already behind schedule if we want to bake all the cookies today," her mother scoffed. Two enormous shopping bags rattled beside her as she moved, and Shelly noted they were overflowing with cookie tins. Lilly grabbed one and carried it into the kitchen.

"You know Mom gets up at o'dark thirty." Susan shifted her own shopping bag to her other hand. Hers was filled with ingredients. A red hat was pulled down over her mousey-brown hair, and her green eyes sparkled mischievously beneath it.

"Come on in! I'm just getting breakfast on the table for Lilly and

Brad." Shelly stepped to the side to allow Susan to pass.

"Brad?" Susan asked as they entered the house, removing the hat from her head and shaking out her hair. "Who is Brad?"

Just then, Brad entered the family room and stepped forward, sticking out his hand. "That would be me. Brad Collins. I'm renting the in-law apartment from Shelly."

As she took his hand, Susan gave him a quick once over. "Hi Brad, I'm Susan Evans, Shelly's sister. It's nice to meet you." She turned to her sister with raised eyebrows. "Shelly didn't mention she had a guest staying for the holidays."

"It was an unexpected development," Shelly said, shifting uncomfortably.

"Oh, really?" Susan and her mother exchanged a glance as they removed their coats and handed them to Shelly. "How so?"

"I was on Shelly's last flight," he explained. "We got to talking and learned we grew up near each other. I'm just moving back to Maryland, and Shelly saved me from trying to find a hotel room amid the holiday season."

Shelly shot him a grateful look. "Brad recently retired from the Marines and has a job with the federal government, starting after the first of the year."

"A Marine?" her mother asked, her emerald eyes scrutinized him. "I should have known. You have the look of one. My Jimmy was the same way: clean cut, solid." She pursed her lips. "Although you don't strike me as the strong, silent type."

Brad laughed. "Wow, you sure have me pegged. I'm afraid I'm a bit of a talker. I've certainly talked your daughter's ear off." His face broke into a smile, and he shot a wink at Shelly, causing her stomach to flip.

"I don't think she minds," Susan muttered. Shelly elbowed her sister before hanging their coats on the rack.

Lilly came back into the room. "He was a tremendous help bringing our tree here."

"Ah, at least you've decorated a bit in here." Her mother glanced at the tree before inclining her head toward the front door. "The outside is another story entirely."

"We had planned to have everything decorated before you arrived," Brad said. "I'm happy to take care of it while you ladies catch up."

"That's all right, I can come with you." Her mother made a move to retrieve her coat.

"Actually, Mom, why don't you let Shelly show Brad where

things go?" Susan gave a conspiratorial wink at Shelly. "While they're doing that, Lilly can help us set everything up in the kitchen."

"Before anyone goes anywhere, Lilly and Brad need to have their breakfast!" Shelly declared, waving everyone into the dining room.

Her mother narrowed her eyes, but Susan quickly grabbed her hand and dragged her toward the kitchen. Shelly lifted the pan off the stove and served the eggs then returned a moment later with the cinnamon rolls.

"Did you and Mom want to join us?" she asked Susan as Shelly poured Lilly a glass of milk. "I can make more eggs."

"Oh please, you know Mom. She ate before the sun came up." Susan laughed. "Besides, we wouldn't want to waste the eggs. We're going to need a lot of them for the cookies."

Shelly, Brad, and Lilly gobbled up their breakfast. There wasn't time for leisurely conversation this morning, for which Shelly was grateful. She was still reeling from the discussion she had with Brad the night before. The intimate revelations were a lot more daunting to think about in the bright light of the day.

When they finished, Lilly washed her plate before assisting her aunt and grandmother with preparations. Brad helped Shelly clear the rest of the table, then headed to the family room. As Shelly left the kitchen, her sister wagged her eyebrows suggestively, and Shelly gaped at her before shaking her head. Desperate to escape her sister's teasing, she followed Brad outside.

"You didn't tell your family you had a guest?" he asked when they were safely out of earshot.

"I haven't talked to my mom much. We texted a bit about plans for today, but I thought it was a conversation better had in person," she said.

"Do you think it will bother them I'm here?" He began unpacking the box. There were strings of blue and white icicle lights, a set of candy cane yard ornaments, and a couple of wreaths.

"They are aware I rent the room. My mother doesn't approve, but she usually bites her tongue because she knows the extra income helps."

He nodded. "If it will make them uncomfortable, I'm happy to go back to my room while they're here. I don't want to intrude on your family time."

"But Lilly and I were excited to bake cookies with you!" His blue eyes softened, and a tingling sensation swept up the back of her neck. "I mean, it's the least we can do after using you to get the biggest Christmas tree ever. Besides, I'm sure they won't mind. We bake a *lot* of cookies, and they would never decline an extra pair of hands."

"I appreciate that." With a chuckle, he turned toward the house. "So, I assume the icicle lights hang from the roof?"

"One string should cover the roof of the garage, and the other should hang off the roof over the bay window," she said, pointing. "The wreaths go on the front door and on the hook outside of the garage door, and the candy canes line the sidewalk."

"Makes sense." He gestured to the door. "If you would like to go help your family, I can take care of this. I'll join you when I'm done."

"Are you sure?" It didn't strike her as fair to have him out there in the cold alone while they enjoyed the warmth of the house.

"Absolutely! Besides," he shot her a roguish grin. "I'll be a lot less anxious if I don't have a perfectionist supervising me."

Had there been snow on the ground, Shelly would have thrown a snowball at him for that comment.

"You might regret that choice when my mother inspects your work later," she retorted before spinning on her heel and going back inside. The sound of murmured voices stopped abruptly when the screen door slammed behind her. As she entered the kitchen, the air was filled with the tension of an interrupted, heated conversation.

"What's going on?" she demanded, her hands on her hips.

"Nothing." Susan gave a high-pitched giggle and cleared her throat. "What makes you think something is going on?"

"Hmm, I don't know, maybe because of how quiet it got as soon as I came back inside." Shelly glared at each of them, waiting for someone to fess up to the subject of their discussion.

No one said anything and the three of them exchanged guilty glances, confirming her suspicions she was their likely subject. Susan had sent her with Brad for a reason, and Shelly was concerned over what that reason was. While Susan avoided her eyes, Lilly seemed anxious to say something to break the silence.

"We were talking about Brad," she piped up.

"What about him?"

"Susan and I were just surprised you hadn't mentioned him when you texted us," her mother answered instead of Lilly. "You've never hesitated to share when you had renters before, even though you know I don't approve."

"Mom." Shelly sighed, pinching the bridge of her nose between her thumb and forefinger. "We've had this conversation. I need—"

"The money," she finished. "Despite my offers to help you out." She shook her head. "I just want to understand why you kept it a secret. You had to know we would find out about him when we got here."

Shelly lowered her gaze. While she wanted to point it out it was a last-minute decision, that wasn't the only reason she hadn't told them. It was strange because she had struggled to explain his arrival to Lilly as well, even though she never gave the renters a second thought.

After last night's conversation, Shelly was admitting to herself her heart was opening for the first time since the divorce, and Brad was the reason. Nonetheless, she resisted. Telling her family about him risked revealing her growing attraction. She hadn't talked to her mother about dating at all, as her mother had never stepped back into the dating pool after Shelly's father died.

She believed her mother had made the right choice for her children, and Shelly was determined to do the same. Susan disagreed and encouraged Shelly to get back out there. Her sister's view was that their mother held herself back from true happiness as some sort of devotion to their father. Their mother had always said their father was her one true love, and no one could ever replace him.

"I guess I was afraid to tell you because I offered him the room on an impulse. You know I only advertise on websites that do a bit more vetting, and I usually require a deposit." Shelly shot a pleading look at Susan. "He was going to spend Christmas alone, and I think Dad would have wanted me to offer him a place to stay for the holidays."

"You're right," Susan said, and Shelly suppressed a sigh of relief. "Dad would have done the same." Her eyes sparkled with mischief. "Honestly, I don't blame Shelly for keeping Brad a secret. He's not my type, of course. But even I can see he's attractive."

The room was suddenly very warm, and Shelly was pretty sure it wasn't the oven. "That's not why I offered him the room, or why I didn't tell you."

Susan pursed her lips, but she let it go and went back to setting out the ingredients. They had made quite a bit of progress while Shelly was outside. Butter and eggs were sitting on the counter, allowing them to come to room temperature. They'd assembled a small table she kept in the garage and had covered it with measuring cups, mixing bowls, and pans.

"What are we making first, Grandma?" Lilly asked.

The tension in Shelly's shoulders eased and she gave Lilly a grateful smile for the subject change.

"I figured we'd start with chocolate chip, then we can make the fudge." Beatrice scrutinized her list. "After that, we can start the peanut butter blossoms."

"My favorite!" Lilly exclaimed.

"I remember," her mother said, running a loving hand over

Lilly's head. "While the fudge is being made, some of us can get the gingerbread and sugar cookie dough started and it can then chill in the fridge. Then we have oatmeal raisin, pumpkin spice pudding cookies, snickerdoodles, peppermint drops, and peanut butter fudge." Her critical eyes met each of theirs. "It's going to be a busy day!"

"Let's get to it," Shelly said.

They began priming the cookie pans with parchment paper and assigning tasks for the day. Shelly measured the dry ingredients for the cookies while her sister started on the wet. Lilly and Beatrice set up cooling racks on the kitchen table. Once the ingredients were mixed in separate bowls, Shelly and Susan worked on combining the dough. They were all so familiar with their tasks, they made baking into a well-regimented art.

Before long, the house filled with the tantalizing scents of melted chocolate, warm spices, and fresh-baked cookies. The front door opened and closed, then Brad materialized in the kitchen doorway, with a familiar face in tow. He inhaled deeply before giving her a charming smile that stopped her heart. "It smells amazing in here, ladies!"

Her family turned to see Brad and his unexpected companion, Shelly's neighbor.

"Why, Wallace Simmons!" her mother gasped as her hand fluttered to her chest. "What a pleasant surprise. I haven't seen you in a month of Sundays."

"Hello, Beatrice," Wallace greeted her with a warm smile. "Nice to see you. I've been away visiting my grandkids." His gaze moved over them. "Susan, Lilly, you both look well." He nodded at Brad. "Shelly, I saw your young man here hanging Christmas lights on your house and thought I'd give him a hand. He said you were in here baking up a storm with your family. Couldn't resist a visit."

Shelly's face grew hot at the suggestion of Brad being hers. Her mother and sister exchanged a glance but said nothing.

"Are you finished, then?" her mother asked Brad, her hands cracking an egg over the side of a bowl.

"Yes, ma'am," he said. "We have put the lights up per Shelly's specifications."

After wiping her hands on her apron, her mother started toward the door, forcing Brad and Wallace to move aside. Shelly met Brad's gaze and rolled her eyes as her mother headed out to inspect his work.

"Oh, Mom!" Susan called after her in exasperation. "I'm sure Brad did a fine job."

"'A fine job' is not acceptable in this family." The slam of the screen door perfectly punctuated her mother's retort. Wallace followed soon after.

"Wow, you weren't kidding when you said she was a perfectionist," Brad said. Shelly just shook her head and sighed as she moved toward the front door.

"Lilly and I will keep an eye on the cookies during Mom's inspection," Susan promised.

Shelly and Brad arrived in the front yard, where her mother was scrutinizing the men's handiwork. It was difficult to read her face to know whether she approved. Brad shifted uneasily beside Shelly, and she patted his arm. As much as she loved her mother, quirks and all, she wished, for once, her mother could smother her obsession with decorating and just thank Brad and Wallace for their willingness to help.

"I vaguely recall how Shelly decorated the house last Christmas." Wallace pointed to a string of lights over the garage. "It looks right to me."

"What's the verdict, Mom?" Unable to mask her irritation, Shelly tapped her foot and crossed her arms. "Does it meet your Christmas standards?"

Her mother's sharp eyes met Shelly's. "You know, sarcasm doesn't become you." Then, studying the house, she nodded. "You men did a good job." She turned back to them. "Thank you, you've earned yourselves some cookies."

"It was my pleasure, ma'am." Brad gave an exaggerated bow. Wallace chuckled softly and dipped his head as well.

"Let's get back inside," she said, rubbing her hands over her bare arms. "It's freezing out here, and those cookies aren't going to bake themselves." With that, she marched back to the door like a general readying the troops for battle as Wallace trailed behind. Brad and Shelly exchanged an amused look.

"Your mom is quite a character," he mused after her mother and Wallace disappeared into the house.

"Thank you for doing this," Shelly said, admiring his work. "You didn't have to, but I greatly appreciate it." She wrapped her arms around herself and gazed up the street at her neighbor's decorations. "At least now we won't be the neighborhood Scrooge."

He laughed. "I doubt you could ever be that. Besides, Mr. Simmons was a great help. He must know your mom well."

"They've become good friends since she's been spending so much time here helping me with Lilly." She shivered as the cold bit through her thin sweater.

"We better get back inside before your family thinks you've abandoned them."

"I can only imagine what they're saying about us right now," she muttered.

"About us?" he asked as they walked back to the door.

Her throat constricted and she swallowed. Why did she say that? The last thing she wanted was for him to learn about her family's speculations concerning their relationship. "There's been some, uh, speculation." She shifted her weight as she stared at the ground, avoiding his gaze. "About why I offered to rent you the room."

His finger slid under her chin, lifting it until she met his eyes. "Whatever the reason was, I will always be grateful for it, and for you." He dropped his hand from her face and opened the door, gesturing for her to go ahead of him.

Shelly went back to the kitchen, her head swimming and her heart fluttering as much because of his touch as his words. *How does he do that? I'm a grown woman, but with him, I'm like a lovesick schoolgirl!*

When she entered the kitchen, Susan took one look at her and gave a knowing smirk. Shelly's face must have betrayed her feelings. With a quick glare at her sister, she went to bury her head in a recipe book until she could regain control of herself.

The chocolate chip cookies were done, and the fudge was mixed and ready to cool. Shelly busied herself with preparing the fudge pan with grease and parchment paper. Now and then, she glanced up from her work to check where Brad was.

After organizing the tins and Tupperware containers on the table, he had set up a station to transfer the finished cookies to the cooling racks. Wallace was helping him, though Shelly could swear he was eating as many cookies as he was setting to cool. She hid a smile.

Once the pan was ready for the fudge, she went over to help her mother with the next batch. While she was outside with Brad, Lilly connected her phone to a Bluetooth speaker, and the joyful sound of holiday music filled the air.

Shelly absentmindedly hummed along with the tune as she measured the flour according to the altered recipe. Her family always doubled the recipes to ensure they could share the fruits of their labor with friends and neighbors. Cookie baking day was her favorite holiday tradition. No matter what she was going through, she could always lose herself in the warm sweetness of making Christmas treats.

Brad ventured into the kitchen, leaving Wallace to man the cookie transfer alone. Without being asked, he took it upon himself to tackle the dishes piling up. She caught his eye as he filled the sink with soapy water and gave him a warm smile. It touched her how much he helped without ever being asked.

Perhaps it was unfair, but she couldn't help comparing his actions to Carl's. When her mother and sister came over to bake in the past, he would make himself scarce, often leaving the house entirely. Her preoccupation had allowed him to meet up with Deborah. At one time, this understanding might have caused Shelly pain, but now, she was only embarrassed by her own naivety.

She took the empty bowl over to the sink, where Brad was making progress. Hesitantly, she laid her hand on his arm. His blue eyes met hers, and they were filled with such warmth, her heart skipped a beat. She opened her mouth to say something when she was interrupted by her cellphone ringing. Bewildered, she pulled it from her pocket.

"Hello?" she answered.

"Hey lady."

"Oh, hi Kylie," Shelly said, stepping away from the bustle of the kitchen. "I thought you had a flight today?"

"We have delayed takeoff because of the weather. We'll be back in Baltimore later this afternoon, then I'll be officially off the clock until after Christmas!"

The familiar sounds of the airport hubbub were audible in the background as her friend navigated the terminal. "I'm glad you're taking a break. You deserve it."

"Do I ever," Kylie said. "And speaking of breaks, we'd talked about getting together over the holiday, and I was wondering if you wanted to meet for dinner tonight?"

"Um…" Her teeth worried her bottom lip as she glanced back toward the kitchen. "It's cookie baking day, and my mom and Susan are here. We might go to the tree lighting tonight." She scratched her head. "I'm making a big dinner for everyone, though. You're welcome to join us."

"That would be wonderful. I haven't seen your mom in ages," Kylie said. "Hold on a sec." A familiar male voice Shelly couldn't quite place said something in the background, though she couldn't make out what was being said. Kylie sighed, and irritation tinged her voice. "Would you mind if I bring someone?"

"Of course not," Shelly said, trying to decipher who Kylie might bring. As far as she was aware, her friend wasn't dating anyone exclusively. "I always make too much food."

"Okay, great. I should land around three, then I'll come by right after."

"Sounds good. See you then."

As Shelly entered the kitchen her mom was just inserting the first tray of peanut butter blossoms into the oven. Lilly and Susan were starting on the oatmeal raisin. Wallace had joined Brad and was helping to dry the dishes. They made significant progress, though it was a never-ending chore on baking day.

"Who called?" her mother asked.

"Kylie."

"How is she? We haven't seen her in so long." Her mother unwrapped Hershey kisses.

"You'll get to ask her yourself. She's coming to dinner tonight, and she might join us at the tree lighting later." Shelly stopped short, realizing she hadn't asked her mother if she was going. "Are you staying?"

"Of course, she's staying," Lilly declared from behind them.

"I guess that's decided then," her mother said with a chuckle. "Can't disappoint my only grandchild."

"And you're coming, too, right, Aunt Susan?" Lilly asked.

"Wouldn't miss it for the world." Susan stepped away from Lilly to pull Shelly over to the small table in the kitchen and asked in a low voice: "Is your Marine coming as well?"

"He's not my Marine!" Shelly grumbled, swatting at her sister. She peeked at him before continuing. "But Lilly and I invited him."

Susan glanced at Brad, who had been watching Shelly throughout the exchange. When he caught Susan's eye, he pivoted back to the sink. "Are you *sure* he's not yours? He seems like he wants to be."

"It's too soon!" Shelly insisted, as much to her sister as to herself.

Throwing up her hands, Susan shook her head. "Shelly, it's been a year. And if you're honest with yourself, your marriage was over long before Carl walked out that door." She put her hand on Shelly's shoulder. "Don't you deserve to be happy?"

"I am happy!" she retorted with a frown.

Susan raised an eyebrow before bursting out laughing. When Shelly realized how contradictory that statement was, she joined in.

"He seems like a good man," Susan said, as she accepted the bowl Lilly handed her and began stirring. "He's been more helpful today than Carl ever was. And he likes you."

"You don't know that," Shelly protested as she scooped a cupful of dry ingredients into Susan's bowl. "You only just met him."

"Oh, Shelly," Susan said, her voice filled with concern as she stopped stirring. "Carl clearly did a number on you if you can't see how Brad feels about you from the way he looks at you to the things he does for you. Perhaps he is just a genuinely nice guy, but I doubt he'd have gone so far out of his way if he were only being nice." Her gaze swept over Brad again, who kept sneaking glances at Shelly. "I understand your caution, but not your outright denial of his interest. Or your own feelings, for that matter." With that, Susan went to help her mother trade another tray of cookies for the oven.

Shelly was conflicted because her sister knew exactly what she was struggling to hide, even from herself. Yes, he had told her the night before he believed something was growing between them, and he expressed an interest in seeing where things might go. To her, that meant he was attracted to her, but it didn't mean his feelings went any deeper than that. *We've only just met* was an ongoing refrain in her mind.

The rest of the afternoon passed in a blur. Wallace left with a promise to join them for dinner. They ate lunch in shifts to hit their goal of finishing the cookies by the late afternoon to give Shelly plenty of time to make dinner before they needed to be at the tree lighting. The ringing of the doorbell made them all jump, and she went to answer it.

She greeted Kylie warmly but froze as her gaze met Kylie's guest. "Hi, Kylie! Eric, wh-what a surprise!"

"Hi, Shelly." Kylie tucked a lock of her wavy brown hair behind her ear as her dark eyes danced mischievously. "Eric was the co-pilot on my last flight and wanted to come visit you over the holiday." Her triumphant grin made Shelly's stomach churn and she bit back a grimace. While Kylie had always loved to stir the pot, Shelly worried this time, she might have taken it too far.

"Hey, Shelly," Eric pushed past Kylie to give Shelly a hug. "It's good to see you."

"Wel-welcome, both of you," she said, stiffening as his arms closed around her.

If he recognized her greeting was less than friendly, he gave no indication.

After she stepped back to allow them to enter, she stood awkwardly beside the door as she processed the situation. "Um, let me take your coats. Everyone is in the kitchen working on the last two batches of cookies."

They passed her their coats, and Kylie headed toward the kitchen, where a chorus of voices welcomed her. Eric hung back and stood so close to Shelly she could smell his aftershave. With a tight smile, she led the way into the kitchen.

As she recovered from her initial shock at seeing him, frustration welled up inside her, both at Kylie for not telling her who she was bringing and Eric for barging in on her family's holiday festivities. Shelly chided herself for extending an invitation without knowing who the recipient was, but she had trusted Kylie and never dreamed she would bring Eric.

Before Shelly could rejoin her family in the kitchen, Kylie grabbed Shelly's arm and yanked her back toward the family room. When Eric started to follow, Kylie waved him away, making it clear she wanted to speak to Shelly privately. She was bewildered, but thrilled to escape Eric, who reluctantly wandered into the kitchen.

"Why is that man from the plane in your house?" Kylie demanded once they were out of earshot.

Shelly explained the story for what felt like the umpteenth time.

Kylie's eyes widened throughout the retelling, then she shook her head in disbelief. "I can't believe you let him stay here. I mean, there was a definite vibe between you on the plane, but I never imagined you, of all people, would act on it."

"Act on what?" Shelly asked, drawing her brows together in confusion. Then Kylie's meaning dawned on her. "No! It's not like that. He just needed a place to stay."

"Uh huh," Kylie drawled, unconvinced. "He's gorgeous! How can you not see that?"

"I mean, I—" Shelly struggled to find the words. "He is attractive, but that's not why I rented him the room." She sounded like a broken record. Why did everyone keep questioning her motives? *Had* there been another underlying reason to why she offered him a place to stay?

"Whatever you need to tell yourself. But this will be priceless. Eric is going to be so jealous!"

Shelly shook her head. "I still can't believe you brought him, but if Eric came here expecting something from me, he's delusional."

"I tried to tell him that, but he insists you're into him. He was standing right there when I called you, and he wanted it to be a surprise." Kylie shrugged unapologetically, her face animated with amusement. "I figured I'd let him come just to watch him crash and burn. I just didn't realize how *epically* that would happen."

They went back to the kitchen together, and Eric was leaning against the half wall with his arms crossed, glaring at Brad. Eric must have recognized Brad from the airport and was unhappy to see him there. For once, Shelly was grateful for the assumptions swirling around about her and Brad, because they might help her quash Eric's persistence once and for all.

She took advantage of his misunderstanding of the situation and slid next to Brad. "Thank you so much for doing the dishes. It's really helped us to keep things moving."

"Your family is like a well-oiled machine," he said, with awe in his voice. "I thought they were overly optimistic about the different batches of cookies they planned to make, but they're on the second to last batch."

"We've had practice," Shelly mused.

She brushed back a stray lock of black hair that had fallen onto his forehead and she had the satisfaction of seeing Eric's eyes flash in her peripheral vision. Hopefully, he would take the hint.

What she hadn't counted on was Brad's blue eyes melting at her touch. Her breath caught in her throat as he grasped her hand in his. He gave her hand a squeeze and started to say something but was interrupted by someone clearing their throat.

"We haven't officially met," Eric said, holding out his hand. "I'm Eric, a pilot who works with Shelly."

"Brad Collins." Brad shook Eric's hand.

He winced, and Eric's knuckles whitened as he gripped Brad's hand. His eyebrows raised, but Eric's eyes were on Shelly. Understanding dawned on Brad's face, and she worried he would misunderstand her relationship with Eric.

When he glanced over at her, whatever expression was on her face must have put him at ease. He smiled at Eric, releasing his hand. "Ah, I remember you. You were at the airport when Shelly returned my wallet."

"That's correct," Eric said with an icy tone. "What brought you to Shelly's house?"

"I'm staying here," Brad said breezily.

Eric's eyes narrowed, but she decided not to dwell on the exchange. Instead, she showed Kylie to the dining room, where she could help Shelly's mother with packing up the cookies. The bustle in the kitchen was winding down as Lilly and Susan mixed the last batch. Lilly's stirring had lost some of its enthusiasm and Shelly took over so she could take a break. She and Susan kept a steady stream of trays going in and out of the oven.

Once the last of the cookies were ready for the oven, Shelly encouraged Susan to go relax while she made dinner. Shelly planned to roast a chicken, but that tiny bird was no match for the number of hungry people in her home. Instead, she opted to make a pasta dish, which was sure to feed everyone.

With the baking over and most of the cookies put away, the kitchen cleared out except for Brad, Eric, and herself. Lilly had gone upstairs and the rest of her family, and Kylie moved into the family room. Their laughter wafted into the room from time to time, but Shelly couldn't hear their conversation.

The tense standoff in the kitchen was creating an uncomfortable atmosphere. Brad was at the sink, finishing up the last of the dishes. Eric leaned against the back wall, and she had the distinct impression he didn't want to leave her and Brad alone. She stifled a sigh as she began dinner preparations. If Eric couldn't take a hint, this was going to be a long evening.

Chapter Seven

Eric was still hanging out in the kitchen, and Brad chuckled to himself. He had pegged Eric from the moment he'd introduced himself, partially because of the firmer than necessary handshake. This guy had a clear interest in Shelly, and he didn't like the idea Brad might be his competition.

Brad couldn't tell if there was any history between them, though based on everything she had said, he doubted it. However, he reminded himself that just because she hadn't dated since her divorce didn't mean she wasn't interested in anyone.

Eric wasn't winning any points by standing in the way and not offering to help either of them. For the most part, she seemed content just to ignore him. Her movements reminded Brad of his first night there, when she seemed to dance around making dinner. It looked like another Italian dish, this time something with pasta. Whatever it was, it already smelled amazing, and he snuck glances at her out of the corner of his eye.

"That pan is clean enough," Eric growled behind him. Startled, Brad glared at him. He glanced at Shelly, but she didn't appear to have heard.

"Just trying to be thorough," he muttered.

Man, this guy was persistent. So far, it wasn't paying off. If memory served, she had been eager to leave Eric when Brad offered to walk her out at the airport. Had she invited him over? She received a call from Kylie, but he didn't recall her speaking to anyone else. Kylie had walked into the kitchen with Eric, so perhaps they arrived together.

"If you wouldn't mind," he continued in a low voice. "I would like a moment alone with Shelly."

Brad took his time rinsing the pan, prolonging his need to remain in the kitchen. While he wasn't sure what Shelly wanted, the tension coming off Eric was making the room claustrophobic, which was ironic, considering how many people they had crammed in there all day. But he seemed to suck all the air, and joy for that matter, out of the room.

Sliding the towel off his shoulder, Brad meticulously dried the pan and drained the water from the sink. Eric huffed in frustration, and Brad grinned to himself as an idea came to him while he crouched to put away the pan.

"Would you like me to set the table?" he asked Shelly as he stood, pointedly ignoring Eric's grumbling.

She turned, her emerald eyes lighting up. "I would appreciate that." She nodded toward the small table her family set up that morning. "If you move that next to the table in the dining room, we can put enough chairs around both. It'll be a tight fit, but we should be able to squeeze in everyone."

Brad lifted the table and maneuvered it into the dining room, pulling out chairs so he could slide the two tables together. It took effort, but he tried not to eavesdrop on their conversation while he set the table.

The minute they were alone, Eric pounced, but she angled her body away from him, toward the cabinets. While Brad recognized this change immediately, Eric seemed oblivious. Brad assumed Eric was asking her out, but then he caught words like "inappropriate" and "stranger." Was Eric warning her about *him*?

"Well, it's none of your concern, is it, Eric?" she retorted, her voice rising. "This is *my* house, and he is *my* guest."

Brad caught Eric's glare at him and pretended to be engrossed in his task, but he was glad he decided not to head into the living room with the rest of the family. The Marines had taught Brad to follow his instincts, and they rarely let him down. It touched him she was defending her choice to rent the room to him, though he doubted it had as much to do with him as it did her need to preserve her ability to make her own choices.

Despite Shelly's attempts to move away from Eric, he managed to remain close beside her. She removed a glass casserole dish from a bottom cabinet. Worried Eric was making her extremely uncomfortable, Brad fought a battle within himself. His protective side wanted to interject, but he stopped himself because Shelly didn't strike him as a damsel in distress.

Eric must have realized his approach wasn't working because he softened his tone. Her posture remained tense, but her face cleared. Her voice was firm, but calmer. Did she match Eric's tone because she wanted to preserve her relationship with him? Or was she trying to maintain her self-control since he was a guest in her house?

Either way, her altered demeanor only encouraged him. "I care about you, Shelly," he said with a raised voice, which Brad assumed was for his benefit. "And I'm concerned for your well-being." Eric glanced over his shoulder, and he smirked when his eyes met Brad's. "Do you think it's wise to have your daughter around some man you barely know?"

If Eric had been paying attention to Shelly, he would have seen the way her jaw clenched and her green eyes flashed at his words. But he was too busy enjoying Brad's reaction to realize Eric just crossed a line.

"Did you seriously just bring my daughter into this?" Shelly's voice shook with anger. "My daughter who, until this afternoon, you had never met yourself?"

His eyes widened, and he spun around. He lowered his voice, and Brad couldn't hear what he said, but Eric's tone became pleading and apologetic. The sound of loud voices and boisterous laughter spilled in from the living room, drowning out the argument in the kitchen.

"Well, you know what, if you don't like it, you are welcome to leave!" she snapped.

Eric recoiled like she'd slapped him. "You don't mean that."

"Oh, believe me, I do." She yanked the oven door open and shoved the pasta in before slamming it shut. As she rounded on Eric, Brad didn't need to see her face to know it was as red as her hair. "We work together, Eric, and that's all. I don't date coworkers, and I *definitely* don't date ones who believe they have some sort of say over how I live my life or how I raise my daughter."

"B-but you invited me."

"Actually, I didn't. You invited yourself."

"Fine! If that's how you feel." He stormed out of the kitchen, almost knocking Brad over as he was on his way to the cabinet to grab plates.

By this time, the escalating argument caught the attention of everyone else, judging by the sudden silence in the next room. With the plates in hand, he hurried back to the dining room just as Eric reached Kylie.

"We need to go," Eric demanded, his hands balled into fists at his side.

Taken aback by his tone, she jumped and leaned away from him. Color rose in her face, but she took a deep breath and closed her eyes, as if she was trying to regain her composure before responding, "Uh, I'm not going anywhere. If you don't want to stay, you can go ahead." Her gaze darted around the room at Susan and Beatrice's stunned faces. "I'm sure I can find my own ride home."

He glowered at her and grabbed his coat from the rack. After sending one last withering glare at Brad, he yanked the front door open and slammed it behind him. The rest of Shelly's family stared at each other in shock.

"What was that about?" Susan asked, breaking the tense silence.

"My guess is Eric just realized he and Shelly have very different views about their relationship," Kylie said, flipping her long hair over her shoulder. "He's a pilot, and I guess he finally found a woman unimpressed by that fact."

One of the plates in Brad's hand slipped and clattered to the floor. All eyes turned to him, and he blinked like a deer in headlights. He scooped up the dropped plate, ducked into the kitchen, and set it in the sink. As he was heading back to the dining room, two fingers tapped him on the shoulder.

"I'm sorry you had to witness that," Shelly said with a sigh. "He's not the only one to question my judgment about renting the room, to you or anyone else, for that matter." Her mouth pressed into a thin line and the color rose in her cheeks again. "But I can't believe his nerve. Bringing Lilly into it? Implying my decisions make me a careless mother?" She shook her head slowly, as if trying to clear it. "That's just something I will not tolerate."

"For what it's worth, you handled it well."

She gave him a small smile. "Thanks, but I'm sure this isn't the last I'll hear about it." When she turned and opened the fridge, removing a head of lettuce, he took that as his cue. As he headed into the dining room, she whispered. "And thank you for staying close by."

He breathed a sigh of relief, happy he had made the right decision. Shelly was a strong, capable woman. At the same time, everyone needs someone in their corner sometimes. If she needed him to intervene, he would have, and not just because it would have given him some satisfaction. Although, it didn't hurt to know she had no interest in Eric.

Kylie wandered into the dining room as Brad placed the napkins at each place setting. The weight of her scrutiny was heavy, and he wondered what sort of relationship she had with Shelly. Were they friendly coworkers or did they hang out often outside of work? Shelly had spoken little about her social life, aside from her family.

"Fancy meeting you here," Kylie drawled, her brown eyes sparkling. "It's not every day I meet a former customer at a colleague's house."

"Shelly was very kind to allow me to stay," he said.

"How long will you be around?"

He shrugged. "I'm not sure, honestly. This isn't the best season to be apartment hunting, and I am hoping to get a better lay of the land. Figure out what the commute would be like. That sort of thing."

She nodded, then came around to stand close beside him. She lowered her voice. "And what are you hoping for in the meantime?"

"Hoping for?" He raised an eyebrow.

"With my girl, Shelly," Kylie said, as if her meaning should be obvious.

He froze, his mind scrambling. The way she referred to Shelly as "her girl" implied a close friendship, which probably meant she was concerned about Shelly's best interest. However, she had also just spent a significant amount of time with Shelly's family, so there was a chance they sent her on some sort of recognizance mission to discover his true feelings.

Recognizance mission? he chided himself. *Get a grip, you're not in the military anymore.*

"I don't have any expectations," he finally said. "I'm just grateful to have a nice place to stay, and the welcome from Shelly and Lilly has been warm."

"So you're not interested in her?" Kylie asked, crossing her arms and fixing him in her stern gaze.

His eyes widened, and he second-guessed his earlier dismissal of her true aims. Maybe she *was* performing some surveillance after all! "I mean, I-I, uh, well, she's a beautiful woman."

"She is," she agreed, then waited for him to continue.

Is everyone interested in Shelly's love life?

When he didn't respond, Kylie pressed on. "Shelly is not just my coworker, she's one of my closest friends. I assume you're aware of what happened with her ex." She narrowed her eyes, and he nodded. "Despite all she's been through, she can be a trusting person, as evidenced by her willingness to rent a room to a perfect stranger. Her family has filled me in on some suspicions they have about your relationship with her, and I would like you to clarify your intentions."

He lifted his hands in surrender. "I have no intentions. She is a beautiful, intelligent woman, and I have enjoyed spending time with her, but she's also made it clear she's not interested in dating anyone right now." When Kylie didn't respond, he lowered his hands and rested them on the back of a chair. "And I get it. She and Lilly have been through a lot."

"They have," Kylie said, her steely gaze giving way to concern. She blew out a breath. "But Shelly deserves to be happy. I thought maybe she was opening herself up again, letting you stay here. When she met you on the plane, she seemed lighter, then when I saw you here, it gave me hope."

It touched his heart that multiple people in Shelly's life were rooting for her, and him, for that matter. He would never pressure her, and he hoped her family wouldn't either. She had plenty of reasons to be cautious.

"I realize I don't know you," Kylie continued. "But I think you're good for her. Beatrice and Susan said you basically spent the day washing the dishes, and you've been helpful around the house. I'm happy someone is taking care of her for once instead of the other way around." She frowned. "Though you still didn't answer my question."

"I told you I have no intentions." Brad ran an agitated hand through his hair.

"Not that, my first question: are you interested in her?"

Debating what to say, he rubbed the back of his neck. "I'm not really in a position to date anyone right now."

She shook her head, her furrowed brows betraying her frustration. "That's not an answer either. Quit being evasive and just answer the—"

"Yes," he admitted quickly.

Her face lit up. "Good to know!"

She left him standing alone in the dining room, wondering whether admitting that was the best decision. Fortunately, Shelly was still busy preparing dinner and did not appear to have overheard any of the conversation. Unfortunately, he could hear whispering in the family room and assumed Kylie was sharing her discovery with Shelly's entire family. Well, everyone except Lilly, who was still upstairs.

With a sigh, he prepared himself to face them as he needed to take their drink orders. The room went eerily silent as he entered, and he shifted his weight from foot to foot, though he was a little relieved when Wallace met his eyes and gave him a brief nod of understanding.

While Susan greeted Brad with a warm smile, Beatrice had an air of skepticism about her. Perhaps he wasn't what she hoped for in a match for her daughter. Lilly and Shelly called her a perfectionist, after all.

"What would everyone like to drink?" he asked.

"Aren't you a gentleman?" Susan gave him a wink. "I'll take a glass of white wine, if Shelly has it. If not, water will do fine."

"Ice water," Beatrice said.

"Same for me." Wallace bobbed his head.

"Wine sounds good to me," Kylie replied.

Brad nodded and entered the kitchen. Shelly was pulling the pan from the oven when he came near. Several glasses had been set on the counter, and he wondered if she had perhaps been paying closer attention to the conversations going on around her house than he first suspected. He cringed as he recalled his conversation with Kylie. Would it bother Shelly that he admitted his attraction for her to her friend? If she overheard, she did not let on.

"There's a bottle of white wine chilling in the fridge," she said, pointing. "Lilly gets milk. I would like a glass of wine myself, please."

Not only had she stopped protesting his efforts to help her; she seemed to welcome it now. He took that as a sign of progress. Grabbing the wine and the milk from the fridge, he worked to get everyone's drinks squared away. As he poured the wine into the glasses, he wasn't sure who would sit where.

Susan appeared and came over to help him. After taking the glass of milk and two glasses of ice water to the dining room, she came back for two of the glasses of wine.

"We can squeeze everyone at the dining table, but we need a couple more seats. There are some folding chairs in the garage." Without waiting for his response, she went back to the dining room.

He dutifully retrieved the chairs from the garage, setting them up per her instructions.

"Dinner's ready!" Shelly called out.

Beatrice, Wallace, and Kylie came in to find their seats. A door opened on the second floor, and Brad could hear Lilly trudging down the stairs to join them. Susan and Lilly sat beside each other, leaving two seats for Shelly and Brad. If Shelly minded the seating arrangements, she said nothing. Her family engaged in lively conversation as they ate and Brad was relieved it centered on topics unrelated to him and Shelly, like the tree lighting that evening. He enjoyed learning more about her family and seeing her interact with them. The cautious, guarded woman he had first met on the plane had completely disappeared, and he marveled at the changes in her.

When dinner was over, he prepared to man the sink again, but Beatrice stopped him. "You've done enough. You and Shelly have been on your feet all day while we took a break before dinner. Why don't you two go relax in the family room until we're ready to go?"

He nodded, although he had the distinct impression this was just a part of her family's plan to set her up. Susan grabbed a plate from Shelly's hands and appeared to be suggesting the same thing. When she turned toward him, she had a bemused expression on her face. Was it because of whatever her sister said? He sank down onto the couch as soon as he reached it and heaved a sigh.

"My sentiments exactly," Shelly said as she sat beside him. "I love baking, but I'm exhausted after being on my feet for so long."

"It still smells amazing in here."

"It does." Her forehead wrinkled. "You're not too tired for the tree lighting, are you?"

"I'm getting my second wind," he said with a wink.

Kylie and Wallace came in at that moment, having been kicked out of the kitchen as well. Wallace brought a chair and some of the bounty from the day's work with him and handed them each a cookie. The cookies tasted even more delicious than they smelled.

"So, Brad, how does it feel to be out of the Marines?" Kylie asked as she settled on the couch on the other side of Shelly.

"It's all rather new to me. I haven't been a civilian for twenty years, so I'm a bit of a fish out of water."

"You struck me as a military man," Wallace said. "I was a Marine myself, many years ago now. What brings you to the area?"

"A job mostly," Brad replied. "I grew up not far from here, but I start working for the feds in the new year."

"This is a great place for commuting." Wallace took another cookie. "It is further out than some folks like, but you won't find a nicer town."

"The people have been very welcoming," Brad said, casting a furtive glance at Shelly.

"I'm amazed you're still single," Kylie said. Shelly sputtered, nearly choking on her cookie, but Kylie ignored her.

"I, uh, I guess I just never found that special someone." He wiped his palms on his pants, uncomfortable with the sudden change in conversation.

"Most women love a man in uniform though, don't they, Shelly?" Kylie teased, then jumped. Shelly's foot retreated from Kylie's leg.

"Having never seen Brad in his uniform, I wouldn't know," Shelly retorted, then bit her lip when she realized what she had said.

"I still have my dress blues if you'd like to see them," Brad joked as he raised his eyebrows. She avoided his eyes and didn't respond, but his chest swelled when she flushed a deep shade of red.

"I wouldn't fit into mine." Wallace chuckled, patting his stomach. "These cookies sure don't help that."

Luckily for Shelly, Beatrice, Susan, and Lilly came into the room at that moment, effectively ending the discussion. It was time to leave for the tree lighting. Shelly blew out a heavy breath, which Brad interpreted as a sigh of relief, and he hid a smile.

Susan insisted they could all pile in her minivan, but Wallace stated he would drive himself. He offered Shelly's mother a ride, but she gave a quick shake of her head and turned away. Was there something going on there? Brad tried not to speculate.

He waited patiently as the women climbed into the vehicle. Beatrice took the front passenger seat, Lilly and Kylie claimed the middle seats, leaving the back seat for Brad and Shelly. He couldn't help shaking his head and laughing to himself about the overt meddling. If nothing ever happened between him and Shelly, it wouldn't be from a lack of effort by her family.

The tree lighting was occurring in the town square, and parking was going to be an issue. Susan drove as close as she could, but they had a bit of a walk ahead of them. After being in a hot kitchen all day, he was eager to breathe in the crisp, fresh winter air. It hadn't snowed yet, but the air was heavy with anticipation.

The weather report suggested it might snow late tomorrow night or early Monday morning, just in time for a white Christmas. He couldn't remember the last time he had seen snow as he'd been stationed in the southern half of the country for his final years in the Marines. There had been a few ice storms, but Camp Lejeune was so close to the coast it wasn't as affected as the rest of North Carolina.

They strolled in twos, with Beatrice and Susan leading the way. Kylie and Lilly were chatting about their Christmas wish lists. It seemed Kylie was almost like another aunt to Lilly. Shelly was beside him, rubbing her eyes and unusually quiet. The day in the kitchen must have taken a toll on her. She stumbled over a dip in the sidewalk, and he caught her. When she recovered, he debated releasing her hand, but instead tucked it into the crook of his arm.

"You can lean on me if you need to. I'll keep you steady," he promised.

She tilted her head with questions in her eyes, and he realized the double meaning that could be construed behind his words. He simply smiled, letting her come to her own conclusions. There was no point in denying how he felt now, with his admission to her friend earlier. He was falling for her, and he only hoped, in time, Shelly might allow herself to feel the same way toward him.

As they came up to the center of the square, a large crowd gathered around the tree. The area was lit up with streetlamps, twinkling lights on each of the storefronts, and a few small spotlights directed at the tree itself. Rich evergreen wreaths accented with large red bows hung on the doors.

He marveled at the mammoth tree, decorated in sparkling silver and gold ornaments. There was a stage set up behind the crowd, and people kept glancing back at it, as if waiting for someone to step up and start the festivities.

Shelly hadn't let go of his arm as she waved toward friends and neighbors with her free hand. A few speculative looks came their way, but she either didn't notice them or no longer cared what people thought.

Lilly came back to stand next to them and, to his surprise, put her hand through his other arm. He squeezed her hand against his side and smiled at her. Her eyes filled with a childlike excitement, and she bounced in place, whether from joy or to keep warm; he wasn't sure. Susan stood beside her, and she gave him an amused look over Lilly's head. Beatrice and Kylie stepped up to Susan's other side just as a hush fell over the crowd. An older gentleman climbed up to the stage and raised a megaphone to his mouth.

"Greetings, everyone! Welcome to Eagle Harbor's annual Christmas tree lighting ceremony. For those new to our town, I'm Mayor Sampson, and I'm so glad to host tonight's festivities. I'm glad to see we have quite a good crowd this evening, and I know everyone is eager to get to the main event. I hope afterwards you all will stay and enjoy the carnival the town has put together. There are lots of fun activities and delicious treats for the whole family." He signaled to someone at the edge of the stage. "Without further ado, let's start the countdown!"

The air filled with festive anticipation as the crowd began counting down from ten. As everyone called each number, Lilly's hand clamped tighter and tighter on Brad's arm, and he wondered if he would have any circulation left when this was over. When the crowd yelled one, the brilliant glow from the tree momentarily blinded him.

Awed voices murmured around him, then everyone began singing the carol "Oh Christmas Tree." Shelly and Lilly joined in, their sweet voices filling his ears on either side. When he added his own voice to the mix, the three of them harmonized well together.

The mayor stepped back up to the microphone. "Now, as a special treat, we'd like to invite the stars of our Christmas pageant to the stage to give a preview of what they've been working on."

Brad gave Shelly's hand a brief squeeze before he and Lilly headed up to the stage. The town brought a guitar for him to use, so he didn't have to carry his around the festival. The children took their places, and he slung the strap over his shoulder. As he strummed the first chords, the crowd seemed to hold its collective breath, then Lilly's strong soprano filled the air with a sweet sound.

She sang the first verse of "Silver Bells" on her own before the rest of the children joined her in the refrain, continuing through the rest of the song in a lovely harmony. When they finished, they were met with a thundering applause from the town, and the children took a bow.

The crowd soon dispersed as everyone wandered over to the carnival. He allowed himself to be led by the delectable scent of kettle corn and roasted chestnuts. Lilly ran off with a couple of young girls who he assumed were her friends. Wallace arrived by this point, and he offered Beatrice his arm before escorting her over to the craft booths.

Kylie, Susan, Shelly, and Brad wandered around the square, commenting on what the town had put together. It was as if he were escorting celebrities. The three ladies seemed to know everyone, while the only person he recognized was Donna from the grocery store, standing next to the mayor. The look she gave when their gazes met told him Shelly was likely in for another embarrassing conversation during her next shopping trip. He made a mental note to warn her.

They found Lilly trying to win a stuffed bear at a bottle game. She had thrown two of her three balls but had only hit the top bottle.

"I clearly lack hand-eye coordination," she moaned as they approached her.

Brad picked up her last ball.

"It's more about how you are using your wrist," he said. He took her hand and put the ball into it, miming cocking his wrist back, then moving it fluidly forward with his arm. "Try that."

"If it doesn't work?" she asked, her brown eyes full of doubt.

"Then I'll buy you another three balls to try again for practice."

She laughed. "Deal!" With the ball in her hand like Brad instructed, she flicked her wrist at the end of her throw. To her and Shelly's astonishment, she hit the bottles right in the middle of the stack, and they all fell to the floor. Everyone cheered, and Lilly's eyes danced with joy.

"Outstanding job, Lilly!" the woman running the game exclaimed. "Which bear would you like?"

After choosing a brown bear with a red and white ribbon tie that resembled a candy cane, she hugged the bear happily and then turned and threw her arms around Brad. "Thank you!"

"Happy to help," he said cheerfully.

Lilly grabbed Kylie and Susan's hands; they ran off together to find more games.

He noticed the female game runner was staring at him with interest and figured he should introduce himself. "Hello, I'm Brad Collins. I'm new to Eagle Harbor."

"Oh, nice to meet you, Brad." The woman smoothed her blonde hair and gave him an appreciative once over. "I'm Daisy Reynolds, Lilly's English teacher. What brought you to our little town?"

"A job. I just retired from the Marines."

"The Marines." Daisy batted her lashes. "Well, we're glad to have you. If you need a tour of the area, I'd be happy to provide one!" As she flipped her hair over her shoulder, her smile widened.

"That's very kind of you, but Shelly and her family have got it covered."

Her smile fell as she turned to Shelly, almost as if she was noticing her for the first time. "It's so good to see you and Lilly here."

"Are you enjoying your break from school, Daisy?"

"Very much," Daisy said. "I love my kids, but it's nice to have some time to rest after a hectic first semester. I'm hoping to enjoy a bit more of a social life before school resumes. By the way, Lilly is excelling in English. I'm excited to have her in my class this year."

"Your class is her favorite." Shelly glanced over her shoulder. "We'd better go so we don't hold up your booth. If I don't see you, have a Merry Christmas!"

"Merry Christmas!" After giving Brad one more wistful smile, Daisy turned to her next customer.

"I believe you have an admirer," Shelly said when they were out of earshot.

"An admirer?" He frowned.

"Daisy," Shelly said in a tone that implied it was obvious.

"You think so?" He stared back at the booth, then focused on Shelly. "I hadn't noticed."

Her eyes softened, and the slow smile that lit up her face rendered him speechless. He took her hand in his as they meandered along, checking out the rest of the booths. There were more games such as ring toss, beanbag toss, and one he'd never seen before involving rubber ducks.

He was fascinated as several small children picked up a random duck and were given a choice of prizes based on the color of the dot on the bottom of their duck. It seemed everyone was a winner. They passed several food trucks, including one selling funnel cakes and hot chocolate, but Shelly wasn't interested in either. There was a firepit arranged for people to warm up and roast marshmallows near the edge of the square. They had set up a photo booth with Santa and people were also taking family photos in front of the tree.

Brad opted for the fire, as she kept shivering. They each grabbed a stick and a marshmallow before settling on a bench. She sat very close to him and, at one point, leaned her head against his shoulder as she rotated her marshmallow in the flames.

"I'm glad you came with us tonight," she said, her voice low and husky.

"Thank you for inviting me."

"And thank *you* for all you did today." She nudged him with her shoulder. "I'm not used to having someone so willing to help me."

"It was my pleasure," he told her sincerely.

She lifted her head, the firelight dancing off the side of her face. Her green eyes were unreadable, and a familiar hum of electricity crackled in the air between them. Her lips parted as the moment intensified, and he had the strongest urge to take her into his arms, kiss her, and let the rest of the world melt away. Searching her eyes for whether she felt the same, he slowly lowered his head to hers.

"Shelly! Brad! Mom wants to get photos by the tree," Susan called, causing them both to jump and drop their sticks, their marshmallows falling into the fire. He caught Susan's smirk before she disappeared.

"W-we should go." Without another word, Shelly bolted.

His brain was still hazy from their almost kiss, and he only nodded in response. He picked up their sticks and tossed them back into the bucket before following her. She moved so quickly he struggled to keep up. Was she embarrassed that Susan had seen them? Or had he misread what Shelly wanted?

Not even twenty-four hours after she told me she wasn't ready for a relationship, and I'm already overstepping her boundaries. If I don't respect her choices, then how can I see myself as any better than Eric?

As they neared the center of the square, he slowed, deciding it might be best to hang back and give her the time with her family. Wallace and Kylie were facing the enormous evergreen where Shelly's family stood. Brad noted the blush had faded from her cheeks as they situated themselves for the photo. She was smiling and laughing as they tried different poses, some serious, most funny.

"Brad! You need to get in these pictures," Susan called.

Shelly's gaze briefly met his before she dropped her head, her hair hiding her face.

"I don't want to intrude." He stood beside Kylie. "But I'm happy to take a few with Kylie in them."

"It's not intruding if you're invited," Kylie scoffed. "Just get in the photo!"

He hesitated, his gaze straying to Shelly, who shoved her hands into the pocket of her coat and turned away. When he didn't immediately acquiesce, Kylie tossed her phone to Wallace and dragged Brad into the picture. She and Susan moved everyone around until they were satisfied with the posing. They placed him with Shelly and Lilly, one of his arms around each of them.

When everyone was situated, Wallace snapped the picture. Brad sensed Beatrice, Susan, and Kylie stealthily step away, leaving him, Shelly, and Lilly alone. Wallace gave an amused grin and took a few photos of the three of them.

After Kylie had a variety of images, Brad stretched and winced, his back sore and stiff from manning the sink all day. Lilly was yawning and leaning on her mother while Beatrice kept glancing at her watch. She and Susan had a bit of a drive ahead of them.

The crowds seemed lighter, and the festivities were winding down as well. Wallace bid them farewell, and everyone else agreed it was time to go. Beatrice and Susan led the way back to the car while Shelly joined her daughter, leaving Brad alone with Kylie, bringing up the rear.

"She likes you, too, you know," Kylie said.

His heart filled with hope, but he tamped it down. "I'm not sure if that's true."

"It is, trust me." Kylie sighed. "She's just scared. Even though her marriage to Carl wasn't great, being left like that really affected her."

"I understand, and I don't want to pressure her into anything."

"You're right, you shouldn't pressure her." Her eyes held a mischievous glint. "But... everyone needs a little push now and then."

Brad laughed. "You're relentless!" His thoughts were muddled as he tried to articulate his concerns into words. "I'm not sure any such 'pushing' should come from me, though. It wouldn't be appropriate."

Kylie pursed her lips. "No, you have a point." Her hand on his arm startled him, and they stopped to let the others get a little further ahead. "I just don't want you to give up on her."

"I don't believe I could even if I wanted to," he said, running a hand through his dark hair. "Believe me, I definitely don't want to."

"Good!"

They resumed walking. Breathing in the frigid air, he replayed the almost kiss. Shelly had seemed like she wanted it too. She hadn't leaned away from him when he moved toward her. But what if he misread what she wanted? What if she was just caught up in the moment? Maybe her sister's interruption caused her to realize she'd almost made a mistake.

He wanted to kiss her. His entire body was on high alert whenever she was around. The rest of the evening replayed in his mind. Her questioning look when she stumbled, and he caught her. How she let him hold her hand and seemed to welcome it. The way she rested her head on his shoulder at the fire. He had imagined none of that, but it was possible he misinterpreted her gestures. Had he only seen what he wanted those actions to mean?

When they arrived at the car, Lilly joined her mother in the backseat, which left Brad and Kylie in the middle seats. Nobody spoke, making for a quiet and uneventful drive. Once back at Shelly's house, he said a quick goodbye and escaped to the quiet sanctuary of his room. He didn't want to intrude on the family's farewells, and he needed some time to himself.

The moment by the fire had made things awkward between him and Shelly. They could both use some space from each other to sort things out. Admitting the strength of his feelings not only to Kylie but also to himself made him more vulnerable than he was used to. He wanted to believe Shelly shared his feelings, but he worried she would talk herself out of it to protect her heart and Lilly's.

As he got ready for bed, he knew it would take time to convince her she could trust him, that he was not the type to run from commitment. He had given half of his life to the Marines, and while it wasn't quite the same thing, there was no doubt in his mind when he found the right woman, he would have no problem providing that same level of loyalty and devotion to her. It was too soon to tell if Shelly was that woman, but he feared he wouldn't get the chance to find out.

Hopefully, he hadn't messed everything up before it even had a chance to start. One thing he was sure of, no matter what happened, he wanted Shelly and Lilly in his life, and he wanted to start his civilian life in Eagle Harbor.

Chapter Eight

Shelly hadn't slept well the night before as she replayed the evening with Brad in her mind, always wincing when she recalled their almost kiss. If Susan hadn't shown up, would they have kissed? Shelly didn't know, but she had wanted to, at least at that moment.

In the end, she was more than a little relieved Susan had interrupted them. They had just had a conversation where Shelly told Brad she wasn't ready, and kissing him last night would have given him the wrong impression. Despite her growing attraction to him, deep down, she needed more time to sort through her feelings.

She promised to take Lilly Christmas shopping, and Shelly dressed with that activity in mind. It would do her and Brad good to get some distance from each other, and she was excited to spend quality time alone with her daughter. Lilly was in a rare, good mood, and Shelly could only hope it would last through the rest of her holiday break.

As she went downstairs, she flicked on lights and started the Keurig. After her rough night, she'd be needing some serious coffee this morning. She considered the options for breakfast and decided on French toast. Grabbing eggs and milk from the fridge, she worried about how awkward things would be when Brad arrived. Would he act like nothing had happened? Would he try to talk to her about it? She cringed. That was a conversation she hoped to avoid, forever if possible.

She set up the skillet and started grilling the bacon and sausage. A sharp knock at the door startled her, and she took a deep breath, steeling herself before answering. Brad stood on the other side, his features barely visible in the early morning darkness. She stepped aside to let him in, and he gave her a warm smile which didn't quite reach his eyes. After murmuring greetings, he went to sit at the table, and she busied herself in the kitchen. While she was relieved he was willing to pretend it never happened, a part of her was disappointed.

Lilly joined her in the kitchen a little later, and Shelly's heart sank when she caught the dark scowl on her daughter's face. But her concern was short-lived as Lilly beamed, clearly pleased with the breakfast Shelly was making. She was surprised when Lilly wrapped her arms around her before she began gathering dishes to set the table.

Once the food was ready, Shelly placed it on a platter and carried it into the dining room. Brad's eyes met hers, and the air thickened with the tension between them. Shelly dropped her gaze and prayed Lilly wouldn't notice the pregnant silence stifling the room.

"Are we still going Christmas shopping today?" Lilly asked, her expression hopeful, though there was a hint of concern in her dark brown eyes.

"If you want to," Shelly said.

"Is Brad coming?" Lilly gestured toward him, but Shelly refused to look in his direction, afraid of what she would find there.

"I, uh, need to focus on apartment hunting," he replied.

Lilly snuck glances at both as her brows lowered, but mercifully, she didn't ask questions. However, she did seem to rush through her meal as if she couldn't wait to escape the strained atmosphere. After she finished eating, she put her plate in the dishwasher and shot her mother a quizzical look before bolting up the stairs.

Alone with Brad, Shelly wasn't sure what to do. Should she try to make polite conversation? She couldn't very well bring up last night without risk of addressing the elephant in the room. He didn't seem to be any more eager to discuss it than she was, and they finished their breakfast in uncomfortable silence.

"I can take care of this," he told her as she stood to help him clear the table.

She nodded and gave him a small smile before turning to head up to her room. While she was relieved he wasn't pressuring her to discuss what happened, they couldn't avoid it forever. Maybe by the time she and Lilly returned, she would have a better idea of how to handle things.

She brushed her teeth and pulled her auburn hair back into a ponytail. There were bags under her green eyes, and she debated putting concealer on her dark circles, but she didn't have the energy to make the effort. Hoping Lilly wouldn't be against starting their shopping trip early, Shelly tentatively knocked on her door.

"Come in," Lilly called from within.

Shelly blinked in surprise. "Oh, you're dressed. That's good because I noticed last night a few stores on the town square have extended hours since it's so close to Christmas. Would you mind if we left now?"

With a vigorous nod, Lilly scrambled off her bed, seeming as eager to leave as Shelly. She grabbed her shoes and motioned for Shelly to go down the stairs ahead of her. The tightness in her stomach eased upon discovering the downstairs was empty. Brad must have already gone back to his room, which meant she could avoid an awkward goodbye. They put on their coats and went out the door.

The morning traffic was light, making the drive to the square much easier than the night before. There was plenty of parking on main street, and they found a spot close to the stores. As they walked by the tree, Shelly marveled at how different it appeared in the daylight. Its lights were extinguished, causing the ornaments to lose some of their luster, but its imposing size still took her breath away.

The festival booths were mostly cleared, with a few people breaking down the remaining ones that morning. Many of the lights she had seen in the windows last night were still twinkling, though the affect was more subdued in the morning sun. There were wreaths adorned with lovely red bows on many of the doors, as silver and gold garlands snaked around the windows.

Their first stop was an electronics store, where Shelly hoped to find a gift for Susan. They wandered around as Shelly searched through the various options, considering what Susan might want. Her sister was always one of the toughest people to shop for, as she was very tech savvy and often bought the latest gadgets as soon as they were released. Eventually, they made their way over to the section of the store for cellphones and accessories.

"Aunt Susan's last headset broke," Lilly offered, pointing at the blue tooth earpieces.

Shelly nodded absently and perused the options. Once she made her choice, they continued to roam throughout the store. They meandered along aisles of televisions and laptops, but when they reached the video game section, she stopped and studied the selection.

"Are you shopping for someone at work?" Lilly asked, her brows furrowing.

With a nervous laugh, Shelly shook her head. "I was debating on whether we should buy a gift for Brad." She glanced at Lilly out of the corner of her eye, then went back to browsing the shelves. "He'll be here for Christmas. It would seem rude not to include him, wouldn't it?"

"Does he even play video games?"

Shelly shrugged. "I don't know, but I figured it couldn't hurt to check out what they have."

"I'd like to get him a gift as well," Lilly said. "As a thank you for saving the Christmas pageant." She flipped through the games on the shelf in front of them. "I'm not sure what he'd like, though."

"It's hard to shop for someone you barely know." Shelly pursed her lips. None of the games struck her as something he would like.

"Is everything okay between you two?" Lilly asked, her voice low and tentative.

Shelly blew out a breath as she debated her answer. This was not a discussion she wanted to have with, well, anyone, but especially not Lilly. Their situation had been tenuous since the divorce. Her daughter was still healing not only from Carl leaving, but also his decision to remarry almost immediately. Would she feel even further betrayed if Shelly started dating again? It wasn't a question she was ready to address.

"It's complicated," she said, stifling a sigh.

Lilly nodded as if she understood and, did not pursue the subject further. Frustrated, Shelly pinched her lips together. There were too many taboo subjects in her life. They finished their browsing and made their way to the cashier. She gave up on finding something for Brad in the electronics store and was ready to move on. The longer she was away from the tension in the house, the more relaxed she became. Her arms, which she had hugged tightly against her body, eased to her sides. One of her favorite Christmas carols was playing on the store's overhead speakers, and she hummed along as her mood improved.

Their next stop was a craft store, which was filled with people. With only two more shopping days until Christmas, the whole town was in a mad rush to find the perfect gift. They checked out throw blankets for her mother.

"We'll have to get a gift receipt." Shelly rolled her eyes as she folded the blankets over her arm. "You know how your grandmother is."

Lilly choked on a giggle, and Shelly grinned. As they moved to another section of the store, someone called out to them. When they turned around, her heart stopped. There, standing in all her southern glory, stood her ex-mother-in-law, Cindy.

Her bleached blonde hair was perfectly coiffed in curls around her face, and her irises were so dark they were difficult to distinguish from her pupils. The bright purple pantsuit she wore was a harsh contrast against the backdrop of red and green Christmas decor. To say Shelly was shocked at Cindy's sudden appearance was an understatement. Last she'd heard, Cindy moved back to Texas, though it wouldn't surprise Shelly if she was there to visit her son. What she was doing in Eagle Harbor; however, was anyone's guess.

"Well, hello there," Cindy drawled as she sauntered up to them. "Fancy meeting you two."

"Hello, Cindy," Shelly said stiffly as the tension that dissipated mere moments before returned in full force, and her fists clenched at her sides.

Cindy gave her a cursory once over before focusing her attention on Lilly. "And how are you, sugar?"

"Okay, Nana."

"Don't I even get a hug? I haven't seen you in so long."

As Lilly gave her grandmother an awkward hug, Shelly noticed Lilly moved her face farther away from Cindy than was natural. Shelly assumed it was to avoid her Cindy's heavy make-up. When Shelly's eyes met Lilly's, she worked to keep her face neutral to hide her emotions and avoid causing Lilly more undue stress.

"Your daddy tells me he's been emailing you about a visit, but you haven't responded," Cindy said with an accusing glare at Shelly despite clearly addressing her comment to Lilly.

Shelly felt like she'd been punched in the stomach. Carl emailed Lilly? More than once? But... why? And why hadn't Lilly said anything? Her mind reeled with this information as Lilly's chin dipped lower and her hair curtained her face.

"Y-your dad emailed you?" Shelly stammered. Lilly's shoulders hunched forward, which only added further confirmation to Cindy's words.

"A few times," Lilly mumbled as she stared at her feet.

"Are you saying you weren't aware?" Cindy directed this question to Shelly.

"No, I'm afraid not." She kept her gaze on Lilly, who continued to stare at the floor.

"Hmph." Cindy's skepticism was obvious in her voice. She smiled at Lilly. "Why don't you run along for a minute, sugar, while your mama and I have a word?"

Defiant, Shelly glared at Cindy, vowing to deal with Lilly later. Right now, Shelly was mentally preparing herself for the onslaught of insults.

As soon as Lilly walked away, Cindy turned on her. "You're telling me you knew nothing of Carl's emails?"

"That's what I said." Shelly struggled to keep her voice even.

"Some mother you are."

"What's that supposed to mean?" Blood boiled in her veins, but Shelly worked to maintain control.

Cindy pulled herself up to her full height and looked down her nose at Shelly. "It means if you were a better mother, you'd have a firmer grasp of your daughter's online activities."

"Or perhaps I believe in talking to my daughter rather than

spying on her," Shelly shot back.

"Talking, huh?" Cindy gave a haughty laugh. "Guess Carl never came up during these 'talks.' Otherwise, wouldn't Lilly have told you about the emails?" When Shelly didn't respond, Cindy sniffed and nodded, as if Shelly's silence proved her point. "As you can see, I'm in town for the holidays and Carl was trying to determine when Lilly might come visit. Now that you're *aware* I expect you will speak with Lilly about the importance of maintaining a relationship with her father."

"I'll talk to Lilly," Shelly said through gritted teeth.

"You do that." With that, Cindy spun on her heel and headed over to the Christmas decorations where Lilly was searching through the stockings.

Shelly glowered at Cindy's back as her ex-mother-in-law approached Lilly. They exchanged a few words and another hug before Cindy strolled away. Lilly slowly came back to where Shelly stood, dragging her feet.

Shelly wasn't sure what to say to her. Seeing Cindy again had shocked her system and Shelly fought to rein in the anger clawing up her chest at the way her ex-mother-in-law spoke to her. But even more than that, she was so disappointed in Lilly and hurt her own daughter hadn't confided in her. What did that say about their relationship?

They continued their shopping trip in silence. She was too angry to say anything without causing a scene, and the last thing she needed right now was the whole town to know about their problems. It was hard enough after the divorce with the sideways glances and the whispers. She was sure anyone who was close enough to overhear her conversation with Cindy would spread gossip all over town, but Shelly didn't need to fuel the fire by getting into an argument with Lilly too.

"I can't believe you," Shelly began when they were alone in her car. Her voice shook as she wrestled with the emotional hurricane festering inside of her. "Cindy said your dad has sent you multiple emails, and yet you haven't said a word."

"I'm sorry, Mom," Lilly said. "I was trying to process it myself, and I wasn't sure how you'd react."

"All this time, I was angry with him for abandoning you, and now I come to discover he didn't abandon you at all." She glared at Lilly before putting the car in gear. "What were you thinking?"

"I was thinking a couple of emails didn't make up for what he did," Lilly cried out, her own frustration rising to the surface.

"He's your father!"

"That doesn't excuse his behavior."

Shelly glanced over at her daughter as they drove back to the house. "Perhaps not, but he's family, and you do *not* ignore family. I raised you better than this. The least you could have done was respond saying you still needed time. To completely ignore him..." Her hands gripped the steering wheel. "What I wouldn't give to talk to *my* father again."

"It's not the same!" Lilly retorted, crossing her arms over her chest.

"Be that as it may, one day you'll regret your choices."

Lilly huffed and scowled out the window. Shelly forced herself to focus on driving. This conversation wasn't over, but it wouldn't help if they got into an accident because they were too busy yelling at each other for Shelly to pay attention to the road.

She struggled to decide which she was angrier about: Cindy's insinuation she was a negligent parent for not monitoring Lilly more closely, or Lilly's decision not to confide in her. The latter caused Shelly more pain than anger. She hoped they were becoming closer, but if today's incident was any indication, she was sorely mistaken.

When they arrived home, Brad came down to help them carry in their packages. By the expression on his face, Shelly wasn't hiding her anger well. He glanced at Lilly. When she shook her head at him, Shelly's tenuous hold on her temper snapped.

"While we were shopping today, we ran into Lilly's paternal grandmother," she blurted out, her voice dangerously even.

"Oh?" he asked, hesitantly. His face brightened until the meaning behind her words sunk in, then his forehead creased in concern. "Uh, how did that go?"

Before Lilly could say anything, Shelly continued, "She only informed me Carl has been emailing Lilly for months and Lilly hasn't bothered to respond." She leveled a steely gaze at Lilly. "Or tell me, for that matter."

"Ah," he said, shifting his weight from foot to foot. His mouth opened and closed as if he was debating his next words. Then he pressed his lips together and ducked into the trunk to remove their bags.

"Can you believe she's been lying to me all this time?" Shelly pressed on.

A part of her knew this wasn't something she should involve him in, but her anger was overruling the rational side of her brain. She was hurt, confused, and enraged by the situation, and she was desperate for someone to validate her.

"Th-this sounds like a conversation you need to have between the two of you." He set the bags down and took a step away from them.

"It's too late for that; now her grandmother has weighed in.

Please enlighten us with your thoughts," Shelly countered.

Lilly, who had been gaping at her, now balled her hands into fists at her side and glared at the ground as her face grew red. For a moment, Shelly regretted her choice to involve him, but then her mind recalled the image of Cindy's haughty expression, and her temper flared again.

"Is this true? Has your father reached out?" he asked, and Lilly looked up at him with raised eyebrows.

"He has," she said. "He started emailing me four months ago, after eight months of acting like I didn't exist." She shot those last words at Shelly, but she was undeterred. Of course, Carl should have communicated before then, but two wrongs didn't make a right in this situation.

"I'm not ready to forgive and forget," Lilly said.

Shelly stared at Brad expectantly as he seemed to mull over what they had each said. He studied Lilly for a long moment. When he spoke, he directed his words to Shelly, but his attention never left Lilly.

"It sounds like you had a rough conversation," he said, his voice low. "I'm sure this is not how Lilly wanted you to find out. But it sounds like Lilly was blindsided herself by his first email. Perhaps she didn't handle it the way you would have, but she's young and understandably hurt by his neglect. She handled it in the best way she knew how." He faced Shelly. "Her father has a lot to answer for, and it's not fair to judge Lilly for not responding to an email from him after what he's done."

Shelly's mouth fell open, not believing her ears.. He was taking *Lilly's* side? A sharp pain twisted in her stomach, like a knife. Without another word, she grabbed the bags and stomped toward the house.

~ * ~

Well, that had clearly been the wrong move. Brad wished he had just refused to engage and stayed out of something which was none of his business. Lilly was silent beside him, her face still flushed.

"Mr. Ryan called while you two were out," he said, breaking the tense silence. "He's going to come pick us up a bit early to get some practice in before the dress rehearsal this evening. He said he'd be here around three."

She nodded but didn't speak. Brad wasn't sure if he should say anything to her or give her some space. After a few moments of continued awkward silence, he made a move to go to his room.

"Thank you," she said, so softly he almost wasn't sure she had spoken.

When he turned, she was looking at him, and he shrugged. "My sister had similar feelings when I left her to join the service after our parents died. Like your dad, I had a lot to answer for, and I'm still making amends. My sister and I aren't close, but we're getting there. Maybe someday, when you're ready, you'll rebuild a relationship with your father too." With a glance at the house, he swallowed the lump in his throat. "But your mother doesn't appreciate my opinion."

"To be fair, she forced it out of you."

"I don't think she was expecting my answer." He pursed his lips. "That said, I can appreciate your mother's side as well. She lost her father, and having lost both my parents, I get that desire for just one more day, one more conversation, with someone you loved." His eyes closed as he remembered similar conversations from his past. "When my friends in the military would complain about their parents, I struggled to empathize because I would give anything to have parents to complain about, but their relationship with their parents was not mine." He opened his eyes and sighed. "Not every situation can be resolved with a simple apology. If your father is trying to apologize now, that's great, but the choice to accept it or not is up to you. No one else can dictate the terms of your relationship with him."

"I wish she could see that." Lilly kicked a rock down the driveway.

"Give her time," Brad said. The sound of an engine coming up the road caused them both to turn.

A black SUV parked at the end of the driveway and the passenger window rolled down. Mr. Ryan leaned over and smiled at them. "Afternoon! You both ready to go?"

Brad nodded. "Just let me go grab my guitar." As he turned to go, he gestured to Lilly. "You might want to tell your mom what's going on."

Lilly rolled her eyes as she pulled out her phone. "I'll just text her."

His lips twitched as he hid a grin and ran up the stairs to his room. It might be good for both Shelly and Lilly to get some distance from each other, and he understood why Lilly was in no mood to talk to her mother right then. When he returned to the driveway, Lilly was already in the car. He jumped into the passenger seat and stole a quick glance at the house. A curtain moved in the second-story window as they drove away. Was Shelly watching them the whole time?

The theatre was dark and empty when they arrived. Mr. Ryan told them to set up onstage. Brad was a little nervous now the reality of performing was settling in. If only he had more time to work with the children before the pageant. But he had practiced a lot whenever he could and was quickly memorizing the sheet music.

When Mr. Ryan offered him and Lilly some extra time at the theatre before the dress rehearsal, Brad jumped at the chance. In retrospect, he should have talked to Lilly and Shelly about it first, but he'd assumed they wouldn't mind. At this point, he doubted he could dig the hole he was in with Shelly much deeper than it already was. He hoped they'd have a chance to talk this evening and clear the air, but he was happy to order takeout if he wasn't welcome to join them for dinner.

Lilly changed into her costume, which was a spoof of a vintage Hollywood director's outfit, complete with khaki pants and a black beret. The pageant was a hilarious play called "The Worst Christmas Pageant Ever." Lilly, as the lead, played the director, who was desperately trying to stop the annual Christmas pageant from being a complete disaster.

Some of the hijinks included eight moose instead of reindeer, the naughty and nice list getting lost, and Frosty being made of ice instead of snow. It sounded adorable. They had interspersed plenty of carols to help with scene changes.

The stage had a backdrop of what was supposed to be a small town, but there were several issues with it to add to the humor of the play. It was purposefully unfinished, for one thing, with one house only half painted in. They painted the streetlights upside down, and even some of the set pieces were wrong. He couldn't wait to see how it all came together.

Brad and Lilly rehearsed several of her solos, then she ran through a few of her scenes with Mr. Ryan. While they practiced, some of the crew rehearsed the lighting changes, which was as disorienting as it was amusing. The spotlights were always shining in the wrong place, and the background lights never quite fit the scenes. By the time the rest of the cast arrived, both Brad and Lilly were a lot more confident in their roles. They relaxed together as everyone else changed into their costumes and prepared to perform the entire production.

"I can't tell you how much I appreciate you doing this," she confided in him as they sat on the steps to the stage, waiting for the dress rehearsal to start.

"It's no problem." He glanced over at her. The clouds that dispersed while they were practicing gathered in her dark eyes again. "You okay?"

"I keep thinking about my mom," she admitted. "She didn't really say much in response to my text, and I hate the idea of her alone right now." With a heavy sigh, she leaned back against the step. "I'm still angry and upset at how she handled the situation, but I'm also worried about her."

"I get that," he said. "But it's good she has this time to cool off.

I'm hopeful once she has a chance to see things calmly, she'll realize her mistake and apologize. Then the two of you can talk about the actual issue of your dad and how to handle his reappearance."

"I hope you're right," Lilly said, though there was obvious doubt in her tone. She snuck a quick glance at him. "I think there're some things the two of you need to discuss as well."

His eyes widened in surprise. "What do you mean?"

"Just that things seemed tense between you this morning at breakfast."

"You could say that." While he'd hoped Lilly hadn't noticed, he supposed the tension that morning was thick enough to cut with a knife.

"When you both are on good terms again, you should ask her out," she said with a sly smile.

"What? Like, on a date?" he asked as he gaped at her.

She nodded. "I believe she would like that." With one hand, she lifted the beret off her head while smoothing her hair with the other. "She was so happy last night with you. It's been a while since I've seen her smile."

Brad wasn't sure what to say. It pleased him that someone else noticed the lift in Shelly's mood the night before; well, at least, the way she was before their almost kiss. She had seemed lighter, less weighed down. But after the way she acted since she left the fire, he wasn't sure asking her out was the right decision.

"Your mom has made her boundaries pretty clear," he finally said.

"Never hurts to ask," Lilly countered as she stood.

Before Brad could respond, Mr. Ryan had called for everyone to go to their places, effectively ending the conversation.

Chapter Nine

Shelly lay on her bed for hours after Lilly and Brad left to go to the dress rehearsal. The scene in the driveway played on repeat in her head. Just when Shelly was finally getting the hang of motherhood, something had to come in and shatter her confidence.

It shocked her when Brad defended Lilly's stance. Having lost both his parents, Shelly expected he would share her view of the situation. That if he had the chance to talk to his parents again, he would take it in a heartbeat. While their situations differed vastly from Lilly's, family was family, and you didn't turn your back on them, no matter what. Shelly sighed as she realized how wrong she was. It was clear he had a different perspective than she did, and she couldn't help envying how he had empathized with Lilly in a way Shelly couldn't.

If she was honest with herself, she was less upset about Lilly not responding to her father and more upset with the way Shelly had learned he'd reached out. Her relationship with her mother-in-law had always been strained, no matter how much she tried to please her. It should have been more of a red flag the way Cindy would go to visit Carl at work, then stop by the house, all the while talking about how amazing Deborah was.

Back then, Shelly brushed it off, but now she wondered if Cindy had always hoped Carl would wise up and leave Shelly. They married rather young. Her mother had taken it in stride, having married young herself, but Cindy believed Carl was made for bigger things, which apparently didn't include a wife and a child in his early twenties. When Cindy had moved back to Texas, it had been such a relief.

Seeing her today brought up a lot of resentments, which were only compounded when Cindy implied Shelly was a careless mother. Since Lilly hit her teen years, Shelly walked a fine line between giving her daughter privacy and keeping her safe. She monitored her social media and regularly discussed internet safety, trusting her daughter would be honest with her. While it hurt that Lilly had kept this big secret from her, Shelly understood why.

Lilly vocalized how conflicted she was about her father the other night, and she was likely still working through her emotions. If only she had at least shared she had heard from her father, it might have saved them the pain and embarrassment of the encounter with Cindy. Yet, there was no way Lilly could have known they would run into Cindy in Eagle Harbor's town square, of all places. When Carl left, he had not only left the home and the life they shared, but the town as well. The divorce documents suggested he moved into Deborah's apartment, closer to the city. Shelly couldn't help wondering if Cindy shopped at the town square with the express intent of running into them.

Shelly glanced at the clock. It was almost time to feed Newton and start dinner. The dress rehearsal was supposed to last until around six. Tonight, she figured she'd make the chicken she had planned for yesterday before Kylie and Eric came over. There would be quite a few leftovers, since now only three people would be eating it.

Well. She grimaced. *Possibly only two, as I will understand if Brad doesn't want to join us for dinner.*

Between the almost kiss the night before and her dramatic departure from the confrontation in the driveway, she wondered if whatever was developing between herself and Brad was over before it had a chance to begin. Things were extremely uncomfortable at breakfast this morning, then she had to go and involve him in an argument that should have stayed between her and Lilly.

Thinking about him brought back memories of the previous evening. Butterflies had been careening nervously around in Shelly's stomach as they walked around the festival together, but at the same time, his attentiveness brought warm and fuzzy feelings. He was kind and caring, not only to her, but to her whole family. His patience in showing Lilly how to throw the ball touched her heart, then his pure pride in her success at winning the bear had her contemplating what a wonderful father he would be.

The latter of these brought a fresh rush of blood to her cheeks, and she was relieved he hadn't been looking at her at the time. Finally, by the fire, it had felt natural to lay her head against his shoulder, breathing in his scent of pine and vanilla. The butterflies had gone into overdrive, whizzing around in her stomach when their eyes met. As he leaned in to kiss her, she thought she would burst out of her skin. But, of course, her sister just had to choose that moment to come find them. What would it have been like if her sister hadn't interrupted? Would she have kissed him back? Would things have changed between them?

Things certainly changed between them since then, but not in the way she expected. She told him she wasn't ready for a romantic relationship, but last night she had briefly forgotten her hesitations and protestations, for once allowing her heart to steer instead of her head. What she realized was she enjoyed being with him, and more than that, she wanted to be with him. How he held her hand, the way his eyes bored into her very soul. Whether or not she wanted to, she was falling for him.

But now, I might have ruined everything

Her phone rang, and the screen lit up with her sister's name. With a dejected sigh, Shelly picked it up, although she wasn't in the mood to talk to anyone. "Hello?"

"Hello yourself. How did shopping go?"

"Not well."

"Uh oh. What happened?"

Shelly twirled a strand of her hair, debating whether to get into it, but she figured Susan would hear about it soon enough. So, Shelly shared the entire story, including the confrontation between her, Brad, and Lilly in the driveway.

"It wasn't my finest moment," Shelly said. "I wish I hadn't involved Brad, but I was just so angry. I wasn't thinking straight."

"Sheesh, what a mess," Susan said. "I can understand your feelings, especially since Cindy has always known how to push your buttons and get under your skin. I'm surprised Lilly didn't tell you, though. It seemed like you two had gotten closer since the divorce."

"We have." Shelly's voice was filled with sadness and regret. "She was probably afraid to tell me because of how I might react, and I'm sure my reaction today just confirmed her fears."

"How do you feel about the possibility of Carl being back in your life?"

"I don't know. On the one hand, I'm happy he's at least trying to reconnect with Lilly. But on the other hand, it's too little, too late." Wracking her brain, she tried to find words to describe how she felt. "It'll be hard to see him again. I believe I've finally moved on from our marriage, and I don't miss him in that way anymore, but it's much easier to say that now, when he's not standing in front of me."

"I can't tell you how glad I am to hear you say you're moving on," Susan said, her tone sincere, then she laughed. "Would the handsome Marine living in your guest room have anything to do with that?"

Shelly's cheeks warmed, and she was glad her sister couldn't witness it. "Maybe," she murmured.

"Maybe?" Susan jumped on the admission. "Well, that's progress."

"Is it though? I think I screwed everything up," Shelly said, biting her lip.

"Why do you say that?"

"Things were weird between us before the argument with Lilly. You kind of, uh, interrupted what would have been our first kiss."

"Ha, I thought so!" Susan giggled. "If only I had delayed myself a few moments more." When Shelly said nothing, Susan continued, "But if he wanted to kiss you last night, odds are that desire didn't go away after one argument."

"But I was distant this morning." Shelly pushed herself off the bed. "We barely said two words to each other." Frustrated, she ran her hand through her hair as she paced the floor of her room. "Maybe I'm more drama than he can handle."

"I doubt that," Susan said. "Just talk to him. He was a Marine, after all. He doesn't strike me as the type to run from a challenge."

"I should talk to Lilly first," Shelly hedged, wanting to delay the conversation with Brad for as long as possible.

"Don't stall for too long."

Shelly smiled. Susan saw through her, even over the phone. "Yeah, yeah. I'll give you a play-by-play later."

"You better! I'm living vicariously through you right now."

"Will Annabelle be home for Christmas?" Shelly gnawed on her bottom lip, knowing this was a sore subject.

Susan sighed. "I hope so, but you know how her career is."

Her sister's frustration was palpable through the phone. "If she is, you must bring her up. It's been so long since we've seen her."

"I'll drag her by her hair if I have to." Susan cleared her throat. "Speaking of, I wanted to tell you, Annabelle and I have come to a decision. We've decided we want to have a baby."

Shelly almost dropped the phone. "What?"

"We've been talking about it for a while, and now, with another election year ending, it might be a good time."

"Uh... wow," Shelly said. "I'm thrilled for you both." Her chest felt lighter as she broke into a wide grin. "That's amazing. I can't wait to be an auntie!"

Susan blew out a breath that sounded like a sigh of relief. "I'm so glad to hear you say that. I haven't told Mom yet."

"I'm sure she'll be thrilled for you." Shelly reassured her. "She always wanted more grandchildren."

"That's true. Keep me posted about how things go with your Marine."

Shelly laughed. "Sounds good. Bye, Susan."

She sat back on her bed with a groan. There was going to be a lot of eating crow in her future, but at least her stomach didn't flip when she considered what she would say to Lilly. With a heavy sigh, Shelly left the sanctuary of her room and went downstairs to feed the cat and get started on dinner.

~ * ~

When Lilly arrived home a couple of hours later, Shelly was surprised and disappointed to find her alone. Brad must have gone back to his room. Did he think he wasn't welcome anymore? Lilly went straight to her room without so much as a mumbled greeting, and Shelly stifled a sigh as she grabbed a white towel and climbed the stairs. She tapped on the door.

"Come in."

As she opened the door, she waved the towel in front of her like a white flag. "Truce! Truce!"

Lilly was lying on her bed, playing on her phone. Her smile was small, and Shelly's heart sank. She entered the room and sat on her daughter's fuzzy purple chair. Her hands balled the towel as she debated how to begin.

"I'm sorry I yelled at you," Shelly finally said. "If I'm being honest, you are not the person I'm truly upset with."

"Nana?" Lilly asked.

"Yes and no." Shelly unraveled the towel and twisted it. "I'm upset with myself because you felt you couldn't come to me." Her stomach churned as she looked at her daughter. "I understand why you hesitated, though, and I imagine my reaction today was what you feared."

When Lilly nodded, Shelly's heart squeezed. "I'm sorry. I let my own emotions cloud my judgment. You and your dad are in a totally different place from the relationship I had with my father, and I shouldn't confuse the two." Her fingers fiddled with her hair as she tried to think of how to explain her reaction. "Objectively, I understand how his leaving differs from my father dying, but every day I wish I could have one more conversation with my dad. I shouldn't have projected this onto you."

"I understand," Lilly said, her voice filled with sympathy.

"But that's not fair of me. Brad is right, your dad has not done right by you." Shelly rolled her head back and stared at the ceiling. The glow-in-the-dark stars they pasted there ages ago were faded and barely glowed anymore. "And yes, being scolded by your grandmother didn't help things."

"I don't understand why she scolded you," Lilly snapped. "She hasn't contacted me, either."

Shelly snapped her head back down in surprise. "Really? The way she acted, it sounded like you weren't responding to either of them, which just didn't seem like you."

Lilly shook her head. "I haven't heard from her since my birthday."

A fresh surge of anger erupted in Shelly, but she clamped it down. What was the point? Cindy did what she wanted because, no matter what anyone said, she always believed she was right. It made Shelly feel a little better about some of the accusations laid against her. Maybe she wasn't such a terrible mother after all.

"I read Dad's latest email," Lilly continued. "I have just been deleting the others without opening them, but I decided to give him the benefit of the doubt."

"Oh?" Shelly asked. Her curiosity got the better of her, though she didn't want to pry.

"He talked about Nana's visit and said I could have lunch with her without seeing him, though I wouldn't put it past him to just show up." She glanced at her mother. "He also told me to give you a hug for him."

The emotional storm that went through Shelly must have been clear on her face because Lilly giggled. First, she was in disbelief, then angered, followed by bewilderment and irritation before she landed on exasperation. That man had nerve.

"I'll take that as a no?"

"I will always accept a hug from you," Shelly said. "But I'd prefer to not have one passed on from your father."

"Only me?" Lilly asked, a little too innocently.

"Hugs from family are the best!"

"What about from people who are becoming like family?"

Shelly narrowed her eyes, but Lilly simply blinked at her, betraying nothing. Did Lilly suspect, as the rest of her family seemed to, there was something going on between Shelly and Brad? Was she bothered by the prospect? The last thing she wanted to do was put her daughter's world in further turmoil at the thought of her mother dating.

"I accept hugs from family and friends." Shelly side-eyed her daughter.

"Does Brad count as a friend?" Lilly lifted her chin.

"He is... an acquaintance who is becoming a friend," Shelly said, then grimaced. "Or at least, he was." She fell against the chair, dejected. "I'm not sure if we'll get the chance to be friends."

"He wants to be."

Shelly stared at her. "Why do you say that?"

Lilly shrugged. "We talked while we were waiting for the dress rehearsal to begin. He was pretty upset."

With a groan, Shelly pinched the bridge of her nose between her forefinger and thumb. "He's next on my apology tour."

"Don't let me hold you up." Lilly jumped up and yanked her mother toward the door.

"Wait!" Shelly planted her feet, and Lilly stopped, an annoyed scowl on her face. "Are we okay?"

"We're fine, Mom. I'm sorry I didn't tell you about Dad's emails. I knew how you'd react, but really—I just wanted to protect you."

"Protect me?" She tilted her head. "Protect me from what?"

"From Dad, from his coming back into our lives. Things are getting better; we're fitting into a routine now. I didn't want to let Dad to interfere with that."

"Oh, sweetie, you don't have to protect me," Shelly said. "If you decide you want your father back in your life, we'll make it work. But I shouldn't factor into the decision." She hugged Lilly close.

"I understand that now, Mom, I do." Her arms tightened around Shelly.

"We both have a lot of… feelings concerning your father and your grandmother," she said, an idea forming in her head. "Would you be open to seeing a therapist to work through everything?"

"Uh, yeah, Mom. Obviously, we need therapy," Lilly deadpanned.

Shelly blinked in surprise, then laughed. "Okay then. I'll search for a therapist for us to meet with after the holidays."

Lilly playfully pushed her toward the door. "Now go finish your apology tour!"

With a laugh, Shelly left and closed the door behind her, but she didn't immediately head over to Brad's room. First, she needed a little more time to determine what to say and how to say it. So, okay, she was stalling. The butterflies that had gone to sleep while talking to her daughter started fluttering around her stomach again. Would she be able to find the words to explain her sudden change toward him so he would understand?

Her mind drifted to the evening before, and a flood of images entered her head, including the way he searched her eyes before he leaned toward her by the fire. He had hesitated, as if trying to gauge what she wanted, and she closed her eyes, preparing herself for when his lips would touch hers.

She shook her head, trying to clear the images in her brain as she went to the kitchen to check on the chicken. It wouldn't be helpful if she was fantasizing about kissing him while she was trying to apologize. But how should she approach him? Would it be wrong for her to just go to his room?

Perhaps, but it wasn't a conversation she wanted to have over dinner, and she didn't want dinner to be a repeat of the uncomfortable breakfast they shared. Besides, he might not even come to dinner if he believed he wasn't welcome.

The chicken still had about thirty minutes to cook, so she closed the oven door. She could always invite him to go for a walk with her, as there weren't many places to sit in the in-law apartment. But should she risk any of her neighbors overhearing their conversation? No, and she didn't want him to think she was afraid to be alone with him, especially after she had avoided him since last night.

With a deep breath, she forced herself to leave the kitchen and head out the front door. The closer she got to his room, the more her apprehension grew. Her heart pounded in her chest as she climbed the stairs, and each step became heavier as she feared the reception she might find on the other side of the door. It took all the strength she had to lift her hand and knock softly.

The door opened, and Brad's face registered surprise. He didn't speak but stepped back to allow her to enter. For someone who always had a ready smile for her, his lack of one was not a good sign, and Shelly's heart sank. Was she too late? Had he decided she wasn't worth it?

They stood uneasily in the room together, the tension thickening the air. A warmth spread through her chest as she noted he had made himself at home. He'd neatly put away his clothes. The bed was made, and the room was warm. His things were well organized and put together in direct contrast to the chaos occurring within her.

He indicated she could sit on the bed, and he leaned against the wall, as if bracing himself for another argument. The barrier that had built up between them fortified as the silence stretched on, and she hoped she could break through it if only she could find the right words.

"I'm sorry," she blurted out, forgetting all the carefully worded apologies she rehearsed in her head.

"For what?" he asked, his voice and face expressionless.

"Putting you in the middle of an argument with Lilly, for starters."

He shrugged, but the hurt he was trying to hide showed through in the stiff way he stood. The night before seemed like a thousand years ago with how distant he was now.

"I realize now I was more upset by my ex-mother-in-law's commentary than Lilly not telling me or not responding to her dad," Shelly tried again.

He remained unmoved, and she wished she knew what he was thinking or how to reach him. Was he upset about her putting him in the middle, and her apology just wasn't sufficient? Or was his behavior because of the strained space between them since the previous evening?

"Regardless, I shouldn't have brought you into it. You came outside to help us, and-and I—" she babbled. "It was unfair and wrong. Then I just—" With a deep breath, she tried to calm herself as she frantically sought for the right words that would break through his stony silence. "I stormed off and left you both outside. I've talked to Lilly, I-I apologized to her, and we-we're good. Now, I want to try to make things right with you."

His face remained impassive, and all her butterflies from earlier seemed to have collided with each other, forming a solid ball in the pit of her stomach. It felt like she had already lost him, but could you lose what you never really had?

The scene was becoming devastatingly familiar, and she was grateful this time, the argument was happening outside of her home, her sanctuary. Deciding she had little left to lose at this point, she figured she might as well address the elephant in the room. At least she could tell him how she felt, even if it didn't make a difference or change his mind.

"I-I've made things awkward, s-since last night. And I know..." Unbidden tears pricked behind her eyes, and she furiously blinked them back. No, she would *not* fall apart in front of him. This time would be different. It had to be. "Th-that's my fault. I wanted, I mean, I thought I wanted—" The words were coming out all wrong.

Was he going to leave too? All her resolve to not break down dissolved as the tears spilled over her cheeks. The perfectly ordered room mocked her, and she covered her face in her hands to avoid seeing his cool, indifferent eyes looking back at her. If she had the strength, she would have run away, but she was too weak and vulnerable from the emotional upheaval she had already gone through. The idea she was about to be left behind, again, by someone who had come to mean a lot to her in such a short time was more than she could handle. Her attempts to maintain her boundaries and to protect herself from more heartache appeared to have been in vain.

Through her sobs, she registered a shift in the bed, then a warm arm wrapped around her shoulders. Another gentle hand drew her hands away from her face but didn't release them. Though her eyes were blurred with tears, it was clear Brad's had lost their apathy, and in its place was only concern. He still said nothing, but he didn't let go either.

As her sobs subsided, she realized he was waiting for her to continue and swallowed thickly before forcing herself to face him. "Brad, I am sorry. For this afternoon, for last night—for everything."

Brad closed his eyes and sat in silence for what seemed like an eternity. When he opened them, they were guarded, and he seemed to take great care in choosing his next words. "What, exactly, are you sorry about regarding last night?"

"The way I acted after..." She hoped he would catch her drift without her having to say the words out loud.

"After?"

She huffed in frustration. "After Susan came to get us f-from the fire." Was it possible she imagined the entire incident into existence?

But then she caught him smiling. Was he was teasing her about not remembering? This was hardly the time for jokes. Just as she was about to call him on it, he lifted his finger and touched it to her lips.

"I'm not trying to be difficult," he began. "But I was afraid you were going to say you were sorry about everything that happened last night, that you regretted the time we spent together and how close we were." Her head tilted and she pursed her lips, not understanding his meaning. "The night we decorated the tree together, you made your boundaries very clear, and I was afraid I upset you because I wasn't respecting them or you." He looked down at their intertwined hands. "I was afraid I'd overstepped."

"Oh," Shelly said, a realization dawning on her. She told him she wasn't ready for a relationship, but her actions, even before the moment by the fire, implied something different. "I've been sending you some mixed signals."

"I get it," he rushed on, as if to reassure her. "When you told me you weren't sure if you were ready, that you and Lilly were still raw from the divorce, I completely understood, and I told myself, whatever happened, I would follow your lead, go at your pace. I was happy just becoming your friend. But then, at the festival, I thought you'd changed your mind. When your sister came to get us, you withdrew so abruptly I was sure I'd crossed a line that I misread what you wanted. And I get you may even be confused yourself about what you want." He searched her eyes. "I just want you to know this is new to me. I didn't expect any of this. I didn't expect you."

Relief washed over her as she squeezed his hand and smiled. It all made sense now, his cool demeanor when she came over here, his silence at breakfast. She wasn't the only person who had a heart to protect, but while he was protecting himself from further hurt, he was also trying to read her, to understand what she wanted from him. His concern for her welfare, despite his own stake in the matter, touched her.

"Are you okay?" he asked when she didn't say anything. "Today has been a tough day for you."

She nodded. "I am now. And I'm sorry f-for the waterworks." A shaky laugh bubbled out of her throat. "For a moment, I was afraid you were planning to stay at a hotel, after all." Her tears blurred her vision, and she lifted a hand to wipe her eyes. "I guess you could say I have abandonment issues."

He frowned and shook his head. "I would not do that to you, or Lilly. If I were to decide to go, I would talk to you first. I would not just leave."

"I appreciate that. With everything that happened, I would have understood if you wanted nothing more to do with me."

"Shelly." Brad cupped her cheek. "Regardless of what happens with us, I care about you. I understand we've only known each other a short time, but you and Lilly matter to me. Besides, that would be a rather poor repayment of your hospitality." His forehead creased. "Do you want to tell me about your conversation with your former mother-in-law? It seemed like what she said really upset you."

"If you'll come back to the house with me. I've got dinner in the oven." Her mouth was dry, and she licked her lips. "It's chicken, if you want to join us again."

"I'll never pass up a home cooked meal," he joked as he jumped up and slipped his feet into a pair of shoes before they descended the stairs.

Dusk was gathering outside, and an icy wind blew as they hurried into the warmth of the main house. Once there, Shelly left Brad in the family room and went to check on the chicken.

Alone with her thoughts for the moment, she breathed a deep sigh of relief. She was thrilled to have cleared the air with him and to have a better understanding of where they both stood. Her heart was full of the knowledge he not only cared for her, but he was willing to be patient as well. She quickly covered the chicken before sliding it back into the oven, eager to return to his side.

Chapter Ten

Brad relaxed on the couch and listened to Shelly moving about in the kitchen. He was overwhelmed with relief after their conversation. When she came to his room, he half expected her to throw him out, especially after he had stuck his nose where it didn't belong. Sure, Shelly asked for his opinion, but it was clear she hadn't expected his answer. He was glad to hear she and Lilly had made up. It was too close to the holiday for the mother and daughter duo to be fighting. They'd been through enough this year.

With his eyes closed, he leaned his head back on the couch, marveling at the way Shelly's tears had broken through all of his resolve to keep his distance. When had he gone soft? Where was the stoic Marine he had been just a short time ago?

If my unit could only see me now! There was no helping it; seeing Shelly distraught cut him deeply. The ability to maintain emotional distance that he perfected during his years as a Marine evaporated at the sight of her tears.

A sound caught his attention, and he opened his eyes to find the cat stalking toward him. He lifted his hand to be sniffed, and Newton pushed in his furry gray head. It was fascinating, petting a cat. They did the work for you. All he had to do was hold his hand out and the cat would move his entire body under it. Newton climbed onto his lap, nuzzling his face and purring up a storm. While Brad had never been much of a pet person, and definitely not a cat person, Newton was an exception.

"I believe you've made a friend," Shelly said as she came into the room. She sat on the opposite end of the couch as Newton circled Brad's lap a few times before lying down.

He scratched Newton's ears, then motioned for her to scoot closer. "Come, tell me about your conversation with Lilly's grandmother."

Without hesitating, Shelly slid beside him. "Leave it to Cindy

Harris to ruin a perfectly good Christmas shopping trip."

As Shelly relayed the things Cindy said to her, including the implication that Shelly was a horrible mother for not closely monitoring Lilly's emails, the corners of Brad's mouth pulled down. He understood how hard it was to walk a fine line between protecting her daughter and respecting her privacy.

He did not envy her position. "Does she not understand the harm her son did to both you and Lilly?"

Her lips lifted in a sardonic smile. "That would imply she cares. Perhaps she does, about Lilly at least, and maybe that's the real reason Carl started reaching out. Maybe she pressured him to. But she doesn't care about me. We never got along. She was thrilled he left me for Deborah."

"I'm sorry," Brad sympathized. "That must have been hard."

"Honestly, if one good thing came from the divorce, it's that she's no longer in my life." With a heavy sigh, Shelly sank deeper into the couch cushions. "Today was a rough day."

"Perhaps we can end it on a cheerful note," he said as he gazed past the tree out the window. "Some of the cast members were talking about going ice skating tonight. Would you and Lilly like to go?"

Shelly's face lit up. "We would both love that!"

Every time she said yes to him, it elated him beyond description. Yet, he was afraid to ask her out, as Lilly suggested. Shelly apologized for pushing him away, but he still wasn't sure how she felt about him despite how open he was about his own feelings. The last thing he wanted to do was upset her again by not respecting her boundaries or pushing her beyond her comfort zone. It was important to him that they go at her pace. Besides, her family had put enough pressure on them as it was with their amateur matchmaking.

A buzzer went off in the kitchen, and Shelly jumped up to check on dinner. Brad gently encouraged Newton off his lap, then followed her to set the table. The room was filled with the earthy smell of herbs and roasted meat. His stomach growled. He hadn't eaten anything substantial since breakfast. After the cold welcome he received that morning and the argument in the driveway, he had had little of an appetite. But now, with the delectable scents wafting through the air, he anticipated another delicious home-cooked meal. He could get used to this.

The thought made him stop short. If he was being honest with himself, he hadn't been as actively searching for a place to live as he should have. While he could make the argument it wasn't the best season for apartment-hunting, the reality was he was happy there. He couldn't rent a room from Shelly forever, but he was in no hurry to leave.

He grabbed the plates and silverware before taking them into the dining room. As he set the table, he examined his lack of effort in finding a place. It wasn't just that he was enjoying his time there; he was still out of his element. He'd lived on his own before, in off-base housing, but the military vetted it. Shelly offered to help him find an apartment, and although she would never recommend somewhere she wouldn't stay in herself, he was hesitant to ask her. It felt like home, and it was that feeling he was resistant to lose.

"Brad, would you mind carving the chicken?" Shelly interrupted his thoughts.

He nodded and followed her into the kitchen, where the chicken was set on a carving board with a fork and knife. An empty platter sat next to the board. He lifted the knife and cut into the chicken as she busied herself behind him with making gravy. There was also a pot of stuffing and green beans on the stove to round out a balanced meal.

Lilly wandered into the kitchen. "It smells fantastic, Mom."

"Hopefully it tastes just as good," Shelly joked.

"It looks perfect." Brad sliced cleanly through the meat. Newton was sitting on the floor, staring at him like a predator watching prey, and he tossed a couple of small pieces onto the floor. The cat gobbled them up, then returned his expectant gaze to Brad. He grinned. "Newton approves!"

Newton meowed, as if in agreement, making them all laugh. Brad finished carving and soon everything was on the table. They sat down together as they had done every night since his arrival, and he was pleased that the uncomfortable tension from the morning had dissipated. It occurred to him if someone peered through the back door and saw the three of them together, they likely resembled a family. His heart swelled. While his brothers and sisters in the Marines were his family for a long time, this was different.

"I can't believe Christmas is only a few days away," Lilly said as she served herself.

"Were you able to get your shopping done?" he asked.

"I think so."

"What about you?" Shelly asked him. "Did you need a ride to the store?"

"I've shipped some things to my sister, but I wouldn't mind picking up a few more items."

"We can go tomorrow if you'd like."

He smiled and started to respond when an unexpected pressure hit his shin, causing him to jump. It took a moment for him to realize Lilly had kicked him. She gave him a meaningful look and inclined her head, her intent clear. He swallowed around the sudden lump in his throat and snuck a peek at Shelly. Would it be inappropriate to invite her to dinner now? Lilly nudged him again with her foot and he chuckled to himself. Apparently, *she* believed now was the right time.

"I would like that," he said as he tried to find the right words. "In fact, I was, uh, wondering if—" his voice broke. A different tactic occurred to him, and he cleared his throat. "You've been very kind to me, cooking every night I've been here, and I was wondering if you would allow me to take you out to dinner Tuesday night, as a thank you." Lilly gave him a quick thumbs up, then ducked her head to hide a grin.

Shelly's mouth fell open. "You mean just the two of us?" Her wide eyes glanced at her daughter. "What about Lilly?"

"I have plans." Lilly cut in before Brad could respond.

"You do?" Shelly asked with raised eyebrows.

"Aunt Susan and Aunt Annabelle are picking me up, and we're going caroling together."

Now Brad hid a smile of his own. Her family really was a bunch of amateur matchmakers. He suspected Lilly told Susan about their conversation at the theatre, and Susan helped concoct the caroling plan to allow Shelly and him some time alone. Though he wondered who Annabelle was. As far as he was aware, Shelly didn't have any other siblings, but perhaps she was a close friend, like Kylie, who was like family.

"Well," Shelly said, her cheeks pink. "In that case, yes, I would love to have dinner with you."

Lilly nudged him once more under the table, and she held out her hand, palm up low enough so her mother couldn't see. He discreetly tapped his palm to hers in a modified high five. It was comforting to know her family and friends were rooting for him, but no matter how much the people in her life pushed them together, the future of their relationship was ultimately up to Shelly.

"I'm glad to hear Aunt Annabelle will be back in town by then." She changed the subject.

"Aunt Susan said they were given leave to come home for Christmas, but she'll have to go back to Georgia before the new year," Lilly said before taking a bite of her chicken.

"Who is Annabelle?" he asked.

"Aunt Susan's wife," Lilly said.

"I didn't realize your sister was married." He lifted his glass. "Why didn't she join the cookie baking?"

"Annabelle works as a campaign consultant, and she was recently hired for the special election in Georgia. She's been gone since

120

Thanksgiving. It's a tight race, and we weren't sure if she would be home for Christmas."

"I'm glad she's back. I bet Susan is thrilled," he said.

"We all are," Shelly agreed enthusiastically. "Annabelle is a riot. She's got quite the sense of humor."

"I imagine you two have a lot in common with all the travel for work." He speared his last piece of chicken onto his fork.

"The difference," she said, "is Annabelle enjoys the travel, whereas I don't. And she gets to experience the cities she travels to, sometimes for months on end, while I'm usually only there for a few hours."

This was not the first time Shelly had implied she was unhappy in her job. But he wasn't clear on why she hadn't pursued other opportunities before. His mind mulled over how he could help her. She mentioned an interest in journalism. Maybe there was a program that would allow her to pursue her dream.

As with every night since he arrived, Brad cleared the table and washed the dishes. They told Lilly about their plans to go ice skating, and she excitedly agreed to join them. He had become accustomed to living there, and he no longer needed Shelly to show him where things went, but he appreciated she still assisted him with the cleanup, as it allowed them to spend more time together.

"How has the apartment search been going?" she asked.

"Uh, not well." Guilt dampened his good mood.

"Are you still struggling to decide where you want to live or are there just few openings?"

"Can I be honest with you?" he asked, glancing over at her.

"Of course."

"I'd, uh, like to make my home here," he said, then when she frowned, he hurried to clarify. "I mean, here in Eagle Harbor."

Her hand cupped her chin. "There aren't a lot of complexes around here."

"Don't worry, I'm sure I'll find something," he said with a grin. "I promise not to overstay my welcome."

"No danger of that," she responded with a shy smile in return. "You're welcome to stay as long as you like."

After she spoke, she broke eye contact and tucked a lock of hair behind her ear. Her words touched him. Little by little, the walls she built were coming down. Sometimes it caught him off guard with how short of a time they had known each other. Already they had created a domestic routine, which they had fallen into as naturally as breathing.

When they finished cleaning up after dinner, Shelly went

upstairs to get Lilly. Brad put on his shoes and coat while he waited for them. As he opened the front door, he was surprised by the snowflakes drifting down in the light from the porch lamp.

"It's snowing!" he called as Shelly and Lilly's footsteps sounded on the stairs.

"What? Really?" Lilly rushed to his side. "We're going to have a white Christmas."

"If it sticks." Shelly squinted at the flakes. "We rarely have snow on Christmas."

"Maybe it's our lucky year."

Shelly frowned as she stared out the door.

"Did you still want to go ice skating?" he asked.

Beside her, Lilly bounced and gave a vigorous nod. Shelly laughed. "I don't have much choice. But we should bundle up."

She and Lilly donned heavy coats, scarves, and mittens. They left the house and climbed into the car. As they drove along, he enjoyed the lights of the neighboring houses. It was truly beautiful.

"Ooh," Lilly cooed from the back seat. "Look over there. It's an inflatable snowman!"

He gazed out the window and chuckled. The snowman took up most of the yard and was large enough to hide the house behind it. "If the snow keeps up, maybe we'll be able to build one of our own."

She clapped her hands. "Oh, I hope so. I love the snow."

"It's been a while since I've seen snow," he said. "I've been stationed in the south the last few years."

"Did you go to war?"

"Lilly!" Shelly admonished as her gaze flicked to the rearview mirror, but Brad wasn't bothered.

"I was deployed multiple times. I served for a couple of years when 9/11 happened. First, I went to Iraq, and then Afghanistan. Working in IT, I was usually on base in a 'safe zone,' er, well, as safe as one can be in hostile territory, I suppose. Not every Marine, or every person in any military service for that matter, sees combat. It just depends on where you're deployed and what your mission is. My mission was to keep our technology operations running, and that's what I did."

Shelly was quiet during his explanation, and he squeezed her hand in understanding. Her answering smile didn't quite reach her eyes. He assumed she was remembering her father, and he recognized he was lucky in ways her father wasn't. It hurt his heart that she was in pain, and he wished there was more he could do to ease it.

When they arrived at the skating rink, there was quite a crowd of people already there. Shelly went to rent their skates, and Lilly must have recognized some of her friends as she rushed over to a family nearby.

"Stacy," she cried out.

"Lilly," the other girl gushed, and they crashed into each other.

Lilly's wavy brown locks seemed to tangle with Stacy's thick black braids, and it was hard to tell where one girl ended and the other began.

Shelly returned a moment later with three sets of skates in hand. After handing one set to Brad, she put Lilly's down on the bench beside them.

"Do you know them?" he asked, nodding to where Lilly was standing with her friend.

"A little," Shelly said. "I'm afraid, with my job, I'm not around enough to make lasting friendships outside of work or family. We've met a few times, when Lilly was little, at birthday parties or school events, but I haven't seen many people since Carl left." She shrugged. "Part of me was ashamed my marriage ended, so I've isolated myself."

The other couple cast curious glances at him, but otherwise made no move to approach them, either. It dawned on him in that moment she was lonely. Her reasoning for distancing herself from people saddened him. He was amazed and humbled she had taken in a complete stranger for the holidays.

She'd truly made him feel at home. "Were you close with anyone in town before the divorce?"

"Not close, per se, but I was friendly with several people. Many were fellow parents I met through Lilly." She laughed half-heartedly as she laced her skates. "I was more social before the divorce, but I guess I've always been a bit of an introvert."

"Being a flight attendant doesn't seem like an ideal job for an introvert," he mused as he cautiously stood on his own skates. It had been a while since he'd been ice skating.

"Perhaps not, but I enjoy helping people, and there is something to be said about seeing unfamiliar faces every day and going to different places." Snowflakes melted on her skin as she raised her face to the sky. "After the divorce, I needed professional distance from people and constant change."

Lilly ran back over to them to get her skates. Her excitement bubbling out of her as she asked her mother if she could hang out with Stacy. Shelly hesitated for a moment before agreeing. He imagined she was still a little emotional after the events of the day, and he wondered if she would have preferred to spend more time one-on-one with Lilly.

When it was just the two of them again, he offered Shelly his arm. "Shall we?"

She nodded, and they walked to the entrance of the rink. Couples were flying together flawlessly over the ice, while a few small children held tight to their parent's hands, taking their first tentative steps. He suspected he looked more like the little ones than he did an adult as he carefully placed his feet on the ice, one at a time. She watched him with an amused grin.

"Have you skated before?" she asked.

"Not recently," he admitted as he took her hand. His progress around the rink was slow, but steady.

She gave his hand an encouraging squeeze. He appreciated how patient she was with him. Other couples skated laps around them, but she didn't seem to care. She went at his pace.

Lilly joined a group of friends and every once in a while, she'd fly past them, doing various twirls and jumps, as if she'd been skating her whole life. He was a little envious of how effortless it seemed to be for her.

"I'm going to take a break," he said as they finished their fifth lap around the rink. While he was getting the hang of it, he worried he was holding Shelly back. She started to follow him, but he shook his head. "Stay. I'd love to see what you can do when you're not bogged down by a novice Marine."

Her green eyes twinkled as she laughed. She released his hand and took a few large strides before spinning in a perfect toe loop, landing cleanly.

"Show off," he muttered, which earned him a huge grin as she skated away.

~ * ~

Shelly forgot how much she used to love ice skating. It was something she and Carl enjoyed doing together when they were dating, then Lilly joined them once she was old enough. Though, in the last few years of their marriage, he stopped going, while she and Lilly bonded over their mutual love for being on the ice.

Thinking about it now, Shelly wondered why she never noticed before how much he had changed toward the end of their relationship. At the beginning, he showered her with affection. His family had money, and he never had a problem spending it on her back then. He'd whisked her away for weekends on the beach or to remote cabins in the mountains. Even the proposal and wedding were a surprise and a whirlwind. He'd proposed to her while they were laying on the beach together, and the next day, he'd arranged for them to be married by the ocean. It was like something out of a fairy tale.

But the signs were there. The grand gestures and extravagant gifts appeared less often, especially in the last few years, and the fighting increased. It was slow at first, a harsh word here, a senseless argument there.

It wasn't all bad. There were happy moments interspersed with the painful. It was almost like a recurring cycle, which only got worse when Shelly went back to work. One minute, he'd pick a fight about nothing and the next, he could be the sweetest man, apologizing for his behavior and giving her the world. She lived for those moments, but they weren't sustainable. The tension in their relationship grew thick and hot until she couldn't see a way out over the steam. She remembered when he left; she felt like an overboiled frog, a burnt, mushy mess.

"Shelly!" a voice called, interrupting her thoughts.

She turned, and her eyes widened in surprise. "Kylie? What are you doing here?"

"Swimming," Kylie replied, her voice dripping with sarcasm. She glanced around. "Are you here alone?"

"No, Lilly's there with her friends," Shelly said, pointing at a group of teen girls. "And Brad is somewhere around."

Kylie raised an eyebrow. "I see how it is."

"What do you mean?"

"I've been begging you to go out for ages, and you always have some excuse, but now you have a man again, you're suddenly social."

Shelly froze. While she suspected Kylie was teasing her, she couldn't deny there was some truth to her words. Ever since the divorce, Shelly had been focused on work and Lilly, avoiding the few friends she had.

"You're right, and I'm sorry," she finally said. "I'm surprised you haven't given up on me."

Kylie shrugged. "I figured you'd come out of your shell when you were ready." Her lips quirked up in a smirk. "I should have known it would take some hot Marine to do it."

"I didn't come here for him," Shelly protested as she wondered if her flaming cheeks could melt the ice and swallow her whole.

"Mm hmm," Kylie drawled. "Whatever you need to tell yourself." Linking her arm in Shelly's, she pulled her to the side of the rink. "I've got some news to share."

"What's up?" she asked, assuming Kylie had found a new boyfriend. Her friend was trying various dating apps lately with little luck.

"I'm getting promoted," she gushed, her dark hair bouncing around her as she danced around on her skates. "To supervisor!"

A sudden coldness hit Shelly's core. "Wow! That's amazing. I didn't even know you'd applied."

Kylie rolled her brown eyes and shook her head. "I told you over a month ago I was going to. Honestly, Shelly, sometimes I wonder if you even listen to me anymore."

Shelly bit her lip. Kylie was right; she'd been a terrible friend as of late. A vague memory of her friend sharing her plans to move up came to mind, but Shelly never expected Kylie to go through with it. The coldness formed a knot of ice in her belly, and she struggled to understand it. She was happy for Kylie, wasn't she? Her friend had been a flight attendant for a few years before Shelly joined, and it made sense for her to want to move to a more challenging role. So why did she feel resentful suddenly?

"Hey, are you okay?" Kylie asked as she searched Shelly's face.

"I-I'm fine," she stammered. "Congrats! That's awesome."

"Thanks," Kylie said, her eyes still filled with concern. "Are you sure everything's all right? Susan told me you ran into your ex-monster-in-law and—"

"Kylie!" Shelly admonished. "Wait, you talked to Susan?"

"Yeah, we've gotten close recently." Guilt flickered across Kylie's face as she shoved her hands into her pockets. "We've both been pretty worried about you."

"Oh," Shelly murmured.

"How are you doing after that?"

"F-fine," Shelly said, forcing a smile. Kylie was moving forward in her career, Susan was talking about having a baby, and now the two of them were becoming close friends. It seemed like everyone's life was progressing except for hers. "Lilly and I talked, and we're going to try therapy."

"That's good," Kylie said, putting her hand on Shelly's shoulder. "I hope that helps you both process everything." Her eyes focused on something behind Shelly, and she gave a wry grin. "Anyway, you've got someone waiting for you. I'll catch up with you later."

She turned and Brad was standing behind them. He was still a little wobbly on his skates, and she rushed over to help steady him. They skated together a few more times around the rink before Lilly rejoined them. It was getting late, and they decided to go home.

~ * ~

"Would you like to come in and have some hot chocolate and cookies?" Shelly asked Brad when they arrived back at her house.

"I'd love to."

He followed her inside. Lilly removed her winter gear and

collapsed on the couch, her attention focused on the Christmas tree, lit up in all its splendor. The timer had clicked on while they were out, and it bathed the room in a soft, festive glow. He went over to sit with Lilly while they waited for the hot chocolate to brew. She opened the tin of cookies on the coffee table and offered him one.

"I'm glad you finally asked my mom out," she said in a low voice, taking a cookie for herself.

"You didn't give me much of a choice," he teased. "I probably have a bruise on my leg."

"Aunt Susan told me to make sure you asked her tonight. We've been texting most of the day about our plans," Lilly continued, ignoring his comment. "Where are you going to take her?"

"Huh, I'm honestly not sure," he said as he studied the evergreen, contemplating her question. "We haven't gone out much since I've been here, and I don't recall many restaurants on the square. Any suggestions?"

"Her favorite restaurant is Guardare del Porto. It's an Italian restaurant on the river."

"Sounds perfect," he said. "I'll make a reservation tomorrow."

Shelly came into the room and handed them each a mug before sinking into the couch beside him. The velvety scent of chocolate filled his nostrils, and he wrapped his hands around the warm mug, allowing the heat to penetrate his stiff fingers.

They sipped their hot cocoa and basked in the warm glow of the twinkling tree lights. It was peaceful. His mind drifted again to how different this Christmas was turning out from what he expected. He glanced at Shelly and marveled at how much a simple meeting had altered the course of his life. She must have sensed his gaze as her eyes met his, and his heart skipped a beat. Yes, this Christmas was exceeding his expectations, and he thanked his lucky stars for every moment he got to spend here.

"Mmm, that hit the spot," Lilly said as she stretched and yawned, breaking the silence.

Shelly glanced at her watch. "Hopefully it helps you sleep, as it's about that time for you."

Lilly nodded and stood. While the day was less physically taxing than the day before, Brad gathered both women were emotionally exhausted. Lilly headed upstairs, and he collected the mugs, taking them to the kitchen to rinse and put in the dishwasher. When he returned to the family room, Shelly curled up on the couch, facing the tree. She appeared to be lost in her own world, and he eased down, trying not to disturb her.

"Today is the thirtieth anniversary of the day my father died," she murmured, staring at the evergreen. "And the day after Christmas will be one year since Carl left."

He took her hand in his but said nothing. Her preoccupation suggested she wanted to talk, and he didn't want to risk interrupting her thoughts or anything she wished to share with him.

"Despite all of that sadness, this is the first Christmas I feel at peace," she continued. "I told you earlier I had a strained relationship with Carl's mother. We spent most Christmases with my family, which she hated. Some years we tried to do both families in one day, but it was exhausting. I didn't go last year. It was just as well as Deborah was there. Lilly told me." Her laugh was empty, hollow. "If I'm being honest, deep down, I knew about the affair long before I admitted it to myself. We fought the next day, and then he left."

Brad squeezed her hand. "I can't believe he brought his mistress to Christmas. That would have been devastating to see them together, especially with how difficult this time of year already is for you."

"Oh and Cindy would have loved to rub it in my face," Shelly said through clenched teeth. Releasing his hand, she shook her head, as if trying to clear some errant thought from her mind. "Lilly and I talked this afternoon about going to therapy."

"You both have been through a lot," he said.

"We have, and I hope it will help us process everything. If she decides she wants to rebuild her relationship with her father, having a trained therapist to talk her through it would be good. I know I would like some guidance on how to navigate that situation myself." Her eyes filled with a warmth that took his breath away. "But I can't express to you how much having you here has helped. While I regret dragging you into our argument, you helped me to see things from a different perspective."

"I guess you can say I've been where Lilly is right now, except in a different role. My sister and I aren't close, but we've been working on our relationship over the distance. I'm more in the role of Lilly's father, but I completely understand her perspective because my sister told me how it was for her when I left. I planned to join the service, even before our parents died, but I could have delayed my ship out date." His hands squeezed together, and he avoided her gaze. Would she be as disappointed in his decision as he was? "Truth be told, I didn't want to because staying was too painful, but now I realize I was selfish. My actions have led to the strained relationship." He took a deep breath and lifted his head. "When I applied for my position with the federal government, there were multiple locations being filled with the job announcement. I included a preference for a posting near my sister, in

Texas. DC was my second choice and ultimately, it is the one I was offered."

"I'm sorry you weren't able to be posted near family," she said, patting his arm. "But I'm glad you ended up here."

"Me too," he said with a smile. "I mean, at first, my sister and I were both upset. But even she suspects DC will end up being the better choice after all." He shifted to face Shelly. "I called her after the argument this afternoon. I needed some perspective."

"What did she say?" she asked, her eyebrows knitting together.

"She understood the points I made but told me I needed to keep my nose out of family affairs," he said with a laugh. "She said even if I agreed with you, it was a no-win situation, and I should have just refused to get involved."

"She was probably right, though I didn't give you much choice," Shelly admitted. "But like I said, I'm glad you shared your perspective. It helped Lilly to have someone understand how she felt—that she wasn't alone."

He nodded in agreement. His conversation with Lilly convinced him she just wanted someone who understood what she was going through. It touched him she confided in him.

"My sister also told me I sounded happy," he added shyly.

"An-and are you?" Shelly stammered.

"Happier than I've ever been."

The light that shone from her face at his words was blinding; it outshined the Christmas tree. He would give anything for her to be this happy every day. She deserved all the joy in the world.

After Lilly came down to say goodnight, he walked to the window. The snow had already accumulated about an inch on the ground and was still heavily falling. The sight brought him an awed sense of peace.

Shelly came up behind him, slipping her hand in his, and they stood watching the snow together. He turned away from the window and studied her. When she returned his gaze, the same magnetic energy he experienced the other night at the festival pulled him toward her. Her lips were parted, and her eyes were warm and welcoming, but he stopped himself, conflicted.

As much as he wanted to take her into his arms and kiss her, he was afraid she was caught up in the moment, and she might regret it in the morning. He couldn't bear another tense breakfast, and he didn't want to jeopardize the progress they had made by misinterpreting what she wanted again.

He took a step back. "It's getting late. I should go."

Her green eyes widened, and there was a hint of disappointment in them, but he'd rather she be disappointed in him leaving than in doing something she might regret. He was still holding her hand, and he gave it a squeeze in reassurance.

"You don't have to go yet," she protested. "I'm not tired."

"I am," he said quickly. "It's been a bit of an emotional day, and I'm pretty beat."

Her face fell, her disappointment tangible now. It tugged on his heart and weakened his resolve, but he kept the memory of her chilly reception of him at breakfast fixed in his brain.

He stepped forward and enveloped her in his arms in a warm hug. Hugs were okay between friends and until she decided what she wanted, friendship would be the only thing he would expect. Her arms came up and tightened around him, as if she didn't want to let go.

"I'm excited to play in the snow with you and Lilly tomorrow," he said as he released her.

She grimaced. "I suppose I've been outvoted there."

"You have!" With a grin, he tucked a lock of auburn hair behind her ear. "Until then. Goodnight, Shelly."

"Goodnight." Her voice sounded almost wistful.

It took all his willpower to walk away from her, but he forced himself into the cold night, hoping it would give him a hefty dose of reality. They would have a chance to spend some time alone together soon at least, but if he was honest with himself, neither of them used the word "date." He hadn't wanted to use it because he was afraid it would upset her. It was dinner, a thank you meal for all the things she had done for him. While he hoped it would be the start of something more, there was no guarantee. After all, she was still processing the divorce.

He was glad she and Lilly were going to attend therapy together. His sister had pursued psychology after their parents died, particularly to provide grief counseling. Studying the brain helped her to process her feelings and understand the stages of grief. Knowing what benefits she provided for people who were struggling, a good therapist could do the same for Lilly and Shelly.

He entered his room and closed the door behind him as he considered all that had transpired in the last twenty-four hours. Today was an emotional rollercoaster, and he sank onto the bed in exhaustion. He wasn't lying to Shelly when he said he was tired. Though he chuckled ruefully as he probably didn't appear that way to her because her company was quite stimulating. In the quiet solitude of his room, away from her engaging presence, he wondered if he even had the strength to change into his pajamas.

Groaning, he dragged himself off the bed and began the seemingly arduous task of changing. As he climbed under the covers and lay on the comfortable mattress, he wondered what awaited him the next day. He hadn't played in the snow much since he was a boy, except for one winter when he was deployed to Germany. There had been many impromptu snowball fights between him and his friends during that time.

He laughed as he remembered Lilly could throw a wicked curveball now, thanks to his instruction at the festival. He'd have to watch out for her tomorrow. Would Shelly join in the fun or run for cover?

Chapter Eleven

Shelly woke early the next morning and lay awake, thinking. The day before had brought up a lot of things she didn't know, and she was still processing. Carl was emailing Lilly, Susan and Annabelle were talking about having a baby, and Kylie was being promoted. It was a lot to take in. More than that, it was hard for Shelly to hear how everyone was moving forward without her.

She was jealous of their optimistic futures when her own promised to be a lonely repetitive cycle of routine flights, raising Lilly, and maintaining their house. Sure, Brad had asked Shelly out, but beyond the fact he hadn't called it a date, it was too soon for her to consider whether he'd even be in her future or not.

Thoughts of him reminded her of a comment he made his first night there. He told her to follow her dream of being a journalist, but she brushed it off. The idea of going back to school at her age was difficult to comprehend. People changed careers all the time, but she wasn't sure if she could put herself out there. Besides, when would she find the time to go to classes with her crazy work schedule?

Still, maybe he had a point. While she wouldn't say she hated her job, she was getting more than a little tired of the constant travel, especially now as a single parent. Lilly was entering an important time in her development, and Shelly hated missing out on so much. She wanted to be there for Lilly's first date, or to teach her how to drive. But with her current job, she wouldn't be around for important events in Lilly's life.

Kylie scored a new position within the airline. Maybe Shelly could as well. The idea of starting over was daunting, but she hoped Brad would help her. After all, he wasn't just starting a new career; he had quite a substantial life change, leaving behind the military lifestyle he'd known for the last twenty years. Perhaps he had some words of wisdom he could share.

It couldn't hurt to ask him, and she quickly dressed and headed downstairs to start breakfast. She gathered the ingredients to make apple muffins and set to work. Before long, the muffins were in the oven, and a soft knock came from the front door. Her lips quirked up as she went to answer it.

"Good morning." She took in his appearance. His dark hair was still damp from a shower, and his sweater matched his deep blue eyes. Her breath caught in her throat as she stepped aside to let him in.

Maybe my career isn't the only area of my life he can help me with. Her cheeks burned, and she was thankful it was still relatively dark outside, so he couldn't see. *Get a grip!*

"Morning to you, too," he said with a grin. "Sleep well?"

"Not as well as I'd have liked." She led the way back to the kitchen.

"Something wrong?" He leaned against the doorjamb.

She peaked into the oven to buy some time before she responded. There was no reason to be nervous, but her heart was still fluttering like a hummingbird's wings as she debated how to broach the conversation. Brad had been nothing but helpful since his arrival, and she knew enough about him to know giving advice was something he enjoyed. But this was a tremendous change, and she wasn't entirely comfortable talking about it at all, let alone with someone who was still a stranger to her.

"Kylie told me she's getting promoted," she finally said.

"That's great!" When she didn't respond, he raised an eyebrow. "Isn't it?"

"It is, but it got me wondering about my own life." With a deep breath, she pushed her shoulders back. "I think I need a change, and since you recently took a big leap in your own life, I was hoping you'd share some wisdom you've gained since leaving the military."

He blinked in surprise. "Oh, uh, I doubt I've gained much wisdom. I've only been out for a week or so."

"True, but before you got out, you at least set up a new job." She gestured to the dining room, and they both went to the table and sat down. "I'm considering getting my degree in journalism. I'm afraid I won't be able to attend classes with my schedule. So, I'd like to find something in my current field requiring less travel. It's been years since I've searched the want ads, and I'm not sure where to begin."

"Ah, okay," he said, his blue eyes brightening. "I obviously stuck with the government, but for you, your best bet would be to see what opportunities your airline has. Have you ever looked at their job postings?"

Shelly shook her head, but before she could respond further, a door opened on the second floor, and Lilly's footsteps padded down the stairs. Not wanting to get her daughter's hopes up for something which might not work out, Shelly touched her index finger to her lips as she stood and headed back into the kitchen. They could continue this conversation when breakfast was over.

"Don't you have perfect timing?" she asked as Lilly entered the kitchen. "Would you mind grabbing the butter from the refrigerator and setting it on the table?"

Lilly nodded and did as she was asked. Shelly removed the muffins from the oven and transferred them onto a plate. When she returned to the dining room, Brad was scrolling through his phone. After she set his plate down, he set the phone aside and gave her a conspiratorial wink. She frowned. What was he up to?

"These look delicious," he said as he picked up a muffin.

"My mom is the best baker," Lilly agreed. "Well, except for maybe Grandma."

"She taught me most everything I know, but I have a few of my own tricks up my sleeve," Shelly said as she took a muffin for herself.

"I'm going to need to join a gym if I stay here much longer." He groaned, patting his stomach. "All this good food is hard to resist."

Lilly giggled, then sighed. "It won't last for much longer. Mom goes back to work after Christmas."

"Grandma will make you dinner," Shelly said.

"I know, but it's not the same." Lilly hunched forward, a forlorn look in her brown eyes. "I wish you had a job that was close by."

He caught Shelly's eye, but he seemed to understand this wasn't something she wanted to bring up with Lilly, at least not yet. While she rubbed her daughter's arm, she silently prayed she could soon fulfill Lilly's request.

"Are we still going to play in the snow?" she asked as she finished her muffin.

"That's the plan," Shelly said with as much enthusiasm as she could muster.

Lilly raised an eyebrow, and Shelly knew she wasn't fooling anyone. It wasn't that she didn't enjoy snow. She did from a safe, comfortable distance inside her nice, warm house. Looking at it was one thing, experiencing it up close and personal, and dealing with the inevitable cold, wet clothes was another.

"But we can't play for too long," Brad said. "We have the pageant this evening."

"I can't wait to show you, Mom," Lilly gushed with a wide grin. "This may be the best pageant yet."

"I thought it was the worst pageant ever," Shelly teased.

Lilly rolled her eyes as she stood and took her plate to the dishwasher. After planting a brief kiss on Shelly's head, she went upstairs.

When she was safely ensconced in her room, Brad handed Shelly his phone.

"This will be easier to read on a computer screen, but I found a job that might be perfect for you at your airline. It's an instructor position."

Shelly read through the position description. While she didn't love the idea of teaching, she fit the qualifications. Then again, she'd helped to train countless new flight attendants during her tenure with the airline. How different could this be? The job came with a nice salary bump and, although she'd still have to travel, it wouldn't be near as often as what she did now.

"That sounds great," she said as she raised her eyes to meet Brad's. "I mean, I'm not thrilled by the idea of standing in front of a room full of people, but I might be able to do this at least until I finish my degree."

"Exactly. It gives you a chance to be home more often for Lilly while also allowing you to pursue your dream job. Which reminds me." He held out his hand for his phone. As she gave it back to him, she leaned forward, curiosity getting the better of her. After tapping around, he set it on the table and pushed it toward her. "There's an online program for journalism with a rolling admission at a local university. You can start whenever you want."

Her eyes widened as she skimmed the website he pulled up. The program was almost all online, but there were options for in-person classes as well. She dropped her head into her hands, overwhelmed by the choices in front of her. Was she up for this? There'd already been so much upheaval in her life. She wasn't sure she wanted to risk bringing in more, even if it was a good kind this time.

"Hey," he said softly as he leaned across the table to touch her arm. "No one is saying you have to do this, but it's good to know your options." She glanced at him, and he shrugged. "Maybe you apply for the position, interview, and decide it's not for you. There'll be other jobs. But it doesn't hurt to see what's out there."

"That's true." Her attention focused back on his phone. She had to admit, as scared as she was to take this step, a large part of her yearned to start fresh. Her heart filled with hope as she met his gaze. "Thank you. I appreciate you checking into this for me."

"My pleasure." He began clearing the table, and Shelly stood to join him.

As much as she dreaded playing in the cold, wet snow, she was excited to spend some more time with him and Lilly.

~ * ~

Brad trudged through the deep snow outside the front door as he headed to his room. He was surprised by how much had fallen so early in the season. The pear tree in Wallace's yard was dusted with snow which was reminiscent of powdered sugar on a funnel cake. Shelly's orange car was barely visible under the blanket of white.

It touched him she'd sought his advice that morning. There was nothing he loved more than helping people, and it was the least he could do after how kind she had been to him. The instructor position was exactly what she needed to spend more time with Lilly and have time to pursue her degree. While it was clear her primary concern was for her daughter, he couldn't deny he'd wondered what it might mean for them.

As he climbed the stairs, he tried to kick off some of the excess snow. Shelly didn't keep a broom or a shovel in his apartment, and he didn't want to go rummaging around in her garage. It wasn't the best job he could do, but at least it made the climb less hazardous. A blast of warm air hit him as he opened the door, and he stood just inside the apartment, basking in the heat after being out in the bitter cold.

Figuring Shelly and Lilly might be awhile, he removed his guitar and started practicing again for the pageant. He was more than a little nervous about performing in front of the whole town. The tiny gigs his band played rarely brought in much of a crowd, and the regulars at the bar paid little attention to them. This was different.

The venue, the music, and the people were new to him, and he didn't want to let Lilly down. In the short time he'd been here, he'd become fond of Shelly's daughter. She was still on the cusp between adolescence and childhood, which she demonstrated in the way she still lit up over small things, like chocolate chip pancakes and snow days. Not every child could hold on to their childlike innocence in the face of all Lilly had gone through, but her resilience made her wise beyond her years.

A sudden splat hit his window, and he jumped. Setting the guitar carefully on his bed, he stood and listened, trying to figure out what had made such a strange noise. Two more splats, then a thump against the wall, followed by some giggling.

He crossed to the window and peered out. Shelly was crunching the snow into a ball between her hands as Lilly took aim at his face. The snowball hit the glass right in front of him, and he grinned. Tossing on his heavy blue winter coat, black gloves, and a gray Irish flat cap, he hurried to greet them.

"Are we starting with a snowball fight?" he taunted, kneeling and forming a ball of his own.

"Hey now." Shelly held up her hands in surrender. "We only threw them at your window, not at you."

"Fair enough," he said, rolling the ball in the snow. "Then what do you say we start with a snowman?"

"Sounds good to me!" Lilly came over to help him rotate the ball around as it accumulated more snow, growing substantially in size.

They wheeled it around the yard until they determined it would suffice as a base. Shelly started on a ball for the middle, and Lilly helped her as he worked on the head.

When the middle ball was ready, the three of them carefully lifted it and placed it on the base. Shelly and Brad patted more snow in to seal the seam, and he noticed each time their hands touched, she gave him a soft smile.

Once they were sure they had thoroughly connected the two parts, they moved on to finish forming the head. Lilly found a couple of sticks to act as arms and stuck them into the sides of the middle ball. When the last ball was a decent size and shape, they placed it on top. Shelly ran inside for some accessories, and they added a carrot for a nose, a couple of buttons for eyes, and an old scarf, which they placed around the neck.

"He needs a mouth." Brad stepped back to admire their handiwork.

"I didn't find anything that would work," Shelly said.

Lilly walked to the end of the driveway and crouched in the snow. He exchanged a look with Shelly, but she just gave a shrug. A few minutes later, Lilly returned with her hand outstretched.

"Will these do?" she asked as she displayed an assortment of rocks.

He nodded approvingly. "These will work perfectly." They set to pressing the rocks into the face below the carrot nose, forming a lopsided grin. "There, now he's happy!"

"We should take a picture." Shelly motioned for Brad and Lilly to stand beside the snowman.

"You need to be in the picture, too, Mom," Lilly protested.

They crowded around their masterpiece, and Shelly held the phone out as far as she could. They beamed at the camera, and she snapped the photo. "All right, Lilly, we have a snowman. What's next on our agenda?"

"We should go sledding on Crestview Drive," Lilly said. "It's not a far walk from here."

"We only have the one sled, though," Shelly reminded her.

"Maybe we can borrow one from Mr. Simmons," Lilly said, pointing to their neighbor's house. Without waiting for her mother's response, she ran through the yard.

Brad and Shelly stood in Shelly's yard as Lilly rang the doorbell. While they were too far away to hear what was said, Wallace's enthusiastic gesturing suggested he was willing to loan them the sled.

Lilly rejoined them in the yard and a moment later, the garage door opened, and Wallace came out carrying a bright red wooden sled. It was old, and had seen better days, but still appeared to be in working order. He set it on the ground in front of the three of them.

"It's good to see you both again. How are you enjoying our little town, Brad?" Wallace asked, the lines on his face crinkling as he smiled.

"Very much, sir, though I'm hoping to get to know it a little better."

"You'll be able to see more when I take you Christmas shopping," Shelly told him. She turned to Wallace. "Lilly and I went yesterday, but Brad still has some things to pick up."

"I'm going later this afternoon if you'd like to catch a ride with me," Wallace said, a twinkle in his hazel eyes. "That way there's no peeking."

"I'll take you up on your offer." Brad laughed as he slid his arm playfully around Shelly's shoulders, bringing a pink flush to her cheeks. "I'd love to surprise these two."

"I don't want to keep you young folks from your fun. If I'm not home when you're done, you can just leave the sled on the front porch."

"Thank you, Mr. Simmons. I promise we'll take good care of it." Lilly grinned.

"I have no doubt of that. You all have fun!"

They waved goodbye, then Shelly grabbed Lilly's sled from the house. The two sleds couldn't have been more different. Lilly's was new and built for speed instead of durability. In contrast, the old wooden sled, while it wouldn't win any races, might outlast them all.

Brad was happy to be out and about. It was a chance to get to know Shelly's neighbors and he enjoyed meeting new people. She introduced him as her friend, though he wasn't sure people were buying that based on their skeptical expressions. Eagle Harbor, like many of the small towns he'd visited over the years, had people who liked to talk. So, it didn't surprise him when neighbor whispered to neighbor as they passed.

He was something new and different, and he was sure everyone knew about Shelly's divorce. All he could do was hope it didn't bother her to once again be the focus of the town. Hopefully, with the pageant tonight and Christmas soon after, she wouldn't be the subject of gossip for long.

They spent the morning sledding before heading back home for lunch. Shelly and Lilly's steps were slow as they trudged to the front door, but the smiles never left their faces. While Shelly made lunch, he shoveled the driveway and cleared off her car, making sure it would be all ready for them to leave for the pageant. When he came back inside, she had set out tomato soup and grilled cheese sandwiches.

He sat at the table where she was staring off into space. Her eyebrows knitted together in a frown of concentration, and she barely registered him or Lilly.

"Penny for your thoughts?" he asked.

"I was just thinking about how nice these last few days have been."

"And the day after tomorrow is Christmas Eve!" Lilly clasped her hands.

"After we eat, I'll stop by Wallace's to ask if he's ready to go shopping," Brad said as he dipped his sandwich into the soup.

"I'm still happy to take you," Shelly replied, and he was surprised by how disappointed she sounded.

"I bet you could use a break. You've been running around since I got here. It might do you good to take the afternoon off." He raised an eyebrow. "Besides, I can't very well buy you a present if you're looking over my shoulder."

Shelly squirmed in her chair. "Y-you don't have to buy me anything."

"I know I don't have to; I want to." He glanced at Lilly. "For both of you." He turned back to Shelly. "Relax and enjoy your afternoon."

After they finished their lunch, he helped Shelly clear the table and wash the dishes. When they were finished, she settled on the couch with her computer, and he hoped she would spend some time reviewing the open position at the airline and the journalism program he shared with her. Wouldn't it be a wonderful Christmas gift if she could be home more often?

As he entered his room, his phone chimed, and he rushed over to it, thinking it might be his sister. He missed a call from an unfamiliar number, but there was a message. *"Hi Brad, it's Doug from the Department of Defense. I understand we've got you scheduled to onboard on January 6th, but I wanted to tell you the person who was hired for the Texas position has backed out. While we would love to have you join our DC team, I would completely understand if you preferred to go to Texas instead. The start date would be the same, so I need to know your decision soon. I'm in the office the next two days, then I'll be back the day after Christmas if you can give me a call. Talk soon."*

The phone fell away from his ear. There was a time when this would have been the most welcome news. He and Lisa were both disappointed when he wasn't offered the job in Texas. While their relationship had improved over the years, he'd hoped being in the same city would help immensely. He'd promised to visit her in the spring, after he was settled in his job in DC.

But now he was torn. As much as he wanted to be near his sister, he couldn't deny his growing feelings for Shelly. He'd only known her a few days, but already she had found a special place in his heart. If he left now, would she be willing to give things a shot at a distance? Or would she decide it was too hard, as his last serious girlfriend had done when he received new orders to a duty station on the other side of the country.

He sank onto his bed and let out a slow breath. Complicating matters was the fact he'd just asked Shelly on a not-quite-a-date. Was it wrong to start dating her, even if they weren't calling it that, when he might leave?

A glance at his watch confirmed he needed to get moving if he wanted to catch a ride with Wallace into town. There was no need to decide right now. Brad would think it over and get back to Doug in the next day or so. If Brad went to Texas, it would probably be easier to travel after Christmas, anyway.

He changed into dry clothes and headed over to Wallace's. The door flew open before he rang the bell, and Wallace's wrinkled face broke into a broad grin.

"I saw you coming," he said as he stepped onto the porch. He was dressed for the cold in a black wool coat, gray gloves and a gray Irish flat cap just like Brad's. They walked over to where Wallace's dark blue truck was parked and climbed in.

"Thanks so much for doing this," Brad said as he buckled his seat belt.

"Not a problem." Wallace drove them toward town. "Any particular stores you want to visit?"

"I'm not sure what's available. But I have an idea of what I want to get. Do you have a jewelry and craft store nearby?"

Wallace nodded. "There's a craft store on the square, but we'll need to go to the local mall for the jewelry."

"Is that okay with you?" Brad asked, not wanting to take up too much of Wallace's time.

"Of course. I've got some grandkids to finish shopping for, so it's no trouble at all."

They spent the rest of the afternoon wandering through the local shops and choosing gifts for their loved ones. Wallace told Brad about his two daughters, who tried to convince him to move closer to them after his wife died. But Wallace loved his home and couldn't imagine himself living anywhere else at this point in his life.

"I'm real glad Shelly invited you to stay for the holidays," he said as they climbed back into his truck to go home. "She's had a rough time of it lately, but she seems happier since you came."

"Are you two close?" Brad asked.

"We've been neighbors for years, but I guess you could say we've grown closer over this last year." Wallace gave him a sideways glance. "I'm guessing you've heard about her ex?" When Brad nodded, Wallace continued, "My wife passed away about the same time Carl left her. We leaned on each other a lot. I watch Lilly sometimes after school, and Shelly invites me to dinner at least once a week when she's home." He winked at Brad. "My wife was the cook in our household. I'm lucky if I can boil water."

Brad laughed, but Wallace's words settled into a knot in Brad's stomach. Shelly had already been through so much. Maybe he should tell her about the job opportunity in Texas before they went out. He didn't want to lead her on if there was even a chance he might accept it.

"When do you start your new job?" Wallace asked, breaking into his thoughts.

"About a week after Christmas," Brad said.

He was relieved when they pulled into Wallace's driveway a moment later. After Brad helped Wallace carry his purchases into the house, he said a quick goodbye before rushing back to his room. It was getting late, and Brad needed to make sure he was ready to go for the pageant that evening.

~ * ~

"Just one more picture," Shelly insisted as Lilly rolled her eyes, but obligingly struck another pose.

It was almost time to leave for the pageant, and Shelly couldn't wait to see everything come together. Lilly was already in her costume, and she looked adorable as a vintage Hollywood director.

"Leave my poor niece alone." Susan stepped in front of Lilly before Shelly could snap anymore photos.

Shelly made a face at her sister, but she couldn't be happier to have her there. Susan, Kylie, and her mother stopped by so they could go to the pageant together. They had done this every year since Shelly moved to Eagle Harbor, and she was filled with nostalgia for the happier times before.

For just a moment, she could pretend the last year hadn't happened. After all, with Brad joining them, their numbers hadn't changed, but the vast difference between him and Carl was hard to ignore. Beyond their physical appearances, there was also a distinction in their behavior.

She recalled last year how Carl scowled throughout the dinner with her family before the pageant, then spent most of the actual performance on his phone. He insisted it was business, but Shelly now suspected he had been texting with Deborah.

"Is Annabelle joining us?" Kylie asked Susan, bringing Shelly back to the present.

"I hope so," Susan said, a hint of frustration in her voice. "Her flight was delayed, but she promised to meet us there."

Shelly gave Susan's arm a gentle squeeze. Her heart went out to her sister. It had to be hard having her wife gone all the time.

"I can't wait to meet her," Brad said.

"Enough talk." Her mother stood and slipped her arms into her coat. "It's time we get on the road."

Everyone streamed through the front door and piled into Susan's van. Shelly's family chatted animatedly about the performance, but she noticed Brad seemed unusually quiet. His fingers fidgeted with his guitar case as he stared straight ahead.

"Are you all right?" she whispered as she leaned toward him, not wanting to draw attention to his obvious nerves.

"I just hope I don't screw this up. I know how much it means to Lilly."

She patted his hand. "I'm sure you'll do fine. Just remember you're doing us a huge favor, so nobody is going to judge you if you make a mistake."

He gave her a grateful smile as they drove into the parking lot. As soon as they were out of the car, Lilly grabbed his hand and dragged him to the backstage entrance. Her mother handed the tickets to the rest of the group, and they made their way to the lobby.

Besides the pageant, the fundraiser included a silent auction. The items were donated by local businesses and ranged from a basket of baked goods to high-quality yarn to various electronic devices. Shelly separated from her family as they wandered through the assortment of options set up around the lobby. They arrived early, but the lobby was already filling with patrons.

As Shelly was admiring a basket of baked goods, she sensed someone behind her. She moved a bit to the side to let the person get a better view.

"Shelly?" a deep, devastatingly familiar voice said.

Her heart dropped to her stomach as she spun around. It was a voice she would recognize anywhere and, sure enough, there, standing behind her, was her ex-husband, Carl.

Chapter Twelve

"Carl?" Shelly froze. Then as she processed the situation, her pulse sped up and she glared at him. "What are *you* doing here?"

"I heard Lilly was in the pageant, and I wanted to see her perform," he said.

The nerve. No word for months, and now he dared to show his face? At least Lilly was already backstage. Shelly could only imagine how her daughter would react to her father's sudden reappearance in the flesh.

His dark brown eyes, so like Lilly's, held a hint of sadness as he studied her. "You look lovely."

Still shaken and vacillating between shock and rage, Shelly glanced down at her outfit, which was comprised a form fitting green sweater and a pair of black slacks. It was hardly a showstopper, but green was her best color. She raised her eyes to Carl and worked to compose her expression. His dark brown hair was cut close to his head and his face was scruffy, as if he hadn't shaved in a few days. On some men, it might be unkempt, but it made Carl appear more rugged than she was used to.

Shelly crossed her arms over her chest, refusing to be swayed by his flattery. "I'm surprised you heard about the pageant."

He ducked his head. "I suppose I deserve that. But just because she doesn't respond to my emails doesn't mean I'm incapable of knowing what's going on in her life."

"Where's Deborah?" Shelly struggled to keep the bitterness out of her voice.

She'd imagined many times what she would do if she saw him again, but all those fantasies failed her now that she stood before him with her heart pounding a mile a minute.

His face fell slightly, and he rubbed the back of his neck with his hand. "It didn't work out."

What could Shelly say to that? She couldn't very well tell him she was sorry to hear it because she didn't want to give him the wrong idea and, truthfully, she wasn't sorry at all. In some ways, she felt vindicated.

He stepped toward her. "Shelly, I—"

"No." She put up a hand. "Save it. I don't want to hear it."

"But—"

"Get away from her!" an authoritative voice cried behind Shelly as someone grabbed her arm and yanked her back.

She blinked, and her eyes focused on Kylie and Susan, who were now standing between her and Carl. A glance behind her confirmed Annabelle had arrived, and she was the one who pulled Shelly away. Her sister-in-law's dark brown eyes were almost black with anger, and Shelly imagined her sister and best friend probably had similar expressions.

"I just want to talk to her," he said, raising his hands in front of him.

"You lost that privilege." Kylie jabbed her finger at him. "You need to leave."

"I came to see my daughter's performance." He took a step back from them as his face reddened—from embarrassment or anger, Shelly couldn't tell. "Are you trying to say I can't do that?"

"You haven't cared about anything else Lilly has done in the last year," Kylie countered.

Susan placed a hand on Kylie's arm and shook her head, as if warning her to back off. She turned to Carl. "Nobody is saying you can't see Lilly. But you need to stay away from Shelly."

At first, Shelly worried he wouldn't back down. He clenched his fists at his side as he glared at Kylie and Susan. But after a brief glance at Shelly, he nodded.

"Would you at least give Lilly this?" he asked as he removed a card and a small box from his jacket pocket, holding it out to Shelly.

Her anger ebbed as she accepted it. "Don't you want to see her?"

"I'll watch the performance, but I, uh, don't expect a positive reception from her either." With a sad smile, he spun on his heel and walked away. His shoulders slumped forward, and his usually confident stride was slow and hesitant, as if he was unsure of his direction.

"Are you okay?" Susan asked once he was gone.

Shelly nodded, her heart rate was returning to normal, but she didn't trust herself to speak. Her family converged around her, wrapping her in a circle of love and support. They led her into the theatre to find their seats. She was relieved when the show started soon after they sat down. The expressions of sympathy and concern from her family were jarring, and she wished she had a moment to herself to process seeing

Carl again.

For the next couple of hours, Shelly was able to lose herself in the performance. Lilly was amazing, never missing a line, covering for her fellow cast members when they did, and knocking her comedic moments out of the park. Shelly was impressed by how quickly Brad had picked up all the music for the pageant in such a short amount of time, and his playing brought the play to life. As the cast returned for their final bow, she and her family jumped to their feet as they applauded.

All too soon, the house lights came up and several concerned glances were cast in her direction by various members of her family. Annabelle slid an arm around her as they exited the theatre, and Shelly was surprised by how comforting she found her sister-in-law's presence.

Annabelle was a tall woman, with thick brown hair and a prominent jawline. There was a no-nonsense aura about her, which likely helped her in her work on political campaigns. It amazed Shelly how little Annabelle and Susan butted heads since they both had such forceful personalities, but they made it work to their advantage, and it was impossible to miss the deep love they had for each other.

They met up with Brad and Lilly in the lobby. Lilly's eyes danced with excitement, and Shelly envied her daughter's ignorance of her father's unexpected appearance. It seemed her family had no desire to share the incident with Lilly or Brad, but Susan and Annabelle kept surveying the room, as if they were keeping a watchful eye out for Carl. Thankfully, he didn't show, and Shelly assumed he'd left soon after the performance. At some point, she'd need to talk to Lilly about his unexpected appearance and give her his gift, but Shelly didn't want to risk ruining Lilly's night or starting another argument.

"Hi, I don't believe we've met," Brad addressed Annabelle, holding out his hand. "I'm Brad Collins."

"Annabelle. I've heard a lot about you." She cast a furtive glance in Shelly's direction before continuing, "I'm sorry I wasn't able to join you in the baking extravaganza the other day, but I hear you were quite a hit with the dishes."

"I aim to be helpful," he said with a laugh. His blue eyes met Shelly's, and a kaleidoscope of butterflies fluttered around her stomach.

There were some refreshments served in the lobby, but nobody seemed to want to hang around any longer. It had been a big night, in more ways than one, and Shelly was more than ready to call it a day. She needed time to process seeing her ex-husband again and what it might mean for her and Lilly.

~ * ~

Brad woke the next morning excited and anxious about his date with Shelly. While Lilly helped him choose the restaurant, and he had a surprise in store for after dinner, he was more than a little worried about whether it would go well. Somehow, tonight would be a turning point in their relationship, and he wanted everything to be perfect.

Gnawing at the back of his mind was the phone call from the DOD. He wished he could talk to someone about it, but when they arrived back at the house the night before, Shelly had immediately gone to bed despite it still being relatively early.

He decided he would talk to her about it that evening. She sought his advice on her own job prospects, and it seemed only fair he do the same. Maybe he'd even get some more insight into her feelings toward him through the conversation.

As he prepared to head to the main house for breakfast, he was optimistic about the day ahead. The pageant director had invited him, Lilly, and the rest of the cast and crew to lunch at a local diner. It was a great opportunity to spend time with the people of the town in a more relaxed environment.

Shelly greeted him when he knocked at the front door, but her smile didn't seem to meet her eyes. He didn't want to pry. While she'd confided a lot in him over the last several days, he gathered from the things she did and the way she was with others she was a very private person. If she wanted to share whatever was on her mind, he trusted she would in her own time.

"Lilly's still sleeping," she said as she led him to the dining room where the table was already set with their plates, an omelet on each one.

"Yesterday was a pretty long day," he said, as he took the bottle of hot sauce and sprinkled it on his eggs.

"But the pageant was amazing. I can't thank you enough for jumping in and helping."

His back straightened with pride as he gave what he hoped was a nonchalant shrug. "I was happy to." He took a bite of his omelet and relished the warm savory herbs in the sausage pieces, the gooeyness of the cheese, and the slow heat from the sauce. "What do you plan to do with your afternoon alone?"

Shelly rested her chin on her hand and stared out the back door. "I'm going to apply for the job you showed me." Her gaze briefly met his before she glanced away. "And maybe the journalism program as well."

"Really? That's great!"

"I've just been going through the motions of my life for far too long," she said, "A lot of things have happened which weren't in my control, but this is."

"I'm sure you'll be a shoo-in for the job. I'm rooting for you." Brad's chest expanded when she beamed back at him.

After they finished their breakfast and he had washed the dishes, he went back to his room. As he closed the door, his phone rang, and he pulled it out to check the caller with slight trepidation. He hoped it wasn't the DOD calling to ask about his decision.

He sighed in relief when he recognized the name. "Howie, how the heck are you?"

"Doing good, man. I saw the photo you posted with your guitar. You playing again?"

"Just for a local town pageant," Brad said.

"That's cool. Where at?" Howie asked.

"It's a little place right outside of DC called Eagle Harbor. I just left the service, and I've got a job with the DOD starting in the new year."

"Dude! I'm with the DOD, but in Texas."

"Really?" Brad's head jerked back. "I thought you worked as a contractor."

Howie laughed. "One too many shutdowns, my friend. I needed something more stable. You know Maria and I have quite the brood to put through college."

Brad wasn't sure if going to the feds was more stable since shutdowns were still a thing, but he knew contractors rarely got back pay while federal employees did. His fingers scratched the back of his neck as he debated his next words. Maybe his old pal had some advice for him.

"Funny you mention you're in Texas," he began before proceeding to tell Howie about the job opportunity.

"You should take it," Howie said with enthusiasm.

"I'm debating it, but I'm not sure."

"Isn't your sister here? What's holding you back?"

"I met someone…" Brad said, running a hand through his hair. "I'm renting a room from her. We've only known each other a few days, though."

"I get it, man. With Maria, things happened so fast, but I couldn't be happier. You do what you gotta do, but it'd be great to work with you again."

They talked about their time in the service and what Howie had been up to recently. When they hung up, Brad sat on his bed, contemplating the way things had unfolded for Howie and his wife. They'd met at Howie's last duty station. He had planned to make a career out of the military, just like Brad had, but once he met Maria, things changed. When it came time to re-up, Howie decided not to. He got married and transitioned to civilian life with ease.

Had Brad met someone special, like Shelly, would he have stayed in the service? He'd loved his time in the Marines, but maybe, if he had met the right person, his life would have taken a different turn. Maybe, like Howie, Brad would even have a couple of kids of his own.

It was frustrating that even with more control over his life, he was still struggling with indecision. No one was telling him where to live. He could make this choice entirely on his own. But things were easier in the military because he was told where to go and what to do. Even as he rose through the ranks, there was always someone above him to provide direction. He envied Howie his security in his decision. His friend had never harbored any doubts about Maria, at least as far as Brad could tell.

Howie's situation was different, though. Maria was young, single, and unencumbered. In contrast, Shelly was still recovering from a divorce and had a child to raise. There was also the issue of timing. Maria and Howie had had the time to get to know each other before Howie made the life altering decision to leave the service, but Brad only had a few days to decide.

A horn honked outside the house; Mr. Ryan had arrived. Brad slid his coat on and rushed down the stairs, meeting Lilly in the driveway. She greeted him with a tired smile as they climbed into Mr. Ryan's car and headed off to lunch with the pageant cast.

~ * ~

Shelly spent the afternoon updating her resume and applying to the position with the airline. After debating it for most of the morning, she applied to the journalism program as well, figuring it couldn't hurt to try. When she was finished, the house was still quiet, and she decided to get some wrapping done to distract herself.

Carl's appearance last night had shaken her more than she wanted to admit, and she hadn't talked to anyone about it since, especially not Lilly. After how upset her daughter had been over running into her grandmother, Lilly likely would have given her father a piece of her mind, and the night had already been dramatic enough as it was. While Shelly was surprised Carl opted not to talk to Lilly, he was spot on in his assumption that Lilly wouldn't be happy to see him. Now, if she could just figure out how to tell Lilly.

For Shelly's part, she still wasn't sure how she felt about seeing him. What had he planned to say before her family got involved? It must have been important for him to seek her out. She was still embarrassed by how her emotions had gotten the better of her when he'd approached her.

I was just caught off guard. She went to the garage and gathered gift boxes, bags, and wrapping paper. *It doesn't mean anything, right?*

Of course it didn't. As she'd told Susan on the phone the other day, Shelly was over Carl. She simply hadn't expected him to be there, that was all. She placed everything on the kitchen table, then went to work separating the gifts according to the recipient. As she sorted through the bags, adding to the piles for her sister and mother, she realized she had bought nothing for Brad. The run-in with her ex-mother-in-law upset her so much she'd forgotten and didn't know him well enough to know what he'd enjoy.

What she really wanted to give him, though, was something intangible. His words from the night they decorated the tree echoed in her head: *"My home for Christmas is truly in my dreams, because it doesn't exist anymore."* The yearning and ache in his voice had touched her. She believed, deep in her heart, the perfect place for him to call home was here, with her. But it was too soon to have such thoughts, wasn't it?

She wrapped Susan's headphones as Shelly mulled things over. It wasn't impossible to have feelings for someone after only a few days. Her relationship with Carl had already proved that. This was exactly the thing she'd been trying to avoid, another whirlwind romance.

She wrote Susan's name on a label and pressed it onto the wrapped package. It wasn't like that with Brad, though. He'd asked Shelly out, but he hadn't called it a date. A part of her was relieved. Every time Kylie or Susan mentioned dating to her over the past few months, Shelly had started hyperventilating. It was too soon. She wasn't ready.

Yet, when Brad asked her to a thank you dinner, she was surprised by her disappointment. Somehow, going out with him seemed like it should be more significant, or maybe she wanted it to be more than an outing based on gratitude.

The sound of the front door slamming startled her. Lilly rushed into the room, her brown eyes filled with joy. "Lunch was a lot of fun, Mom! You should have been there." Her smile faded as her eyes swept over the table. "You wrapped without me."

"I'm sorry, but I thought we should wrap these before Christmas," Shelly said. "I didn't wrap the gifts you bought." She gestured to the shopping bags on the table beside her.

"I'll wrap them now," Lilly said as she came to stand beside Shelly and removed the items. "This one's for Brad." She held up a blue stocking with embroidered snowflakes.

"I still need a present for him," Shelly murmured as she cut a square of wrapping paper.

Her stomach fluttered, though she tried to reason with herself that Lilly wanted to thank Brad for helping with the pageant. Still, she worried her daughter was becoming attached to someone who had only been in their lives for a few days.

Lilly raised her brows. "I can think of one thing you could give him for Christmas." She puckered her lips. "A goodnight kiss!"

Shelly's mouth fell open. "Lilly!" This was not the conversation she wanted to have with her daughter, well, ever, but certainly not right now.

"What?" Lilly gave a nonchalant shrug. "I can probably borrow some mistletoe from Aunt Susan to hang up when you two get home."

"Not funny! We're just having dinner."

"Call it what you want. It sounds like a date to me," Lilly countered.

Shelly glanced at Lilly out of the corner of her eye. "That doesn't bother you?"

"I mean, it was a little weird at first, seeing you with another man. But he seems good for you, and I want you to be happy." She taped the gift she was wrapping. "Besides, he saved the pageant, so he gets points for that."

Shelly's fingers fumbled, and she dropped the scissors. Bending to retrieve them, she was thankful she had a moment to hide her face. Lilly thought Brad made Shelly happy? She was okay with Shelly going on a date with a man who wasn't Carl? Well, if she'd been hoping to use Lilly as an excuse to keep Brad at a safe distance, that idea just went out the window. Shelly shook her head ruefully as she stood and set the scissors back on the table.

They wrapped the rest of the presents together as Lilly talked animatedly about the lunch she had gone to. The cast had basically taken over the diner, and they spent hours joking and laughing about the play. Shelly was pleased to hear how much Brad fit in with the group, and she couldn't help hoping he would make his home in Eagle Harbor, regardless of what happened between them.

"You need to get ready for your date," Lilly said as they cleaned up the wrapping paper.

Shelly groaned. "But I have no idea what to wear."

"I'll help you find the perfect outfit. Come on." Lilly grabbed Shelly's hand and dragged her up the stairs.

Lilly directed Shelly to sit on the bed before she went to the closet and started pulling various outfits. Clothes were piled by the armful on the bed. Once she'd emptied the entire closet, she began sorting through them.

"Is there any rhyme or reason to what you're doing?" Shelly

asked as Lilly seemed completely absorbed in her task.

"You'll see," she promised, continuing to sort.

Shelly shifted on the bed, her impatience increasing as the piles grew.

When Lilly was done, she beamed triumphantly. "So, I've divided your clothes based on how you want to appear for your date." She pointed. "This side of the bed is more casual and laid back. The outfits get fancier as you move toward the other side of the bed."

"Do you know where he's taking me?" Shelly asked.

"Guardare del Porto," Lilly responded, her brown eyes twinkling.

"Oh wow, that's my favorite!"

Lilly laughed. "That's why I suggested it to him." Her hand rubbed her chin as she surveyed the pile of clothes. "Some of these won't work because you'll freeze."

Shelly frowned. "I can't imagine I'll be that cold on the walk from the car to the restaurant."

"Let's just say there may be more to your date than just dinner." With a mysterious smirk, Lilly picked a green dress with long sleeves, a fitted green sweater and slacks, a black sheath dress with matching jacket, and a green V-neck body suit with black slacks. "Try these on, and we'll see if one of them will work."

"There's a lot of green," Shelly mused as she examined the options.

"They bring out your eyes," Lilly pointed out.

Shelly tried on the green dress with long sleeves. It was an A-line dress with a sweetheart neckline which flattered her small waist. She stepped out of the bathroom and spun in front of Lilly.

"That is a top contender," she said. "It'll definitely catch his attention."

Shelly scrutinized herself in the mirror and agreed. It was a very flattering dress, but was it too much? The restaurant was considered fine dining, but it was fine dining for Eagle Harbor, not quite the same as an upscale restaurant in the city. Still, she wanted to look nice for Brad.

"Try on the black dress," Lilly said.

Shelly went back to the bathroom and changed into the black dress with the matching jacket. It was very elegant and sophisticated. If she wore this one, she would wear her hair in a French twist. When she returned, she twirled again and waited for Lilly's opinion.

"Hm." Lilly scanned it critically. "A bit too formal." Her eyebrows pulled together as she studied the other options. "I'm still partial to the first dress, but given the temperature, let's try the sweater and slacks."

Shelly was feeling like a barbie doll, but she picked up the outfit Lilly indicated and changed. This time, when she came out, Lilly grimaced. The sweater, while fitted, didn't flatter Shelly's shape, and the slacks were more appropriate for an office, not a date.

"Next!" Lilly called out, clearly not impressed by this choice.

Shelly grabbed the last outfit.

When she emerged in the V-neck body suit and slacks, Lilly tilted her head and waved her hand as if to say it was okay, but not great. Staring at her reflection, Shelly couldn't help but agree the green dress was still the top choice.

"I mean, we can try a few other outfits," Lilly said as she viewed the remaining piles. "But I like the green dress best."

Shelly shook her head, still shocked at how comfortable Lilly seemed to be with the situation. Her instincts told her to try on the green dress again. When she inspected herself in the full-length mirror on her closet door, she had to admit Lilly was right. The deep green material made her eyes pop and contrasted perfectly with her auburn hair.

Lilly came up behind her. "You're beautiful, Mom."

Shelly turned and wrapped her daughter in a warm hug. Lilly left to get ready to go caroling with her aunts. Shelly's hands flitted about her face as she wondered how she should do her hair and make-up. Her nerves were getting the better of her and she decided to leave her hair down in loose curls with a minimal amount of make-up. The mascara brush trembled in her hand, and she took a deep breath to steady herself.

Tonight was significant, not just for what it might mean for her relationship with Brad, but also because she was stepping out of her comfort zone after hiding from the world since the divorce.

The doorbell rang, and her heart leaped into her throat. He was early, and she wasn't ready, in more ways than one. Lilly went downstairs to answer it, and Shelly was immensely relieved when Susan's voice floated up. She sighed and stood to go greet her.

"Wow!" Susan exclaimed as Shelly entered the room. "Hot stuff coming through."

"That dress is killer," Annabelle agreed as she stepped from behind Susan, her brown eyes appraising Shelly's outfit.

Shelly smoothed her dress and gave a self-deprecating laugh. "Thanks." They both gave her a quick hug. "Where are you going caroling?"

"I suggested an empty field where no one could hear me croak, but I was outvoted," Annabelle quipped, a wide smile on her face.

Shelly laughed. "I can't believe you're that bad."

"Trust me," she said with a wink. "They've decided to inflict me on the town square."

Susan playfully poked Annabelle in the side. "And afterward, I figured we'd grab dinner."

Shelly nodded but her thoughts were elsewhere. While they had been talking, the reality of the evening hit her again. Her mind was running a mile a minute, and she twisted the hem of her dress in her hands. Annabelle and Susan exchanged a quick glance.

"Lilly, why don't we grab your coat?" Annabelle grasped Lilly's arm and steered her out of the room.

When they were alone, Susan placed her hands on Shelly's arms and gave her a stern shake. "He's a good man, Shelly, and you deserve nothing less. No matter what happens tonight, just remember that."

Shelly nodded, and she gave a weak smile. "But that's what makes me nervous. He's been amazing to me and Lilly. What if *I* screw everything up?"

"Just listen to your heart." Susan's green eyes softened in understanding, and she touched Shelly's cheek. "Don't get too caught up in your overthinking you ignore what you're *feeling*."

Behind her, there was a soft knock at the door. Shelly's pulse kicked into overdrive, and she feared she might faint. Was she really doing this? Was she ready to open herself up to love again?

It's a bit late for that question, isn't it? You've already opened your heart again, at least to Brad.

Susan opened the door, and Shelly caught a brief glimpse of Brad's face as he greeted her sister and then his gaze wandered over the room until it fell on Shelly. When Susan stepped out of the way to let him in, a play of emotions crossed his face as he took in Shelly's appearance. He was as handsome as ever in a dark blue button-down shirt and gray slacks. His brown hair was neatly combed. For a moment, neither of them could speak as they just gazed at each other.

"You two better go or you'll be late for your reservation," Susan broke the silence, pushing Shelly toward the door.

He grabbed her jacket and helped her into it, just like the first morning when they went to the store. This time, she didn't have to wonder about the tingles spreading through her as his fingers brushed her neck; she knew what they meant, what *he* meant, to her. He offered her his elbow, and she put a trembling hand on his arm. She gave a nervous smile to her family before they walked out the door into the cold winter night.

He escorted her to the driver's side and opened the door for her. She noted his hands were also shaking a little when he reached for the door handle, and it touched her that he was also nervous. After he closed her door, he went around to the passenger side and climbed in, the air filling with the hum of electricity as they sat in close quarters. She started the car, wondering if she should ask him where they were going and pretend to be surprised or just drive to the restaurant.

"We have reservations at Guardare del Porto," Brad said.

With a nod, she put the car in gear, unsure of what to say.

Why am I making this so complicated? She maneuvered through the dark streets, heading toward the harbor. *He's admitted how he feels for me, and I care about him. It sounds simple.*

A hand closed over hers, and she raised her eyes to meet his gaze. Could he read her mind and the war waging inside her head? His thumb caressed the back of her hand, and she relaxed for the first time since he knocked on her door. It occurred to her she hadn't said a word to him.

"I'm sorry. I've been lost in my own thoughts." She smiled at him, and the crease in his brow relaxed.

"I understand." He gave her hand a quick squeeze. "Is the restaurant okay? Lilly said it's your favorite."

"Oh, yes, I love it." She was thankful for the distraction. "In the spring and summer, you can view the sunset during dinner. Their food is amazing, and the owner is an old friend."

"Good," he said, relief apparent in his voice.

Was it because he picked the right restaurant or the fact she was finally speaking again?

They arrived at the harbor and her anxiety dispersed as she took in how beautiful it was, all lit up for Christmas. The way the twinkling lights reflected off the rippling water was mesmerizing. This was her favorite place in Eagle Harbor. She could spend hours just staring out over the river, watching the boats go by. There was just something about being near water. It soothed her soul in a way nothing else could.

A few other shops and a cafe lined the Riverwalk, but only Guardare del Porto was open. After parking the car, Brad escorted her to the restaurant. Once inside, he gave his name to the young hostess standing just inside the door. The table she led them to had a breathtaking view of the harbor, and Shelly exhaled in contentment.

The restaurant was decorated with strings of soft white lights. Splashes of color offset the room in the deep green garlands wrapped around the bar railing and wreaths on the doors. A few balls of mistletoe caught her attention, and she recalled Lilly's comments from earlier, bringing a fluttering of butterflies in her belly. There were several families and couples dining near them. Shelly smiled and waved to people she recognized, including Lilly's friend Stacy's parents.

Brad didn't seem aware of anyone else; his eyes only briefly left hers to peruse the menu. Neither spoke while they determined what they wanted to order. Shelly had a hard time reading through the dinner options as she kept sneaking glances at him when she thought he wouldn't notice, but it didn't matter as she had the menu memorized. The server arrived shortly after they were seated and took their drink orders.

"You look incredible, by the way," Brad said when they were alone again.

"Thank you." She smiled, mentally thanking Lilly for her help in deciding on an outfit. "You clean up nicely as well." The shy grin he gave her sent the butterflies careening around her stomach.

"I'm glad you agreed to join me tonight. I've enjoyed our evening talks in your living room, but it's nice to talk to you without dish soap hands."

Shelly giggled. "I appreciate not having to cook."

"I'll bet. Although this food probably doesn't compare to yours."

"I don't know about that. Eduardo, the owner, is actually Italian."

"Ah, it's authentic, then?"

"You're in for a real treat," she said with a nod.

"I'm glad to give you a break." When he slid his hand across the table, she slipped her hand into it and was awarded with another heart-stopping smile. "You've done a lot for me since we met. I'm not sure how I'll ever repay you for your kindness."

"But, Brad," she protested. "You have no idea how much I've appreciated all the help you've provided." She took a deep breath to stop herself from gushing in hopes of lightening the mood. "I mean, it's been nice having my own personal dish washer."

"I'll gladly do whatever I can for you if it means I get to see you happy," he said with an unexpected intensity in his deep blue eyes.

She gazed at him, as if transfixed, until the server returned with their drinks, breaking the spell.

Brad settled back in his chair. "You should know, though, our evening was not my idea."

"Oh?" She tilted her head.

"Your daughter suggested it, encouraged by your sister."

Her smile faltered as she wondered if this had all been some set up by her family. Was that why he hadn't used the word "date?" Maybe she misread things, and he just intended this to thank her for offering him a place to stay, as he said.

"Not that I didn't want to," he continued, as if reading her mind.

"Believe me, I did. I just wasn't sure it was the right move." He dropped his gaze to their hands. "It's why I asked you to dinner and not on a date."

"And now," she asked, breathlessly. "Is this still just a dinner?"

The intensity came back as he raised his blue eyes to hers and shook his head. "Not unless you want it to be."

"I… I don't want it to be j-just dinner." Her stomach flipped.

"That's good," he said, breaking the intensity. "Because there's more in store for tonight."

She cocked her head to one side, but he just gave an enigmatic grin. Whatever was coming next was a surprise, though she wondered who set it up, him or her meddling family. In any case, she was quite enjoying their interference. She was pleased they liked him, which was in stark contrast to how they had felt about Carl, even before the affair. He'd never meshed with her family. It was as if they'd known all along he would not stay.

"This restaurant is beautiful." Brad changed the subject as he surveyed the room. "I can understand why it's your favorite."

Shelly's heart swelled with pride as she followed his gaze. The owner had tried to incorporate old world Italian architecture into the building when he renovated it. Doorways were expanded to appear like archways, intricately carved columns accented the bar, reminiscent of the colosseum.

Having never been to Italy herself, this was probably as close as she would get, at least for the near future. "The food is even better."

"You said you know the owner?"

"Eduardo is an old friend, one of the first I made when Carl and I moved to Eagle Harbor." She frowned as she flashed back to the night before, but she pushed the image out of her mind. "We came here when he first opened. Carl wasn't a fan, and since then I have only come with my family or friends. They enjoy it as much as I do."

She was glad Carl had only gone with her the one time. Had this been one of their regular restaurants, she might always have a negative association with it. As it was, she only had fond memories of times spent there. Brad seemed to enjoy himself as well, so perhaps they would come back in the future.

A new feeling took flight in her heart: hope. It wasn't something she allowed herself to feel often since the divorce. The concrete, tangible things were what mattered: her job, caring for Lilly, her family. Those were what helped Shelly to get through the day-to-day. Hope was dangerous because it could lead to disappointment, unfulfilled dreams, and heartbreak.

Their food arrived, and the conversation became limited as they ate. If his clean plate was any indication, Brad thoroughly enjoyed his choice of lobster ravioli, and Shelly savored her favorite dish of chicken piccata. The capers added just the right amount of saltiness to counter the acidity of the lemon sauce.

She sipped her glass of wine and regarded him. "I should thank you for connecting me with the journalism program."

Brad leaned forward. "Are you going to apply?"

"I already did, this afternoon." Her fingers fiddled with the stem of her wine glass. "I also applied to the flight instructor position you found."

"I'm glad to hear that, and I hope you get it. Lilly would be thrilled; she really misses you when you're gone."

"Not as much as I miss her. It's a great opportunity."

"Speaking of opportunities," he said. "I wanted to share some news I received the other day."

Shelly arched an eyebrow. "Oh?"

He took a deep breath. "You recall how I told you when I originally applied for my position, I was hoping for the Texas duty station?"

"So you could be near your sister."

"Exactly." He pushed his plate back and clasped his hands together on the table. "The guy who accepted the Texas position changed his mind. They offered it to me."

As the news sunk in, she worked to keep her expression neutral. Was he telling her he was leaving? Her heart pounded in her chest, but she tried not to jump to conclusions.

"A-are you going to take it?" She cringed internally at her stammer, but she was having a hard time keeping her emotions in check.

"I haven't decided," he said, his expression sincere. "I wanted to talk to you about it first."

She wanted to believe him, but the doubts she'd tried to quell resurfaced. Was he just humoring her when he said he wanted this to be more than just dinner?

"I'm not sure what to say," she replied, sounding as small as she felt.

"My sister is important to me, of course," Brad said, seemingly oblivious to the emotional upheaval going on inside her. "And repairing our relationship would be easier if we lived near each other, but. . ." He reached his hand across the table, and she slid hers into it, not sure what else to do. "I believe we might have something good here, and I'd hate to lose it."

Her stomach churned, and she wondered if she had opened her

heart just in time to have it broken again. It came easily to him, talking about the future, being open about his interest in her. She wished she could be more like that, more open to the possibilities he was offering her. But she had built the walls around her heart to protect her from situations like this. He was talking about leaving, and she couldn't go through this again.

"Have you talked to your sister about the offer yet?" Shelly asked, trying to buy herself some time.

"No, I didn't want to get her hopes up if I decide to stay." He signaled to the server for their check. "I wanted to talk to you about it first as I hoped you might have some words of wisdom for me, since you also might be embarking on a new career."

She forced a smile as he paid the bill. "Let me think about it a bit more."

Brad nodded and gestured for her to stand. After he helped her into her coat, he led the way out into the brisk evening together. She headed to her car, but he stopped her, and she raised an eyebrow.

"I've been told we can walk to our next destination from here," he said slyly.

He took her hand in his and led her down the Riverwalk to a path through the trees. She recognized it as a popular running trail which led to Crescent Moon Park.

We're going to a park? She was momentarily distracted from the prospect of his leaving. *It's less than thirty degrees outside, and there's snow on the ground, but he wants to go to a park?*

She shivered. What could they possibly be doing in a park in the middle of December? No wonder Lilly debated on whether she should wear a dress. Shelly was going to freeze. At this moment, all she wanted was to go home, crawl under the covers, and hide away for the rest of her life. But Brad had taken great pains to plan a nice evening for her, and she didn't want to ruin it. He didn't notice her subdued mood since he dropped the bombshell of the Texas position, and for that, she was grateful.

When they reached the end of the path, she was astonished by the number of people in the park. A rich scent of chocolate poured from a hot cocoa truck, and there was a bonfire in the center of the clearing, but the principal attraction was the horse-drawn carriage rides. She had forgotten the town planned this event, having never been before.

Her heart leapt into her throat. It was like something out of a movie. It was easy to lose herself in the beauty of her surroundings, and she decided to do just that. If tonight was all she was going to have with him, she might as well enjoy it to the fullest.

There were multiple carriages going through the park, and they didn't have to wait for long. When their turn came, Brad lifted her into the seat, then climbed in after her, settling the provided blanket around their legs. He hesitated before sliding his arm around her shoulders and pulling her close against him.

"I realize you're not dressed for this," he said, as if trying to explain his actions.

Shelly didn't care why he did it, she just savored the feeling of being wrapped up with him. When she snuggled in closer, he squeezed her shoulder. Her head rested against his chest as the carriage began to move. As they left the lights and sounds of the crowd, she relaxed, enjoying the sway of the horses' trot along the path.

"Thank you for this," she murmured. "Tonight has been wonderful. I'll be sad when it ends."

"Who said it has to end?" he asked, his voice deep and husky.

Tears pricked behind her eyes. *Because you're leaving.*

"You saw the line," she said out loud, trying to lighten the mood. "We can't hog the carriage all night."

"That's not really what I meant."

"I know," she whispered, thankful he missed the tear that had rolled down her cheek.

His arm tightened around her, and they rode on in silence. She had much she wanted to say, but she couldn't help being afraid of how much she liked him. Despite vowing never to get swept up again, there she was, fighting back tears as she was about to lose another man who had stolen her heart, and left when something better came along.

Brad isn't Carl. It wasn't fair of her to hold one man's transgressions against another. Maybe Brad meant it when he said he wasn't sure what choice to make. He'd been honest with her about the job offer, and asked her opinion, but the little voice inside her head needled her with all the doubts she had harbored since her husband left her for his mistress. It said she wasn't worth staying for, and she believed, in the end, Brad would choose the job over her. Maybe he wanted someone with less baggage. He had been willing to walk the fine line between what her heart wanted and what her head allowed, but she worried he'd already tired of that tightrope, and his patience had run out.

An icy breeze blew over them, and she pressed ever closer to him, placing a hand on his chest. She could feel his heart pounding and he took a shaky breath as he laid a hand over hers.

"Shelly," Brad's voice rumbled in his chest, right against her ear. "These past few days have been some of the best days of my life, and I don't want them to end." He took a deep breath, and she swiped away the tear before she lifted her head; his eyes were even more mesmerizingly blue and seemed to bore into her very soul. "It may be too soon to say this, but I need you to understand the depth of my feelings."

Before he could continue, the carriage stopped, and she was relieved the ride was over. His brow furrowed, but he climbed down and offered her his hand. They moved away from the crowd, and she hastened back to the car. She couldn't bear to hear him give her a similar speech to what Carl said when he left. That as much as he loved her, she wasn't what he wanted. Brad grabbed her hand and stopped her.

"Shelly, I'm falling for you." The words tumbled from his lips as if any attempt to slow their release would cause him immeasurable pain. "I understand you're still healing from your divorce, and I'm willing to go at whatever pace you set." He stared down at their hands, tracing circles on hers with his thumb. "Just as long as we're moving forward together."

She froze and a ringing sounded in her ears. This was not at all what she expected him to say. For a moment, she stood there, rubbing her free hand over her arm. How could he say these wonderful things to her while at the same time consider accepting an opportunity that would separate them? It made little sense.

"Then why are you leaving?" she blurted out.

He blinked at her. "W-what? What do you mean?"

"You told me you were offered an opportunity in Texas, and we both know you're going to choose to be near your sister. It was your original plan." The more she spoke, the more upset she became. "Why tell me all this if you're going to leave anyway? Haven't I been through enough?"

Chapter Thirteen

Brad staggered back as if she had slapped him. "I told you, I haven't made a decision yet."

"The fact you're even considering it tells me all I need to know." Shelly spun on her heel and practically ran away from him.

He stood alone on the path, dumbfounded. This was not at all the way he'd imagined this would go. While he knew he should have told her sooner, he never expected this reaction. He told her he was thinking about taking the job, not that he'd accepted it, but it was like all she heard was he was leaving. It didn't make any logical sense.

"Shelly, wait!" he called after her, but she kept going. He raced to catch her as she reached the car. She started to open the door, but he put his hand against it. "Please, just listen to me. Leaving the military was a huge decision for me, and I want to start this next chapter on the right foot. I thought you would understand, since you're making a big change."

"My 'big change,'" she said with air quotes. "Doesn't involve moving halfway across the country. Why would you even start something with me if you weren't sure you were going to stay?" She shook her head, pulling her arms tighter around her body, as if she was protecting herself. "I can't believe this. I never would have gone out with you if I knew you were just going to leave."

Her heartbroken face gutted him. It was clear, as far as she was concerned, he had as good as accepted the decision and was halfway to Texas, despite the fact he was still standing in front of her.

With his hand no longer blocking the door, she wrenched it open and jumped in, slamming it in his face. He blew out a heavy breath and trudged to the passenger side. Shelly didn't look over at him as he climbed in, and she put the car in gear as soon as his seatbelt clicked into place.

He kept quiet on the drive home, hoping by the time they arrived at her house, she would calm down. Nothing he was saying was getting through to her, anyway. The more he thought about it, the more upset it made him. Sure, the changes he was considering were more life altering than hers, but that was just it, he hadn't made up his mind. He'd listened to her when she'd shared her dreams, and he'd helped her find ways to achieve them. Why couldn't she do the same for him? Even if she was right about him telling her before they went out, she had seemed fine at dinner. Had she been stewing on this the whole time they were on the carriage ride?

She parked in her driveway and shut off the engine. At first, Brad didn't speak. Everything he said just seemed to upset her further.

"I'm sorry for not telling you sooner," he said, breaking the silence. "You're right. I should have told you before our date."

"It doesn't matter." She glared out the windshield, refusing to look at him.

"It matters to me. You..." He cleared his throat. "You matter to me."

She turned to him, eyes narrowing. Her mouth opened and he held his breath, hoping he had finally gotten through to her.

A ping sounded in the silence, and Shelly pulled out her phone. Her brows furrowed as she scanned the screen.

"What is it?" he asked hesitantly. He didn't want to pry.

"It's Carl," she said, her voice barely above a whisper.

"Your ex? Wow. When's the last time you heard from him?"

She raised her green eyes to his; her expression was almost... guilty? "He came to the pageant."

"Wait, what? He was there?" Brad ran a hand through his hair as he struggled to process this new information. "You never said anything."

She lowered her head. "It happened so fast. He tried to talk to me, but Susan and Kylie forced him away."

An unfamiliar emotion welled up inside Brad. His fists clenched at his sides, and a flash of heat came up the back of his neck. It wasn't anger, exactly, but related.

"What does he want?" he asked as he tried to keep his voice even.

"To talk. He doesn't say what about, but he wants to meet for coffee tomorrow."

"That strikes me as a bad idea. You shouldn't go alone. I don't have a good feeling about it." Though he couldn't explain why. It's not like he'd ever met her ex to form an opinion on him beyond what Shelly and Lilly had shared. Still, something was suspect about Carl showing up out of the blue and Brad clenched his jaw.

"He probably just wants to talk about Lilly." Shelly removed the keys from the ignition and opened her door, exiting the car.

"Does she know you saw him?" he asked, scrambling after her.

She shook her head. "I didn't want to risk upsetting her."

"Well, that's rich," he muttered.

"What did you say?"

"It's just interesting you were angry with me moments ago for not telling you sooner about the job offer when you saw Lilly's father days ago and she's still unaware."

Her eyes flashed with anger. "That's different."

"Is it? Weren't you also angry with her for not telling you her father had emailed? Is that also somehow different?"

"I don't need to explain myself to you," Shelly said as she moved past him toward the house.

"You're right, but you might need to explain yourself to Lilly," he replied in a low voice.

She spun around and glared at him. "What do you care? You're leaving anyway."

If the situation wasn't so tense, he might have laughed. "You've built up this whole idea in your head about what I'm going to do, you aren't even hearing what I'm saying. I haven't made a choice yet."

"Then let me help you make it," she said, her voice rising with each word. "Why don't you go worry about your family problems, and I'll worry about mine." With that, she turned and stalked into the house, slamming the front door behind her.

He stood on the sidewalk staring after her, barely noticing the cold winter air as anger radiated off him. Shaking his head, he stomped up the stairs to his room. He'd never met a more illogical person in his entire life.

~ * ~

The house was dark and quiet when Shelly stepped inside. It was probably a good thing though, as she wanted to get her raging emotions under control before Lilly returned. She went upstairs and took a shower, allowing the water to wash away the stench of the horrible night and drain away her pain.

Her mind was racing when a car pulled up outside, and Shelly went to the window just as Lilly jumped out of the car. Hoping to avoid a thousand questions, Shelly extinguished the lights in her room and climbed under the covers. She listened as Lilly came up the stairs and tapped at her door. When she didn't respond, Lilly creaked it open, but must have bought the idea Shelly was asleep because the door shut a moment later, and Lilly's footsteps faded as she went to her own room.

In the darkness, Brad's words haunted Shelly. As much as she hated to admit it, he was right about one thing: she should have told Lilly about seeing Carl. How ironic. She was trying to protect Lilly from the truth, just as Lilly tried to protect her. But Lilly deserved to know. They'd talk it over in the morning and decide together what to do. Carl's message could go unanswered until then.

When she rolled over on her side, the cold moon peaked through her curtains. Was it a mistake to meet him tomorrow? He'd seemed surprisingly contrite the night of the pageant, though Shelly had only seen him for a moment before her family drove him away. Still, something was different about him. He wasn't the Carl she knew. Maybe the ending of his second marriage had had a more profound impact on him than his first.

A tear rolled down Shelly's cheek, and she sniffled as her mind recalled the date that wasn't. Whether or not Brad understood her feelings, his words and actions had cut deep. For almost a year, she kept everyone at arm's length: her friends, her family, even Lilly, to some extent. In just a few short days, he had upended her entire life. She'd applied for a new job, she was trying to pursue an old dream, and her heart was opening to love again. The walls she had built weren't strong enough to withstand his attentions.

She flipped to her other side as her blood boiled. He'd done so much to worm his way not only into her heart, but her life as well. Why had he bothered? He was an attractive man; surely, he could have found another woman with less baggage. Was she just some holiday fling, a distraction while he waited for his real life to start?

With a sigh, she rolled onto her back and stared at the darkened ceiling. She wasn't being fair. He had been honest with her about his original plan to live near his sister, and it was only natural, given the opportunity, he'd be driven to accept regardless of how much he liked Shelly. It didn't make it hurt any less, though. It was her fate in life to always be someone's second choice. An option instead of a priority.

She regretted telling him to take the job. While she would never stand in the way of him being with his family, she wished she asked him what his moving meant for them. Was he hoping they could try long distance? Maybe if she stayed a flight attendant, she could book more flights to Texas, and they could spend some time together between her flights.

Some relationship. An hour here or there, a short weekend if she was lucky. That would get old fast, and she didn't want to be forced to make a choice between her dream and her heart again.

Deep down, she knew how things would work out. He would leave, she would stay, and life would go on. They say people come into your life for a reason, a season, and a lifetime. Maybe Brad was her reason, since he likely wouldn't even stay through the Christmas season. He had come into her life and forced her to make changes. She worried she wouldn't have the courage to change things without him. Maybe once she'd had time to grieve what might have been, she would remember their time together with fondness, but right now, she was in too much pain.

She closed her eyes as she tried to push the whole horrible situation out of her mind. But images of the past few days swam behind her eyes. Sleep would be a long time coming, if it arrived at all.

~ * ~

When Brad got back to his room, he checked the time on his phone. It was still relatively early in Dallas. After a moment's hesitation, he scrolled through his recent calls and tapped his sister's number.

The phone rang a few times, but then her cheery voice answered. "Hey Brad! How was your date?"

"Well," he said. "Things started out great."

"Uh, oh." Concern colored Lisa's voice. "What happened?"

He rubbed his hand over his face. "I'd rather not get into it. Besides, it's not the reason I'm calling."

"Um, okay, what's up?"

"I got a call the other day from the DOD. The position in Texas is still open, and they told me I can have it if I want it."

"Oh my goodness, that's amazing news! When are you getting here?" she asked, the excitement in her voice clear.

He smiled. At least *someone* wanted him around. "I haven't accepted it yet."

"What are you waiting for? Isn't this what you wanted?"

"It was, but... I don't know, Leese, things are different," he said, then cleared his throat. "It's not that I don't want to live near you, though."

"Better not be," she teased. "What's holding you back?"

"Shelly," he said. "Tonight was awful, but I'm not sure I'm ready to give up yet."

"Can you tell me what happened?"

He closed his eyes and shook his head, even though his sister couldn't see. "It boils down to a misunderstanding. She's upset I didn't share the opportunity sooner, but then tonight I learned she saw her ex at the Christmas pageant and didn't tell me or her daughter."

"Why should she have told you?" Lisa asked, rather bluntly, in his opinion.

"Wh-what do you mean?"

"You've only known each other a few days, and you've already overstepped in her life once. While you might be right about her telling her kid, I don't understand your entitlement to knowing about it."

"Entitlement?" Brad's mouth dropped open. Did she really think he was acting entitled?

"Yeah. You believe she should have told you she saw her ex. I disagree."

"But that's not fair! Why is it okay for her to get mad at me for not telling her about a job opportunity, but she conceals this information from me?"

"Conceals? Really? I thought you left the military," Lisa scoffed. "And I never said her expectations were okay."

"Oh," he said feebly.

"Did she say why she expected you to tell her?" she asked with an exasperated sigh.

"She said I shouldn't have started something with her if I was planning to leave."

"Ah, that makes sense." As she said it, her tone switched from sister to psych analyst, and he bit back a groan.

"All right, Dr. Lisa, lay it on me." He could almost hear her rolling her eyes.

"I'm not going to analyze a stranger," she said through gritted teeth. "But I do want to get back to her ex. I can understand why her daughter should have been told, but why should she tell you?"

"Maybe I wouldn't have gone on the date myself if I knew she was talking to her ex."

"They have a child together; it's expected they may have to talk sometimes. Why does it bother you?"

He frowned as he considered it. "I don't know. But when she told me, it hurt."

"Is it possible you're jealous?"

Her clinical tone rubbed him the wrong way. "No, stop analyzing me!" The silence on the other end of the line was deafening. He blew out a heavy breath. "Okay, maybe, but only a little."

"Perhaps you should deal with that before you make any rash decisions. Why don't you come here for a few days, get some distance, then you can decide on the job later?"

"But tomorrow is Christmas Eve…"

"True, but it doesn't hurt to check flights. It'd be great to spend Christmas with you!"

He chuckled as he opened his laptop. "I'd love to see you and my nephews as well. I'll check when we get off the phone and get back to you." He had to admit, the idea of having some time away from Shelly was appealing, no matter the cost.

"I'll keep my fingers crossed. You'll love Texas. It's humid, but it's almost always warm."

"I'm sure I will," Brad said, trying to sound convincing, though he was doubtful he'd like the state. After living the last several years in the south, the thought of having actual seasons again made him happy and hopeful. And he'd miss being only a couple hours' drive from the Atlantic Ocean.

A loud screech sounded in the background, and Lisa groaned. "I'm sorry, Brad, but I've gotta go. It's time to put the little monsters to bed."

"Good luck." He stifled a laugh as he hung up. Would Lisa expect him to babysit if he moved there? His nephews were adorable, but he enjoyed being the fun uncle who fed them tons of sugar and then left when the whining started.

There were few flights available, which was unsurprising, and nothing direct. There were other options to get to Texas, but they all involved significant time in traveling, and he didn't want to be alone with his thoughts for that long. He decided to go to bed and check again in the morning. Hopefully, after a good night's sleep, he'd have a clearer head.

Chapter Fourteen

When Shelly woke the next morning, it was as if she hadn't slept at all. She staggered out of bed and splashed some cold water on her face. It had been a long night, filled with tossing and turning as she relived the evening with Brad. Would he even bother stopping by for breakfast or would he eat in his room?

Lilly was still sleeping when Shelly left her room, and she went downstairs, hoping to grab some coffee before she had to face her daughter. The rooms were dark as the sun was only beginning to rise, and Shelly groped along the wall until she located the light switch. She blinked as the light flooded the kitchen, making her head throb. With a groan, she flipped on the Keurig and pulled a mug out of the cabinet.

Moments later, the machine was ready to brew her a cup of much needed caffeine. As the warm liquid poured out, the aroma of hazelnut filled the room, and she sniffed in anticipation. Today was shaping up to be a three-cup day, which was well beyond her normal limit, but she didn't care. If she was going to have to deal with Carl and Brad, she was going to need all the energy she could get.

Too tired to bother with anything else, she grabbed a couple of pastries and tossed them into the toaster. Lilly would be disappointed, but Shelly promised herself she'd make more of an effort for Christmas morning.

A few minutes later, Lilly's soft footsteps thudded on the stairs. Shelly brewed a cup of hot cocoa and set it on the table with a pastry, then went to get her own. Lilly entered the dining room rubbing her eyes.

"Where's Brad?" she asked with a sleepy frown.

"I'm not sure," Shelly lied. Well, it wasn't really a lie. After all, he could have slept in, totally independent of what had happened between them the night before.

"How'd your date go?" Lilly picked up her own pastry and took a bite, but not before Shelly caught the grimace of disappointment on her face.

"Okay," Shelly said. She sipped at her coffee, not bothering to touch her own breakfast. Her stomach was already in knots. "Actually, there's something else I need to talk to you about."

Lilly's brown eyes widened. "Oh? What's wrong?"

"Nothing's wrong... exactly..." She took a deep breath. "Before I tell you, though, I just want you to know I didn't mean to keep this from you. There just wasn't a good time to tell you."

"Um, Mom, you're scaring me," Lilly said as she set her food down. "Just tell me what's going on."

Bracing herself, Shelly slid the card and box across the table. "I ran into your father at the Christmas pageant, and he gave me this." Lilly's eyes widened, and Shelly wiped her sweaty palms on her pants. "We didn't speak long as your aunts and Kylie intervened, but he sent me a text last night. He wants me to meet him today to talk."

"About what?" Lilly's voice held a note of fear, and Shelly's heart sank.

"I'm honestly not sure," she said. "He told me he and Deborah have split up."

"You don't think he wants to get back together with you, do you?" Lilly's eyebrows knitted together as she pushed the card away from her.

"No, I imagine he wants to discuss you," Shelly said. "It would make sense as he's been emailing, and you haven't responded. Though perhaps he's provided some insight into his actions there." Her head inclined toward the unopened card on the table.

With a cautious nod, Lilly picked up the card and opened it. "All it says is congrats on the pageant and he hopes we can get together soon." She opened the box and a slow smile spread across her face. "Mm, chocolates!"

A laugh bubbled up from Shelly's throat. "He sure knows your weaknesses."

Lilly rolled her eyes. "A box of chocolates isn't going to fix everything." Her attention turned back to her breakfast, and she took a bite. "When are you meeting him?"

Shelly shrugged. "I haven't answered him yet. I wanted to talk to you first."

The room was quiet except for the sound of Lilly's chewing. She swallowed and tilted her head thoughtfully. "I mean, I don't like the idea of him coming back into our lives at all. But it's good he's reached out to you this time. It never felt right he emailed me instead of talking to you first."

"So, you're okay if I meet with him?"

Lilly gave a one shoulder shrug. "I guess. I don't like that it's on Christmas Eve, but I guess I'd rather know sooner than later what he wants."

"All right. Your grandmother and aunts were planning on coming this evening anyway. I'll see if they can come by sooner to stay with you."

"I can take care of myself," she said, rolling her eyes.

"I know," Shelly said. "But I hate to leave you alone on a holiday. Besides, I'd like to spend more time with them as well. I have to go back to work soon."

Lilly grumbled in response, and Shelly made out words like "stupid job" and "stay home" before her daughter took another bite of her breakfast. Shelly hid a smile. Perhaps soon, she would have a new job that would allow her to be home more often. She'd decided not to put all her eggs in one basket, and she would continue to search for additional positions that required less travel.

After Lilly had gone back upstairs, Shelly pulled out her phone. Carl hadn't texted again, and she had to admit, she was more than a little surprised. She quickly typed a response, agreeing to meet him at a local coffee shop in town that morning, then she stood to get another cup.

There had been no word from Brad, and she assumed he was keeping his distance today. It was odd, not having him here, but part of her was grateful. She had no idea what she would say to him when she saw him again.

Her phone pinged. Carl confirmed the time and location of their meeting. She took a deep breath, trying to settle the queasiness in her stomach. This wasn't how she anticipated spending her Christmas Eve, but she could sure use some clarity about one complicated situation in her life right now.

~ * ~

The light shining through Brad's curtains changed from a pale pink to a brilliant lavender before fading to a soft amber as he stared at the ceiling. He was pretty sure he hadn't slept a wink. The clock told him it was nearing seven, which was the latest he had gotten out of bed in twenty years. It was tempting to lay there for another hour or two. There didn't seem to be much point in getting up. He had nowhere to be, and he certainly had no plans to join Shelly for breakfast.

At the thought of food, his stomach growled, and he groaned as he sat up in bed, running a hand through his tousled hair. He was glad he had the forethought to buy himself some snacks when he joined her to grocery shop his first day here. The little kitchenette in his room had a small coffee maker, and he bought a small container of cream. He hadn't made much use of either since he'd arrived, having eaten most of his meals with Shelly and Lilly. But even if he were to stay through the holidays, he doubted he'd be welcome to join them now.

He grabbed a granola bar and his mug of coffee, carrying them back to the bed. After setting his breakfast on the nightstand, he opened his laptop and searched flights. To his surprise, there was a direct flight leaving this evening bound for Dallas. Someone must have had a last-minute cancellation. It wasn't a cheap flight, but he had already decided money wasn't an issue.

What he hadn't decided was whether he would stay in Texas, but this morning, in the cold light of the day, he was convinced it was the right choice. Lisa would be more than happy to help him find a place, and he could crash with her if need be. Truthfully, the only thing holding him in Maryland was Shelly and, well, she made her opinion of him pretty clear last night. Somehow, he suspected if he gave her all the time in the world, she'd never be ready to pursue anything with him.

And who knows, she might get back with her ex, anyway. With a heavy sigh, Brad squeezed his eyes shut. Lisa was right. He was jealous. It didn't make any logical sense. Shelly hadn't indicated any residual feelings for her ex, but it was clear Carl had broken her heart. Until then, she had a life and a family with him. Would it be such a stretch to believe there was still something there, even if it was deeply buried?

Then there was the fact she hadn't told Brad. Despite what Lisa said, he didn't believe he was acting entitled to expect Shelly to share such an important development in her life. She shared her career aspirations, her fears concerning Lilly, so much in such a short amount of time. Was there a reason she chose not to tell him about her ex? The thought only fanned the flames of Brad's jealousy.

So, he booked a one-way flight, then spent the morning packing his things. At one point, a car door slammed, and he looked out the window just as Shelly was leaving. He wasn't sure if Lilly was with her, but he assumed Shelly was going to meet her ex.

There was an ache in his chest as he closed his suitcase. Just when he believed he had finally found a home, he was being uprooted again. All he could do now was hope his true home was in Texas near the only family he had left.

~ * ~

Shelly sat in The Daily Grind, her untouched frappuccino sitting in front of her, her toe tapping against the table leg as she watched the door. Her hope was that, in arriving early, she would ease her nerves and give herself a sense of control. It did neither of those things and, if anything, made her more nervous because the longer she sat there, the

172

more she convinced herself Carl wouldn't come. It was an irrational thought. After all, he'd requested to meet; why would he bother if he wasn't planning to show?

The coffee shop was all decked out for Christmas, with garland along the edge of the counter, jingle bells on the door, and a holiday message handwritten on the whiteboard behind the counter. Normally, the festive decor would have a calming effect, but it wasn't working. The shop was rather busy for the day before a holiday, and she wondered if some last-minute shoppers had come for a jolt of caffeine to get them over the finish line. She was lucky to find a table amidst the rush.

Just when her anxiety had risen to astronomical levels, the front door opened, and Carl stepped in. He'd shaved since the night of the pageant, but his expression was still contrite, almost boyish, like he'd been caught stealing a cookie. She waved, and he walked right over, not even bothering to get himself a cup of coffee first.

"Thank you for meeting me," he said as he sat.

"Don't you want to get something?" she asked, gesturing to the counter.

"No, I'm fine. I'm jittery enough without the caffeine," he replied with a soft smile that didn't quite reach his eyes.

She took a sip of her drink as she studied him. It surprised her how much he had aged in the last year. There were dark circles under his eyes and wrinkles around his mouth that weren't there before. His dark brown, almost black hair was sporting more than a few grays.

He cleared his throat. "I'm sure you're curious why I asked you to meet me after so much time." His movements were stiff and robotic as he placed his clasped hands on the table. "My mother told me she saw you and Lilly. To be honest, when Lilly didn't respond, I thought it was because of you. Maybe you hated me enough to keep her from me."

"If you believe I'd keep you from our daughter, you don't know me at all."

"You're right, and of course, I realized that after everything you went through with your dad, you wouldn't do that to me or to Lilly." He leaned back in his chair and finally met her gaze. "I came to the pageant to see Lilly. I had no intention of talking to either of you; I just wanted to see her. But when I saw you standing alone, I couldn't help it. I wanted to apologize then, to tell you how sorry I was for how I treated you. But then, well, your family…"

Shelly bit back a smile. "Yes, my family." Her hands wrapped around the mug as she considered what he told her. He hadn't planned to talk to either of them? On the one hand, she appreciated he respected Lilly enough to not force her, but on the other, it would have been more than a little weird if Shelly saw him there and he avoided her.

"I want to fix things with Lilly. There's no excuse for my actions. I never intended to abandon her. Things with Deborah…" He blew out a breath and rubbed the back of his neck. "Everything just happened so fast, and I got caught up in the newness of it all."

"You couldn't call or even text?" she asked with an arched eyebrow. She couldn't imagine anything being so all-consuming to make her forget her own child.

"I considered it, believe me, I did, but the more time that passed, the more I feared the reception I might receive from her." He scrubbed a hand over his face. "Even before I left, my relationship with her was strained. We fought a lot, maybe more than you realized."

Shelly nodded. "Lilly told me."

"So maybe you can understand why I hesitated, even though I knew it was the wrong thing to do." He spread his hands on the table. "Then Deborah wanted to have a baby. Whether it was a last-ditch effort to save our marriage or because she genuinely wanted to start a family, I may never know." His gaze dropped, and his brows pulled together in a sad frown. "I couldn't imagine starting a new family for many reasons, but the top one was I couldn't do that to Lilly. I'd already hurt her enough."

"Is that why you and Deborah split up?" Shelly asked before she could stop herself. This wasn't her business or concern.

"It's not the only reason, but I guess you could say it was the final nail in the coffin. I moved out about a month ago."

She wasn't sure what to say. This was a lot of information to digest. Carl's aversion to have another child did not surprise her, as she'd hoped to grow their family beyond Lilly. He'd refused, citing finances as the reason, but that was just an excuse. His family had money, and only a few years after having Lilly he had built a successful law practice. Truthfully, Shelly wondered if he even wanted to have Lilly, though he doted on her as a baby. But as the years went by and she got older, his interest seemed to wane, and Shelly was never clear on why.

"It sounds like you had a rough year," she finally said. "But please understand, reconciling with Lilly won't be any easier. You really hurt her by just disappearing. And as you said, your behavior, even before you left, was uncalled for."

His shoulders hunched forward. "Believe me, I know."

She cocked her head to one side. "Can you tell me why? You two were close when she was little. What changed?"

He shrugged. "I guess I did. For me, things were easier when she was younger." His expression seemed focused on something far away, and he smiled. "I was her hero. But then, as she grew older, she started having other interests, opinions." He refocused on Shelly. "She went from wanting to spend all of her time with me to wanting you around more, which makes sense now, but it hurt."

"I get it," she said. "When she was a toddler, and I was home all the time, all she wanted was her daddy."

"Those were the days," he said with a wistful grin. The smile left his face almost as soon as it arrived, and his tone became more serious. "Will you help me reconnect with her? I'm willing to do anything."

She drained her cup as she contemplated her next words. Based on her conversation with Lilly that morning, her daughter hadn't struck Shelly as averse to seeing her father.

"Lilly and I planned to go to therapy in the new year," Shelly said. "Maybe you can join some sessions."

"That sounds perfect," he said, his face lighting with enthusiasm.

She held up a cautious hand. "But whatever we do, we need to take things slow. You haven't spoken or seen each other for a year, and there's a lot of pain there. I need you to promise you'll go at her pace."

He nodded, the shadows under his dark eyes fading. This was the Carl she remembered.

"I'll find a therapist after the first of the year. It'd probably be best if Lilly met with her alone to start, then we incorporate you into later sessions, per the therapist's recommendations."

"That works for me." He leaned back in his chair and relaxed for the first time since he'd walked in. It appeared a weight had lifted off his shoulders. "I'm going to get myself a coffee after all. Do you need a refill?"

She nodded, bemused. Was there more he wanted to discuss? Truthfully, she was in no hurry to return home and deal with the Brad situation.

When Carl returned a few moments later, he set her cup in front of her and resumed his seat. His face was clouded again, and she wondered what was bothering him now.

"Shelly, I—" he said, then stopped himself.

"What is it?" she asked as she leaned toward him.

"I appreciate you being willing to help me and Lilly reconnect. It's much more than I deserve," he said in a rush. "I probably shouldn't be pushing my luck, but I have to at least ask."

Her muscles tensed as she prepared herself for whatever he was going to say. Somehow, this conversation had taken an unexpected turn, and she had a sneaking suspicion she would not like this new direction.

"Would you be willing to take me back?" he asked, his dark

brown eyes boring into hers.

Before she knew what she was doing, she shook her head. It wasn't a conscious action, but she knew in her heart it was the right answer.

"If you'd asked me six months ago, I might have considered it," she said. "Despite its difficulties, we had a good marriage. And while I forgave you a long time ago for leaving like you did, I couldn't risk going through that again."

He nodded, as if he'd been expecting her response. "I figured, but you miss a hundred percent of the chances you don't take." His face broke into a wry grin.

"I'm sorry," she said, automatically.

"Don't be. It was a long shot," he said with a dismissive wave. "I should spend some time alone anyhow."

She didn't trust herself to respond, and instead gave an enigmatic smile. It would be a very smart move for him to spend some time on himself before he delved into another relationship, and it would probably help him focus on repairing his relationship with Lilly if he wasn't also pursuing a new love interest.

"Well, you heard my tail of woe for my second failed marriage," he said, before taking a sip of his coffee. "What about you? Are you seeing anyone?"

An image of Brad's face flashed into her mind, and she blinked, hoping to dispel it. It didn't work. The picture her mind conjured was from the last time she'd spoken to him, and his eyes were filled with anger and pain. She swallowed thickly.

"I was, but I think it's already over," she blurted out. Great. This was not a conversation she wanted to have with anyone, but certainly not with her ex-husband.

"What happened?" he asked, and he sounded so genuinely concerned Shelly found herself relaying the entire story. It reminded her of how much she missed talking to him.

"It doesn't sound to me like Brad was trying to tell you he was leaving," Carl said when she was finished. "He seems conflicted."

She scoffed. "I don't see where you got that from what I told you."

"First of all, he didn't tell you immediately because he was weighing his options. He broached the subject only after you asked for his help in finding a new job," Carl said, ticking each point off on his fingers as he went. "He told you he was falling for you, and he wanted to move forward together." He closed his hand and raised an eyebrow. "It sounds like he was hoping you would ask him to stay."

"B-but I would never do that!" she protested. "And he should know I would never stand between someone and their family."

"I agree, it wasn't fair to put you in this predicament, but honestly, his mind was made up to stay here, with you, if that's what you wanted." He gave her a wistful smile. "I envy him recognizing a good thing when he finds it."

Shelly shifted in her seat. "But what if he regrets the decision one day? We might not work out."

His eyebrows knitted together, and he shook his head. "Okay, this is a part of you I don't miss. You worry too much. He's a grown man, for goodness' sake. As someone currently facing the consequences of his own actions, I say let *him* decide if you're worth the risk." He reached across the table and grasped her hand. "But the thing you're really afraid of is you aren't worth it. I'm sure some of that is due to me. I'm sorry, Shelly. But my leaving was never about you. You were an amazing wife. I just thought I wanted a different life."

She gave him a small smile as she blinked back tears. "Thank you. That means a lot."

He squeezed. "And thank you for meeting with me, but it sounds like there's somewhere else you should be." Her emotions were warring within her, and she hesitated, but he gestured to the door. "Go. At least one of us should be happy this Christmas."

Her heart went out to him as she stood and embraced him. She promised to text him as soon as she had a therapist lined up, then she left. As she jumped into her car and turned on the ignition, she hoped she wasn't too late to talk to Brad.

~ * ~

Shelly's car was gone as Brad left his apartment, and he took a small comfort in knowing he would be able to leave without any uncomfortable goodbyes. He walked to Wallace's door with his luggage and knocked. The door opened, revealing the familiar, wrinkled face which broke into a broad smile.

"Brad, what a pleasant surprise," Wallace said. His smile fell as he took in Brad's bags. "Moving in?"

"Not exactly." Brad shuffled his feet. "I was wondering if you would mind if I hung out here for a few hours. I'm flying to Texas this evening, and I don't want to stay at Shelly's any longer."

Wallace frowned, but stepped back to allow him in. "Of course, you're welcome anytime."

Brad set his bags by the stairs, and Wallace led him into the living room. He gestured to the gray couch against the wall, and Brad sank down, exhausted from his sleepless night. Wallace's house had a similar setup to Shelly's. His living room sported a bay window where he had put up an artificial Christmas tree. There were stacks of presents beneath it. Were Wallace's children coming to visit?

"May I ask what happened?" Wallace asked as he took a seat in the black recliner across from Brad.

Before he knew what he was doing, he rehashed everything, including Shelly's harsh words and the revelation her ex had reentered her life. Wallace sat quietly, listening, his expression neutral, until Brad completed his tale.

"Are you sure this is what you want to do?" Wallace asked, his brows knitted together. "Shelly's been through hell this last year. Maybe if you gave her time—"

"She told me to go." Brad tried to keep the frustration from his voice.

"She's upset, and rightly so. When Carl—" Wallace ran a hand over his sparse white hair. "His leaving was a shock to everyone, and I'm sure you can see the similarities between what he did and what you're doing now."

"That's just it. I hadn't decided," Brad said as he rubbed his hand over his face. His stomach churned with nausea. "She made the decision for me when she told me to go."

Wallace stood. "Why don't I make us some tea?"

Brad nodded and slumped against the back of the couch, his energy sapped by reliving the last twenty-four hours. A few minutes later, Wallace returned with two mugs and handed one to Brad before returning to the recliner.

"My wife was a lot like Shelly," Wallace said as his hands wrapped around his cup. "Stubborn and independent on the outside, but timid and vulnerable within."

"I'm sorry for your loss."

"Thank you." Wallace took a small sip of his tea. "Your situation reminds me of my own courtship. I met my wife at a sort of crossroads in my life."

"How did that go?"

"She was seeing someone else and kept her distance, trying to stay true and all," Wallace responded, his gray eyes wistful. "But there was no denying the magnetism between us. I tried to convince her to choose me." He chuckled. "It went about as well as you'd expect. So, I pursued a career opportunity, which took me out of state."

"What happened? Did you come back?"

Wallace stirred his tea with his left hand, and the glint of gold on his ring finger caught Brad's eye. The level of devotion in Wallace's voice gutted Brad. Wallace and his wife built a life together there, in their home. The evidence of their life was on full display in the array of pictures covering the walls. This was the one thing Brad wanted most of all, and right as he had it within his grasp, it was snatched away.

"I did." Wallace's gravelly voice pulled Brad from his thoughts. "I couldn't stay away for long. The next time I saw her in town, she stopped me. Told me she'd made a mistake. Asked if it was too late." He raised his eyes. "I told her it's never too late. I apologized for trying to tell her how to live her life." His wrinkled face broke into a sly grin as he winked. "Take it from me, son. Never tell a strong-willed woman what she should do."

A lump formed in Brad's throat. He wished he found Wallace's words reassuring, but the truth was, he didn't. There were many complications in his situation that didn't exist in Wallace's. Shelly was a mother, and Brad understood her underlying motivation to provide her daughter with stability. He suspected if he left, there would be no future with Shelly. Even if he came back, it would be too late.

But Wallace's last words haunted him. Had Brad been wrong to call Shelly out on what he believed was a double standard? Had he overstepped again? He recalled what Lisa said about his so-called entitlement. Maybe she had a point.

Throughout his career, he was the person everyone came to when they had a problem to solve. Even in his personal life, his friends often sought his help. But over the past several days, he had begun to suspect not everyone appreciated his advice. The night he upset Lilly with comments on her food choices, Shelly told him to back off. His sister suggested he shouldn't have given Shelly his opinion when she dragged him into her fight with Lilly, then last night, Lisa called him entitled.

On the other hand, Shelly requested his help with her job search. And while she hadn't technically asked him to look for a journalism program, she hadn't seemed upset by his initiative. Was there some balance he was missing? He had missed the signs he was upsetting Lilly at the dinner, but were there other indications he was overstepping of which he wasn't aware?

Wallace didn't press Brad as they sipped their tea in silence. His mind whirled over the events of the last several days. Maybe Lisa was right. He shouldn't have involved himself in Shelly's situation with her ex. His actions were born out of jealousy and pain, and he wished he could take back what he'd said to her.

But that wasn't possible. He could apologize to her, beg her forgiveness, but was that the right move? Would it be better to just leave quietly and not subject Shelly to any additional pain?

He wasn't sure how long he sat there in Wallace's living room, debating the merits of staying versus going. Every once in a while, Wallace would leave the room and bring in more tea, or something for Brad to eat. It all turned to ash in his mouth. He had no appetite. To his credit, Wallace left Brad alone to think in peace, occasionally making small talk to break the silence.

A car door slammed, and he went to the window. He nudged the curtain aside as Shelly exited her car and rushed into the house. She seemed lighter, freer, as if the weight of the world had been lifted from her shoulders, and his resolution to leave quietly strengthened.

~ * ~

Susan greeted Shelly at the door. Her sister gave her a brief hug, then led her to the kitchen table where the rest of her family was waiting. Shelly sank into a chair and gave them a warm smile.

"It went well," she said with a quick glance at Lilly, who settled back into her chair in relief. "Carl is open to attending therapy with you so you can work through your relationship together. He's willing to go at your pace, and he just wants to be in your life again."

"That's excellent news," Annabelle said, as she hugged Lilly.

"Thanks for doing this, Mom," she said as the worry in her brown eyes evaporated. "I'm glad I won't be bombarded with unsolicited emails anymore."

"I'll bet," Shelly said.

"So, we didn't get to talk to you last night." Susan leaned forward, her green eyes focused on Shelly. "How was your date?"

Shelly's stomach churned and her throat constricted as she tried to swallow. "It, uh, wasn't great."

"Oh no," Annabelle murmured. "What happened?"

"He's leaving," Shelly said with a sigh. "Or at least, he has an opportunity in Texas, and I expect he's going to take it."

"Wait, what?" Her mother asked, her gray eyebrows furrowing. "Start from the beginning."

For the second time that morning, Shelly went through the entire tale again. Her family listened intently, and no one said anything for several minutes after she finished.

"Hold on." Susan held up a hand, a wry grin on her face. "Carl told you to ask Brad to stay? Did he have a personality transplant in the last year?"

Everyone laughed, and Shelly was relieved to have a break in the tension. "I think having two failed marriages within a year has sobered him up."

"At least something did," Annabelle said. "Have you spoken to Brad?"

"Not since last night."

"You should go now," her mother suggested. "Clear the air. It does neither of you any good to continue to let this stew."

Shelly's eyes widened with fear, but her mother patted her hand. "We'll be right here waiting for you when you get back."

As she looked around at each of them, they gave her different gestures of encouragement. With a sigh, she stood and made her way to the front door. It felt oddly reminiscent of the last time she went to apologize to Brad. She hoped she would have similar results this time.

However, something was off as she climbed the stairs. She tapped at the door, but there was no response, not even the sound of stirring within. A growing sense of dread filled her, and she reached into her pocket to pull out her keys and found the spare to the apartment. She knocked once more, then unlocked the door.

The room was as dark and cold as it had been when she had first brought Brad there. It was also empty. The picture frame on the nightstand was gone. She ran to the closet, but it was bare. A quick check of the bathroom revealed his toiletries were gone. It was as if he had vanished into thin air.

Her heart in her throat, she raced back down the steps and into her house; the door slamming behind her. She leaned against the door as she tried to sort out where he might have gone. Footsteps sounded from the kitchen and soon her family was standing in the living room, gaping at her.

"Shelly?" Susan asked. "What's wrong?"

"He... he's gone."

Chapter Fifteen

"What do you mean, he's gone?" Lilly's face went pale.

"He left," she said, trying to make sense of it in her own head as she struggled to explain it out loud. "His belongings are all gone, and the room was dark and cold, as if he left hours ago."

"But where could he be?" Lilly asked. "He doesn't even have a car."

"Maybe he called an Uber?" Shelly pressed her fingers to her temples.

"Does he have any old friends in the area?" Susan asked, and when Shelly looked over at her, she could tell her sister was already formulating a plan.

"I-I don't think so," Shelly stammered. "But I'm not sure."

"Is it possible he decided to fly to Texas today?" Annabelle asked.

Shelly's knees gave out and she staggered to the couch. Yes, it was very possible he had done just that. But she couldn't believe he would leave without at least saying goodbye, if not to her, at least to Lilly. No matter how angry he was with Shelly, she couldn't imagine he would do that to her daughter.

"What about Kylie?" her mother asked, breaking into Shelly's thoughts.

"She's not supposed to be working, but maybe she knows who is," she said as she forced herself to focus. "I can call her."

"You do that," Susan ordered. "But it's also possible he found somewhere else to stay. Why don't the rest of us brainstorm where else he might be?"

Shelly nodded and pulled out her phone. Before she called her best friend, she dialed Brad's number and held her breath, praying he would answer. Her disappointment crushed her as the call went straight to voicemail and she hung up. Scrolling through her contacts, she pushed Kylie's name and hoped for better luck.

"Merry Christmas Eve, Shelly!"

"Merry Christmas, Kylie. I, uh, have a bit of a favor to ask."

"Sure, what's up?"

"It's a long story, and I don't have time to go into the details, but do you know someone who is working today who can check if Brad has booked a flight to Dallas?"

"Brad? You mean your new boyfriend?" Kylie's voice took on a teasing tone.

"Yes, that Brad!" Shelly snapped, then covered her mouth with her hand as a wave of guilt washed over her. It wasn't Kylie's fault she was in this situation. Shelly took a deep breath and tried again. "We had an argument, and he left without saying goodbye. I'm afraid he's booked a flight out, and if he has, I need to talk to him before he boards."

"Wow, you need to fill me in on the details, but I'll check the system."

"Wait, I thought you were off until after Christmas?"

"I was, but then someone called out sick, and I offered to fill in. Honestly, I don't mind and can use the money."

"Wow, I'm sorry you have to work through the holiday, but that double time pay sure doesn't hurt. Thank you for checking for me. I promise I'll tell you everything, but I want to find him first."

"Hm, I have him booked on a flight departing late this evening, but I can't imagine he would have left for the airport already. Did you check if all his stuff is gone?"

She pinched the bridge of her nose between her thumb and forefinger. "I did, and it is."

"Hmm, weird. Maybe he's still in the area," Kylie said. "I'm scheduled to be on that flight, so if you don't find him, let me know and I can get a message to him."

"I appreciate it."

"Any luck?" Susan asked, as Shelly entered the kitchen. Not trusting herself, she shook her head.

"All right, we've got a plan," her mother said. "Susan, you and Annabelle go check the tree farm and the harbor while Shelly goes to the town square. Lilly and I will stay here in case he returns."

With a weary nod, Shelly agreed, though she worried she was sending her family on a pointless wild goose chase. If Brad had already gone to the airport, then there was only one way she could stop him from leaving, and even then, she wasn't sure if it would be enough. She followed Susan and Annabelle to the driveway, then headed toward the town square, already convinced she was wasting valuable time.

~ * ~

Brad gazed out Wallace's window as Shelly left her house in a hurry. Where was she off to this time? It didn't matter as he'd made up his mind, and it was time to put some distance between himself and Shelly. A sudden urge to leave came over him as he headed toward his things. Wallace's eyebrows shot up in surprise.

"You don't need to leave yet," he said, gesturing for Brad to sit back down. "There's still plenty of time to get to the airport."

"I know, but I—" He ran a hand through his hair. "I'm sorry. I know you mean well, but I just can't—it's too—" His mind was racing with muddled thoughts. Reaching into his pocket, he pulled out the envelope with the note he wrote and the apartment keys and handed it to Wallace. "Will you give this to Shelly?"

Wallace agreed, his gray eyes solemn. With a heavy sigh, he came around the table and placed a hand on Brad's shoulder. "Take some time. Go to Texas if you must, but don't accept the job just yet, eh?"

Brad gave a noncommittal shrug. While he hadn't accepted the Texas position yet, there wasn't any reason not to. As far as he was concerned, once he got on that plane, there was no turning back. It was better this way. Or at least, that was what he kept telling himself.

After requesting a car to take him to the airport, he shook Wallace's hand and thanked him for his hospitality. Then Brad left and went to wait at the end of the driveway for his ride. It couldn't come soon enough.

"Brad!" a voice cried behind him, and he spun around. His heart sank as Lilly ran toward him. "I was afraid you left!"

"I'm leaving now," he said. His curt tone caused her to falter, and she stopped short. He took a deep breath and tried again. "I have a flight to Texas this evening, and I'm heading to the airport."

"But, Brad, you don't have to go! Listen—"

"I'm sorry, Lilly, but I must." He held up a hand. "I know we talked about spending the holidays together, but I can't stay here. Things between your mother and I—" His voice caught in his throat, and he had to clear it to continue. "Things between us didn't end well. It'll be better for everyone if I just leave."

"But—"

"No, Lilly," he said, his voice firm. "No 'but's.' I appreciate everything you and your mother have done for me, and I will never forget you. Your mom has my contact information. You can call me anytime." He stepped away from her and grabbed his bags. "Tell your mother... Tell her I said, 'thank you.' For everything."

Tears spilled down Lilly's cheek. "Please Brad, just wait! My mom is on her way back and—"

A car parked in front of the driveway. The driver climbed out to help Brad with his bags. It physically pained him to leave her there, alone on the empty, snow-covered street, but it was the right thing for all of them.

"I have to go now," he said again, his voice strained. He gave Lilly a fierce hug. "I'll never forget you." Just as quickly as he embraced her, he released her. "Goodbye!"

He spun on his heel and jumped into the backseat, slamming the door behind him and signaling to the driver to go. Unable to resist, he glanced back as the car drove away and knew, in that moment, the memory of her tear-stained face would haunt him for the rest of his life.

~ * ~

Brad is here. Come home now!

Shelly blinked and rubbed her eyes, not quite trusting the message Lilly had sent. Had he really come back? Her heart leapt into her throat as she put the car in gear. The square was humming with activity, and it took all her patience to wait for multiple pedestrians to cross the street.

The recent snow had mostly been cleared from the roads, but she was cautious while her nerves were on fire. She wanted nothing more than to fly home, rush into his arms, and tell him how much she loved him. Her phone rang, and she hoped he was calling to talk to her.

"Mom?" Lilly's voice came over the speaker. "Brad left."

"What? Why didn't you stop him?"

Lilly heaved a heavy sigh. "I tried, Mom. I tried to tell him you were on your way back and wanted to talk to him, that he didn't have to leave, but then a car came, and he left for the airport. He wouldn't let me explain."

Shelly pulled to the side of the road and buried her face in her hands. He wouldn't give Lilly a chance to explain, and he still left. Why? Had his feelings toward Shelly already changed? What else could she do?

Her head shot up. There was only one thing left to do. She needed to go to the airport and try to stop him from getting on that plane. First, she had to change into her uniform so she could use the Known Crewmember program to get through security. Going home would delay her arrival to the airport, but it was better than trying to fight through the Christmas crowds at security to keep Brad from leaving the state, and her, for good.

"It's not your fault," she finally said. "Thank you for trying. I'll be home in a few minutes."

"What are you going to do?"

"Go after him and beg him to stay."

"Can I come?"

Shelly pursed her lips but shook her head. "I'm sorry, Lilly, but it will take too long to get us both through airport security without boarding passes. I have special clearance. Grandma and your aunts will stay with you while I'm gone."

"Okay," Lilly's voice was dejected. "I just hope you can get to him in time."

"Me too. I'll see you soon. I love you."

"Love you. Bye."

Shelly immediately texted her sister to meet her back at the house, figuring it would be easier to just tell them what happened than to type it all out. After putting the car in gear, she merged onto the road, and headed home, anxious to get to the airport. It was unlikely Brad would be able to find an earlier flight this late in the game, but she didn't want to take any chances.

When she arrived home, her mother and sister were already there. Shelly rushed inside where they were sitting in the living room.

"Do you want me to come with you to the airport?" Susan asked. "I can't go through security, but at least you won't be alone in case..."

Shelly understood her meaning. In case she was too late to stop him. In case she missed her chance to fix what she had broken. For even if she found him, he may not be willing to come back. After all, she told him to go to Texas and had given him no reason to stay. She tried not to let those fears cloud her focus. Even if it didn't stop him from leaving, at least she could share what was in her heart. What he did with that information was completely out of her control.

"I want to do this alone," she said. "No matter what happens."

Susan nodded. "Understood. We'll stay here with Lilly then."

"Well, hurry girl!" Her mother waved her upstairs.

Shelly dashed to her room then removed one of her work suits from her closet, fixing her nametag on the lapel. She changed and ran a brush through her hair. Putting on a pair of matching heels, she hurried downstairs. To her surprise, her family was standing by the open door where none other than Wallace Simmons was waiting for her.

"Mr. Simmons, Wallace, what on earth are you doing here?" Shelly asked.

"Brad was at my house this morning, and he asked me to give you this," Wallace said, handing her a piece of paper.

She took the paper in trembling hands. Time was wasting, but curiosity got the better of her and she opened the note. Her gaze devoured the page, and her eyes welled with tears. It wasn't a long message, but it felt heavy in her hand, weighed down by so much that was left unsaid. She clutched the note to her chest and gave Wallace a watery smile.

"Thank you," she whispered.

"I'm sorry to see him go," he said, his understanding gray eyes offering support.

Her emotions threatened to overwhelm her, but she forced them down. She had to focus. Getting to the airport was the most important thing right now.

"Well," she said, trying to keep her voice even. "Wish me luck."

"Best of luck, my dear," her mother pulled her in for a quick hug. "He'd be a fool to leave you."

"I'm sure just showing up will convince him to stay," Susan encouraged. "There's no mistaking the way he looked at you."

Lilly engulfed Shelly in a fierce hug. "Good luck, Mom. Please bring him home."

Wordlessly, Shelly leaned back and searched her daughter's dark brown eyes, which were swimming with tears. How could she not realize how attached Lilly had gotten to Brad? How attached they were to each other?

"I love you," she finally choked out.

"Love you, too." Then Lilly was pushing her to the door. "Go!"

As she sprinted to her car in the gathering dusk, she knew she was cutting it close, but she hoped and prayed she would catch him before boarding began.

~ * ~

Traffic was snarled on the interstate, and Shelly kept obsessively checking the clock on her dashboard as the minutes ticked down. After what seemed like hours, she inched her way to the exit for the airport terminal.

Surprisingly, traffic around the airport itself was light, and she drove to the hourly parking lot. Before she exited her car, she called Kylie to make sure Brad was still booked for his flight.

"Shelly!" Kylie exclaimed when she answered the phone. "I was just about to call you." Her voice was muffled as she said something to a customer, then she continued in a conspiratorial whisper, "He's here."

"He is?" Shelly breathed a sigh of relief. "Oh, thank goodness."

"I will warn you though, it's a madhouse. Even with your pass, it might take you a while. You'd better hurry. We're at gate B11."

"All right, thanks," Shelly said. "I'm on my way."

With a heavy heart, she climbed out of her car and ran as fast as her heels would allow to the airport entrance. Bypassing the check in counters, she headed straight for security. When she arrived, she inwardly groaned. Kylie wasn't exaggerating. The line for security stretched far beyond the main doors.

She headed for the exit lane for Concourse B to access the Known Crewmember gate. There was a line there as well, though thankfully much shorter. Her impatience grew as each member of airline personnel passed through. There were a few squabbles between those who forgot their uniforms and the TSA agents, but most people were prepared.

When it was her turn, she handed the agent her driver's license and airline ID, which the agent scanned into the system. Once she was cleared, she rushed into the terminal and navigated the maze of Christmas travelers.

As she neared the gate, her eyes darted from face to face, searching the seated passengers for Brad, but he was nowhere in sight. After making two quick passes through the waiting area, she finally went to the information desk. "Kylie."

Kylie turned, and her face lit up. "Did you talk to him?"

"No, I can't find him. Did he leave?"

"That's strange," Kylie said with a frown. "He was sitting right there a minute ago. Maybe he went to the restroom."

"I'll check. If you see him before I do, text me!"

Without waiting for a reply, Shelly sprinted away. She stood by a column where she had a good view of both the seat Kylie mentioned and the restrooms. There was still some time before they would start boarding, but the waiting was proving to be difficult.

Her gaze scanned the area between the restrooms and the seating area, but he didn't appear. She hoped she would see him first, as she was afraid he would try to avoid her. Not to be cruel, but because she imagined he was trying to avoid a painful goodbye. Impatiently, she abandoned the plan of remaining hidden as she paced back and forth in the hallway between the gates.

On one of her treks back toward the column, someone was sitting in the seat Kylie indicated. Shelly's heart stopped, and she rushed over, but as she drew nearer, she realized it wasn't Brad. Someone else had taken advantage of the empty seat. Frustrated, she returned to the information desk.

"Anything?" Kylie asked when she finished with a customer.

"No," Shelly said with a sigh. "I'm being ridiculous."

"You're just anxious. I get it. I wish I could help more, but we're getting slammed." Kylie inclined her head to the line of customers forming behind Shelly.

"Right," she said, pinching the bridge of her nose between her thumb and forefinger.

She shook off her frustration before heading back to the hallway between gates. With the number of people crowding the airport, finding Brad was like searching for a needle in a haystack. If it wasn't against protocol, she'd ask Kylie to page him to the front desk.

"Excuse me, miss?" a deep voice said behind her.

Shelly spun around, her heart in her throat, but the voice belonged to an older man. He wore a business suit and had an air of authority about him.

"Can I help you?" she asked, silently cursing her decision to wear her uniform as she knew, even off the clock, she represented the airline and had to act accordingly.

"I'm looking for flight 382 to Fort Lauderdale. The departure board said it was coming to Gate B13, but that's not the case. Can you point me in the right direction?"

"Let me check, sir," Shelly said, her eyes scanning the area behind the man so she didn't miss seeing Brad. She pulled up an app on her phone commonly used among flight attendants to track gate changes, as well as other important information. "I'm afraid flight 382 has been moved to D13. If you go back—" She stopped short as a tall man with dark hair headed away from her. Resisting the urge to race after him, she forced herself to focus on the customer. "Sorry, if you go back down this hallway and pass Concourse C, you'll arrive at Concourse D. Look for a store called Charm City Market, and you'll know you're in the right place."

"Thank you. Merry Christmas!"

"Merry Christmas," Shelly said distractedly as she headed in the direction she had seen the man walking.

Her nerves were shot, and she tried to avoid eye contact with other customers in hopes she wouldn't be stopped again. When she caught up with the man, she was disappointed when it wasn't Brad after all, and she headed back to the waiting area for the B gates.

As she searched the sea of passengers, she didn't pay attention to where she was going. She slammed into a solid body without warning and almost fell backward from the force.

Strong hands grasped her shoulders to steady her. "Whoa!"

"Oh gosh, I'm s-sorry." Shelly raised her head and met a familiar pair of blue eyes. "Oh, Brad!"

"We need to stop running into each other like this." His tone was light, but his voice cracked.

Unable to laugh, she threw her arms around his neck and burst into tears. Relief and happiness at having found him flooded her entire being. At first, he didn't move, frozen to the spot by either her sudden appearance or her emotional reaction. She wasn't sure which, but she didn't care as she tightened her hold on him, and his arms slowly came around her. They held each other as the Christmas travelers bustled around them.

"Shelly," Brad said, leaning away. "What are you doing here?"

Her mind was all jumbled together. In her rush to find him, she never planned what she would say. She gazed up at him, trying to form words, but no sound came out. It was imperative to her she say the right thing, whatever that was, but now she was there, standing before him, she was tongue-tied.

"Why don't we go sit down over there?" he asked, pointing to an empty gate where a plane had just boarded.

Shelly nodded, still unable to express why she had come. He took her hand and led her through the crowd. When they reached a row of empty seats along the back wall, Brad let go of her hand and sat. She joined him, surprised at how lonely she felt without having that physical connection.

"What are you doing here?" he asked again. His tone was measured, as if under a tight control.

It reminded her of the reception she received when she went to talk to him after the incident with her former mother-in-law. Remembering that scene, she had a better understanding of his demeanor. He was protecting himself, his heart, from further pain.

"I-I," she stammered, then took a deep breath. "You left without saying goodbye."

"I thought that might be easier," he said, simply.

There was an emotion in his blue eyes she couldn't quite place. "Easier for whom?"

"For everyone."

"Easier for you, maybe," Shelly retorted, then regretted her tone. It wouldn't do either of them any good if she lashed out. She tried again. "But not for everyone."

Throwing his hands in the air, Brad let out a frustrated sigh. "Shelly, I don't understand. You told me to leave Maryland, to go be with my family." He ran a hand through his dark hair. "I'm sorry about how things went last night. It wasn't my place to comment on how you handle the situation with your ex and Lilly. I'm sorry I overstepped. And I should have told you about the job sooner." His eyes closed, and lines etched his forehead. "But you wouldn't even give me the benefit of the doubt and let me explain. You shut me out last night, and you didn't try to talk to me this morning before you left..." When he reopened his eyes, the sorrow in them took her breath away. "So, I ask again: why are you here?"

"Because I've fallen in love with you!" Shelly blurted out. He blinked in surprise, but otherwise, his face stayed neutral. "You're right. I should have given you a chance to explain, but I wasn't ready to listen."

When he didn't respond, she went on, uncertain if she was being articulate or not, but needing to fill the silence. "I came by your room to talk, t-to apologize. But all your things were gone. When Lilly texted me she saw you, I rushed home, but you were already gone. So, I came here." She cleared her throat. "I know you have an opportunity to live and work near your family, and I won't stop you from pursuing it if that's what you want." Her eyes filled with tears again. "But I had to tell you how I feel. We've only known each other a few days, but I couldn't let you go without telling you I love you, and I want you to stay."

His expression had softened during her admission. "You mean that?"

"Yes, Brad," she said. "With all my heart."

His hand closed around hers, but he didn't speak. Shelly waited, trying to let him digest everything she had said, but the silence was becoming unbearable.

"I haven't accepted the opportunity in Texas yet," he admitted.

"You haven't?" Her heart skipped a beat.

He shook his head. "I didn't want to decide until I had space and time to get some perspective. I figured I'd spend Christmas with my sister, check out the housing scene in her area, then decide."

"Will you stay?" she asked, trying to keep the pleading tone from her voice. "At least for Christmas?"

He kept his head down as he traced his fingers over hers. When he finally looked up, his blue eyes were shining with love. "I never wanted to leave in the first place. I love you, Shelly."

Her heart was pounding so hard it might burst out of her chest. She stood and pulled him to his feet, wrapping her arms around him. "Then come home."

"Home," he murmured, closing his eyes as if relishing the word. "I like the sound of that."

He brushed her auburn hair back from her face and bent his head toward her. She responded by pushing up on her tiptoes and touching her lips to his. The kiss was soft and delicate. He lifted his face from hers and smiled before passionately pressing his lips against hers again, deepening the kiss. Shelly pressed her hand against his chest, feeling his heart beating in time with her own. All the worry, the fear, and the heartache melted away. He was staying! He was home.

~ * ~

Shelly and Brad stayed up most of the night, whispering and laughing on the couch while enjoying the twinkling lights of the tree. Susan, Beatrice, and Annabelle had gone home soon after Shelly and Brad arrived, promising to come back the next day to celebrate Christmas with them. Brad was glad to see them again and looked forward to spending what he hoped would be the first of many holidays together.

When Shelly and Brad got home, Lilly had already gone to bed, and he couldn't wait to surprise her. He wanted to replace the haunting memory of her watching him drive away with tears in her eyes with a happier one. After leaving Shelly briefly to put his suitcases away and pull out the Christmas gifts he had hidden in his closet, he placed them under the tree, ready for Christmas morning.

As the sun dawned behind the house, the floor creaked upstairs, and he held his breath in nervous anticipation. A moment later, a door opened, and Lilly's footsteps trudged down the stairs. He gave Shelly's shoulders a squeeze as they both sat up straight.

"Good morning, Lilly, and Merry Christmas!" he called as she reached the bottom step.

She snapped her head up in shock, and she rubbed her eyes. Then the tears started flowing, which he hoped were happy, and she rushed over to hug him. "Brad? You came back!"

"If it's okay with you, Brad will be staying with us indefinitely," Shelly said, her green eyes full of joy.

Lilly drew Shelly into the hug. "This is the best Christmas ever!"

A sudden blur of gray sprang onto the couch as an insistent cat joined in on the family embrace.

"Merry Christmas, little Newton," Lilly cooed, as she released Brad and Shelly and petted the purring kitty.

"Sounds like it's time to open presents," Brad said as he stood. "Do you agree, Lilly?"

With an enthusiastic nod, Lilly ran over to the tree. He followed her and retrieved two presents. There was one for Lilly and one for Shelly. Then Lilly handed him their gifts.

"Lilly, you should go first," Brad said.

Lilly ripped the paper off a small box and gasped in delight. Inside was a tiny snowman charm on a chain-link bracelet. Her eyes sparkled as she lifted it to show Shelly.

"Wow, it's beautiful," Shelly said. Her green eyes met his, and she gave him a warm smile.

"I bought it to honor the snowman we built together and to

remember the fun we had that day." Brad pointed at the empty links. "There's plenty of space to add more charms as we make more memories."

"I love it. Thank you." Lilly stood to give him another hug.

"You're welcome." He helped her remove the delicate bracelet from the box and fastened it around her wrist. Then he gestured to Shelly. "Your turn."

He held his breath as she unwrapped her gift. It was a leather-bound book and most of the pages were blank. Lilly leaned closer.

"Is that a diary?" she asked, her brows knitting together.

Shelly shook her head in wonder. "It's a blank recipe book, so I can add my own."

"You'll notice there are already a few recipes in the front. I may have flipped through your other cookbooks in search of things you've made since I've been here." He gave her a sheepish grin.

"I'm sure I'll fill it as I cook for you over the years," she said, her voice full of emotion.

He leaned forward and gave her a quick kiss.

"This one is from Mom." Lilly handed him a box wrapped in green.

He opened it, revealing a framed photo of the three of them in front of the town square Christmas tree. His lips turned up in a slow smile as he remembered that night.

"I love this," he said, his eyes on Shelly. "We look like a family."

"We are a family." Lilly gave him the next present. "I saved the best for last."

He grinned and shook the box, holding it up to his ear and making a show of trying to figure out what was inside. Despite rolling her eyes at his antics, her hands twisted together, betraying her nerves. After ripping the wrapping paper, he lifted the lid off the box and held up the stocking which was inside. A plethora of emotions went through him. It was the perfect present, more than a holiday gift; it was a homecoming.

"Do you not like it?" she asked with concern.

He shook his head. "I don't like it, I love it. It's perfect. Thank you, Lilly."

He stood and walked to the banister where the other two stockings were hung. With great care, he slipped the loop on the top of the stocking over the hook and gingerly laid it against the wall. Shelly and Lilly joined him as they looked at the newest addition to the Christmas decor. He put an arm around each of them.

"Welcome home, Brad." Lilly said.

Brad's arms tightened around them. "Home," he said, his voice thick with emotion. "The best gift of all."

Acknowledgements

First and foremost, I'd like to thank my mother, who encouraged me to pursue my dream of writing from the tender age of eight. I want to thank my husband and daughter, who have provided me with so much love and support throughout the whole process. Thanks to my father, whose quiet observations have led to so many revelations in my life. And a huge debt of gratitude goes to my brother and sister, who never gave up on me, even when I felt like giving up on myself.

I want to thank the teachers who believed in me, from the second-grade teacher who first saw promise in my writing to two influential high school English teachers. Thanks to the MFA faculty and staff at Queens University of Charlotte, who gave me the support, but more importantly, the deadlines I needed to finish this book!

I'd be remiss not to thank Cassie Knight and the staff at Champagne Book Group who brought my dream to reality. Thank you for taking a chance on me and my book.

Finally, thanks to all my friends who have offered feedback on my writing over the years, especially those of you who were unfortunate enough to read my angsty teenage poetry. They say it takes a village to raise a child, and I think it takes at least that, and so much more, to raise a writer.

About the Author

Katie Eagan Schenck has loved writing since she was a child, but she first got the idea of writing professionally after submitting a book report in the second grade to rave reviews. It was there the idea of growing up to be a princess or marine biologist gave way to the lifelong dream of being an author.

Katie put that dream aside for a while after losing her mother to cancer. Instead, she pursued a career in public service at the state and federal levels. But she never fully gave up on her dream of writing. She enrolled in an MFA program for fiction writing and graduated in the summer of 2022.

Having been a single mom herself at one point, Katie holds a special place in her heart for Shelly's struggles parenting Lilly on her own. However, Katie found her happily ever after with her husband, daughter, and their three cats in a town just outside of Annapolis, Maryland. She is currently working on two other novels that also take place in fictional small towns in Maryland and hopes to have a long career in writing sweet romance.

Katie loves to hear from her readers. You can find and connect with her at the links below.

Website/Blog: https://keschenckwrites.com
Facebook: https://www.facebook.com/keschenck
Instagram: https://www.instagram.com/keschenckauthor
Twitter: https://twitter.com/faery_whisper

Thank you for taking the time to read *A Home for Christmas*. If you enjoyed the story, please tell your friends and leave a review. Reviews support authors and ensure they continue to bring readers books to love.

Now turn the page for a peek inside *Saving the Winchester Inn*, a sweet holiday romance by Sofia Sawyer.

What if everything you've been looking for is right where you left it?

Cordelia "Lia" Winchester, a successful marketing director in Boston, is called back to her North Carolina hometown when her parents are injured. Despite her desperation to stay away from the place where she's known as "Little Lia," guilt forces her to hop on a plane to care for her parents and their family inn. What was intended as a short trip soon becomes extended when Lia uncovers distressing news about the inn and town's financial state and decides to stay through the holiday season. She doesn't plan on feeling safe, appreciated, and happy once she's surrounded by the quirky townspeople, who help her put a new spin on some of her favorite Christmas traditions from childhood to boost tourism. She also doesn't plan on falling in love.

Logan MacDermot was ready for a fresh start, and the job at the Winchester Inn came at the perfect time. He may not be from this small town, but its people made him believe he could be one of them. Except Lia Winchester. He's heard plenty of rumors about Lia and is surprised to see a different person than he imagined when they finally meet and ultimately butt heads. But after spending more time together, Logan realizes the big-hearted girl he'd heard about still exists within the stubborn, strong-headed persona of Cordelia. As they team up to save the inn and the town, can Logan help her remember who she is and convince her this is exactly where she belongs?

Chapter One

Cordelia Winchester's phone vibrated across the glass top of her desk, disrupting her from her work. She dragged her gaze from her computer and glared at her cell, noting the area code from her quaint hometown in North Carolina.

"Not today, robocaller," she muttered, hitting the ignore button.

Anyone she needed to talk to from Fraser Hills was programmed into her contacts. If it was important, they'd leave a message. As the director of one of Boston's premier event planning companies, she was too busy for unsolicited calls, real or telemarketing.

Turning back to her laptop, she scanned her endless to-do list, her eyebrows pulling together as she focused on the overwhelming tasks left. Christmas was always crunch time for her company. Holiday parties. Galas. Fundraisers. All extravagant events for clients with deep pockets. They wanted the best of the best, and she was expected to move mountains to give it to them.

More importantly, in less than a month, Cordelia will have pulled off the most prestigious event she'd ever been tasked with. Elizabeth Sinclair's holiday fundraiser was an opportunity of a lifetime, and if all went well, it would seal the deal for the promotion to vice president Cordelia had tirelessly worked for.

Eight years of long days, compromised weekends, and sacrificed free time would mean something.

Everything was riding on this.

She couldn't afford to be distracted. Not even for a minute.

I just have to survive these next five weeks.

Her phone vibrated again. It seemed louder and more annoying than last time, grating on her nerves. She closed her eyes, sucked in some air, and let out a controlled breath before picking it up and checking the display.

A photo of her younger brother appeared on the screen. As much as she loved him, he didn't have a clue as to what was appropriate conversation during business hours. Cordelia had been caught on one too many calls with him babbling about God only knew what. That was the benefit of living at home and working part-time at her family's tree farm. He had all the time in the world to chat.

She, however, did not.

Her boss, Melody Kensie, owner of Kensie Affairs, breezed through the doorway, startling Cordelia. Fumbling with her phone, she quickly hit the ignore button before placing it face down on her desk.

I hate when she does that.

"Melody. H-hi. H-how was your Thanksgiving?"

"Adequate," Melody responded without a hint of emotion. Her skin was wrinkle-free thanks to her permanent Scarlett O'Hara face— not a smile in sight. Ever.

Cordelia straightened and folded her hands on her desk to convey she was the capable and competent professional Melody relied on. "How can I help you?" she asked, forcing her voice to sound confident.

"I want a status update on the Sinclair event. Now." Cutting and direct as always.

Melody was one of Boston's elite, having started her business at the ripe age of twenty. Now in her forties—not that she'd ever admitted it—her high standards and unrelenting expectations could strike fear in even the thickest-skinned person.

Cordelia grabbed her planner from the desk and flipped it open, resisting the urge to wipe her sweaty palms on her slacks. "Absolutely."

If there was one thing she learned from working with Melody, it was to always be prepared. She'd seen colleagues get fired for merely hesitating. Cordelia wasn't about to lose that promotion now, not for something so stupid.

"Cordelia," the sweet voice of the young office manager sounded on her desk phone intercom. "Your brother's on line one."

Cordelia tried not to let her agitation flare at his poor timing and punched the button to respond. "Thank you, Talia, but I'm in a meeting. Can I call him back?" She eyed Melody and noted her slight look of annoyance.

"He says it's urgent," Talia responded.

Melody arched an eyebrow, a simple gesture that always made Cordelia feel small. "My office. Fifteen minutes." She left the room without waiting for a response.

Cordelia clicked a button next to the blinking red light and lifted the receiver to her ear. Cocking her head to peer through the glass door of her office, she spotted Melody speaking to another colleague just outside. Cordelia spun away from the door and ducked behind her desk as if that position would prevent Melody from overhearing.

"Mike, this isn't a good time," she whispered into the phone.

"Lia!"

She winced at her childhood nickname. No matter how many times she told her brother she went by Cordelia now, he still insisted on using it. As much as she wanted to correct him again, she'd have to pick her battles. Right now, she needed to get him off the phone ASAP.

She peeked over her shoulder and let out a breath when Melody disappeared into her office. She straightened. "What do you need, Mike?" she asked in a clipped voice.

"It's Mom and Dad," he started, causing her pulse to spike.

Her parents were getting older. It was only a matter of time before health issues kicked in. Although her family's inn kept them young and spry, as her father would say, there was only so much a person could do to pause Father Time.

"What about them?"

"There's been an accident at the inn." His phone crackled, making the news more ominous.

She stood from her chair and placed a shaky hand on her desk for balance. "Are they okay?"

"They're in rough shape, but the doctor says they'll recover." He sighed. "The inn took a beating too."

"What do you mean?"

"There was a freak storm last night. Mom and Dad were in the upstairs room toward the back. You know, the one that overlooks the big Fraser?"

"Yeah, I remember." Her breath caught in her throat as she waited for Mike to get to the point.

"Well, they were prepping for guests coming the following day, and I guess some rough wind caused the tree to snap. That thing was old, it was going to happen eventually. The top fell onto the roof, and it collapsed. It all came down on them."

Cordelia gasped, hand to heart. "My God. How bad are their injuries?"

"Took a bit to pull them out from the debris. Dad has a collapsed lung and a broken rib. Mom has some bruising around the face and a fractured wrist. All in all, they didn't make out too bad, considering."

She lowered herself into her chair as she processed the news. "That's horrible."

"Yeah. I tried calling from the hospital a few minutes ago to let you know what the doctor said." If Mike was agitated with her, he didn't sound it. If anything, his voice hinted of exhaustion and stress.

Guilt for ignoring the call hit her hard. Cell service was spotty in that part of town, which explained the poor connection now. He likely had to drive a few miles just to get a couple of bars. "Sorry, Mike. I had no idea."

"That's not the only reason why I'm calling." He paused for a minute, his tone more serious than she'd ever heard. "With Mom and Dad out of commission for the next few weeks, we need your help."

"Sure, whatever you need. I'll transfer funds later today. Just tell me how much."

"No, Lia," he said with exasperation. "We need you. Here. To run the Winchester Inn."

"No way." She took a breath and checked her harsh tone. "This is my busy season. I can't leave Boston right now."

"Yeah. We're well aware. You've missed the last couple of Thanksgivings and Christmases because of it."

Was that attitude?

His words only intensified the tightness in her chest. "I have an enormous event to deal with. Coming home isn't an option."

"You know Christmas is our prime season for tourism. With the Winchester Inn needing repairs, we're losing reservations. Things have been tight for the last few years, sis. Mom never told you because she didn't want you to worry, but if we can't pull through this year, the inn's done for. Our family legacy will be gone." There was another pregnant pause. "It will affect the town too."

She had made it a point to walk away from that life years ago, giving them a clear message she didn't want the family legacy to be *her* legacy. She wanted something of her own, and she had stuck to that.

Now, she was getting sucked back in.

Cordelia was lodged between a rock and a hard place, but how could she consider *not* going? Her poor parents were in the hospital, and their inn was struggling.

And the quiet desperation in Mike's voice chilled her. It was rare to see her little brother so serious about anything, which only made the situation that much more alarming.

Sighing, she said, "Let me figure out some things and get back to you."

"Tonight?"

"Yes."

Cordelia hung up, closed her eyes, and rubbed her temples, trying to relieve the tension headache threatening to ruin her day.

It didn't work.

Opening her eyes again, she turned to her computer and scrolled through her jam-packed schedule. Flying home seemed impossible, that was obvious. Her boss had given her the opportunity to prove herself, and although she'd been an exceptional employee, she didn't have the leverage to take time off to go to North Carolina. Not with this high-profile event in the works on top of the other five she was planning simultaneously.

Melody was, in a word, tough. She had high expectations and a low tolerance for "slackers." And it didn't take much for someone to be placed in the slacker camp. Cordelia worried that even broaching the subject would knock her out of the running for the promotion.

But then there was Mike. He seemed...distressed. Her usually affable, easygoing brother was concerned. If he was concerned, then she should be tenfold.

Cordelia stood from her desk and walked to the oversized windows that overlooked the city streets of Boston. Even with the overcast day, enough light filtered in so she didn't need to turn on the harsh fluorescents. She preferred the natural light. It was nice to have a bit of nature streaming in when she spent her days surrounded by skyscrapers and concrete.

She caught her reflection in the glass. Her tailored slacks, silk blouse, and sleek brown hair made her appear poised and sophisticated. Inside, however, she was anything but. If she thought she was stressed before, her levels were now well off the charts.

Looking down from the tenth story window to Congress Street, she watched a steady stream of people walked below on a purposeful mission to wherever they needed to be. Even though it was the day after Thanksgiving, Bostonians were still hard at work, as was she. Most people would argue they were workaholics, but she respectfully disagreed. This was a city of the doers, the innovators, and the ambitious. Things happened in Boston, which was what drew her there for college. It was a far cry from her sleepy hometown, nestled in the mountains. Fraser Hills was quiet, predictable, and boring.

When she decided to leave home, she knew she wanted to be working alongside these brilliant, determined New Englanders with their big ideas and endless energy. It was also one of the reasons she stayed after graduation. The constant buzz of exciting things on the horizon was addictive.

Beyond the bustling sidewalk, families cheered as their children gleefully threw what they pretended was tea overboard the Boston Tea Party Museum ship's railings. Although tourism was lighter in the colder months, Cordelia assumed they were here to catch the last of the autumn leaves or to spend the holidays with family who lived nearby.

Family.

She couldn't turn a blind eye and let them fend for themselves. She loved her parents and brother and respected all they did to keep the Winchester Inn running as the heart of Fraser Hills.

This couldn't have happened at a worse time.

The Sinclair event was for a vocal woman who challenged everything she did. Cordelia often ended her day in bed with a splitting headache, a side effect of her clenching her teeth in a pleasant smile as she tried not to let Elizabeth's constant criticisms get under her skin. It wouldn't be easy to move up to the VP role, but she could have done without the snide remarks. Or those damned pursed lips Elizabeth made whenever she was disappointed.

Which was always, it seemed.

Cordelia straightened and composed herself, smoothing the nonexistent wrinkles from her slacks. She lifted her head in determination.

One week to go home and get things sorted out. Maybe less.

If there was one thing Cordelia possessed, it was impeccable work ethic. She'd proven time and time again she could manage a lot, flawlessly handling the curveballs often lobbed at her. Melody couldn't deny that.

Cordelia'd jump on a flight, check on her parents, find them temporary help, and come back to Boston. She'd convince her boss nothing would fall through the cracks. After all, it was a digital world these days. She'd be accessible 24/7 by email, phone call, text message, or video. Her clients would be none the wiser she was out of town.

One week, that was all. Cordelia would assure Melody that despite the circumstances, she had everything under control.

Dear God, I hope so.

Chapter Two

Two days later, Cordelia stood outside the Asheville Regional Airport. Slipping on her sunglasses to battle the glare of the sunrise, she scanned the area for the car rental stand.

A gust of wind whipped around her, giving her cheeks a healthy sting and offering a not-so-subtle reminder to zip up her jacket. Despite being in the South, it was cold. Not the same cold as in Boston, which seeped deep into your bones and made you think you'd never know what warmth felt like again. Instead, the mountain air here was reinvigorating and intoxicating, inspiring one to get outside and take a hike through the woods or hit the slopes.

Taking a deep breath, she filled her lungs, easing the tension she'd held on to for far too long.

What would it be like to have time to do those things again?

She sighed. This was no time for nostalgia or comparisons. Time was ticking. She needed to get the car, drive the forty-five minutes west to Fraser Hills, check on her parents, meet with the contractors she'd thankfully strong-armed into coming on short notice, ensure the inn was in good hands, and get out.

Based on her schedule, it would take four days, tops. Maybe three if she didn't tap into the contingency time she scheduled for the unexpected.

She prayed she wouldn't need it. Although Melody had allowed her to take the short trip, it was obvious Cordelia was on thin ice. As the lead event planner, the only way she'd been able to convince Melody was by promising she'd be back in time to run point for the Sinclair event at the State Room, a breathtaking venue in Boston.

Craning her head to the right, Cordelia spotted a tiny sign with an arrow directing people to the otherwise hidden rental booth. Beelining for it, she opened the glass door and was greeted by a smiling face.

"Well hello there, ma'am," the young boy said. "How may I help you today?"

It took her a moment to process his accent. Did the people here really have that strong of a twang? No wonder her college roommates poked fun at her, so much so that she tried to tone it down to fit in with the Northerners. Doing it for as long as she had, her Southern accent was now practically nonexistent.

"I have a reservation for Cordelia Winchester." Placing her stylish carry-on on the laminate-tiled floor, she folded her manicured hands on the counter as she waited for the teen to access her information.

"Alrighty. Here we go, ma'am. I see a Hyundai sedan reserved for four days with a drop off at this location." He looked up from the screen and shot her another cheery smile. "Is that correct?"

She nodded and suppressed the urge to tap her foot, her patience already wearing thin. She forgot how slow everything moved here. "Yes, thanks."

"Great." He swiveled the screen to face her. "I'll need you to review this information and sign at the bottom. I'll pull the car out front in the meantime."

"Perfect." She scrolled through the endless forms, opting out of unnecessary add-ons, and signed at the bottom. By the time she was done, the employee was back and handing her the keys.

"Drive safe." He shook her hand enthusiastically.

She gave a tight smile in return. In Boston, you were lucky to get eye contact, let alone a grunt of acknowledgment. All this chatting and grinning was throwing her off.

She grabbed her bag and exited the rental store. Placing her carry-on in the trunk, she slipped into the driver's seat and got situated. Pulling up her map app, she plugged in the address for the Winchester Inn to see which route would get her there the fastest. Every option lit up green.

Hmm, I guess there's not much traffic this early in the morning.

It was a rare occurrence to find traffic moving freely in Boston this close to rush hour. The smooth ride would be a treat.

The drive to Fraser Hills was uneventful, if not productive. As Cordelia navigated the empty roads through small towns and farmlands, she made calls to the office and her vendors, and gave an update to her most important client, Elizabeth Sinclair. By the time she ended the call, she had turned off the highway and taken the exit ramp that led to Fraser Hills Road, the main street that went through downtown.

Her breath hitched as the town came into view. The impeccably clean streets were lined with cute shops, restaurants, cafes, and stores. The center of the main road had a roundabout with a small park. A picturesque gazebo sat square in the middle. But it wasn't the small-town America feel that was appealing, it was seeing it with the Great Smoky

Mountains backdrop. The distant mountain range looked like it was outlined in blue, and the infinite trees lining the hills were now speckled with yellows, oranges, and reds as if someone painted them just that morning. The mountains protected the town, cocooning it in a valley of impenetrable walls.

Maybe that was part of the reason Cordelia left in the first place. She felt safe in Fraser Hills and sheltered in the valley. *Too* safe. If you hiked up far enough, you could see the town, a small speck in an otherwise rural area of North Carolina. Whereas other people thought the open lands were freeing, to her, the nothingness was suffocating, closing in on her each day that passed. The disconnectedness from the world made it hard to envision a fulfilling future.

She wanted more for her life than what would be passed down to her, which is why she purposely traded in mountains for skyscrapers. A future could lie in any one of those tall, shiny buildings. And if not, she could easily hop on one of the many flights around the world to find a new calling. The world was at her fingertips in Boston.

Staying in Fraser Hills would have been too easy. Wasn't life about handling challenges head on to see what you were made of? About discovering you could do more and be more than whatever you'd been pigeonholed into?

Taking the roundabout, she passed by Evergreen Avenue and continued on Fraser Hills Road. She loved this section of the main strip, with the manicured Fraser firs lining the median and the rushing stream that ran under the small bridge, leading to the heart of the town: the Winchester Inn. Her home.

Despite being the largest building in town, it was homey. Off-white cypress siding covered the two-story structure, complete with black shutters that lined large windows. An ornate wrap-around porch dominated the first floor, with a wide staircase leading up to two windowed wooden doors. Rocking chairs painted deep blue and window boxes filled with seasonal flowers gave the inn a pop of color. Smoke floated lazily from the chimney.

Cordelia remembered sitting on those rocking chairs in the fall when she was growing up, wrapped in a throw blanket, a mug of hot chocolate keeping her hands warm. She enjoyed watching the leaves change and the town slow down right before the holiday rush started.

Aside from Christmas, fall was her favorite time of year. Although Boston didn't provide the same serenity as a rocking chair on the veranda did, she embraced the vibrant colors of the trees through the crisp autumn months. During the rare free time she found, she'd visit one of the local parks when the colors were at their peak. Those days, she could breathe.

In the fast-paced life she lived, it was hard to remember to do that sometimes.

She pulled into the circular driveway and parked. Stepping out of the sedan, she made her way to the back of the inn to see the damaged roof, following a stone pathway around the side of the inn, which stopped before it reached where she needed to be. She eyed the soggy ground and then down at the pumps she was wearing.

Not exactly made for off-roading.

Leaning around the corner of the house, she noticed the remainder of the giant Fraser fir towering precariously over the inn. The top had broken off and was now lying on the ground, chopped into pieces. She tilted her head for a better view of the collapsed roof but couldn't get the right angle.

Assessing the muddy ground again, she identified a few dryer spots along the way. If she could make it to those, she would be fine. Kind of like playing the lava game when she was a kid.

She took a giant step, reaching the first dry area successfully, and then a small leap to the next. More confident with her decision, she hopped along to the section she needed to inspect. She was mid-hop to the next spot, but before she could land, something flashed in her peripheral vision and slammed into her knees, causing her to pinwheel her arms to keep her balance. But it didn't work. The next thing she knew, she was flat on her back.

In the mud.

She laid in the cold slop, stunned by what happened, and tried to catch her breath. A moment later, a face hovered over her and gave her a sloppy, wet kiss.

"Willow," a voice commanded from a distance. The dog stopped its frantic kissing and ran to the man who was calling.

Cordelia pushed onto her elbows and took stock of the damage to her body and clothes. Her back was sore and the cold seeped through her slacks and jacket, causing a chill to run up her spine. Her pants were caked in mud—they would be impossible to clean—and one of her pumps stuck out from the mud, doing its best reenactment of the Titanic in its final moments.

A hand thrust in front of her face. She grabbed it without looking up but couldn't help noticing the owner of said hand lifted her with ease. She bent to pull her shoe out of the ground, and her gaze trailed up the length of the man who had helped her.

Work boots. Long, solid legs in dark jeans. Broad shoulders and athletic build. All very nice, but it was his face that had her heart beating uncontrollably. His strong jaw was covered with dirty-blond scruff, and his olive complexion complemented his light brown hair, which still held hints of being sun-kissed from the summer. Blue-gray eyes popped under his thick eyebrows, and full lips hitched up on one side in a boyish smile.

He was ruggedly handsome, not at all like the clean-cut, well-manicured men from the city.

"Looks like you're a long way from home," he noted in a playful tone. His deep voice had a hint of Southern to it, but not from the Carolinas. Cowboy, maybe.

Next to him sat the dog who knocked her over, a shaggy golden retriever mix with random tufts of hair spiking out awkwardly. Her ears were covered in crinkled hair like they were styled after an eighties icon, personifying a bad hair day.

The dog gave a big lopsided smile, its tongue lolling.

"She yours?" Cordelia asked as she tried to shake the clumps of mud off her pants.

"Yup. Sorry about that. She gets excited sometimes. She saw you hopping around and thought you were playing." He patted the dog on the head and pure adoration filled her goofy face. "This your first time here?" Another attractive grin crossed his features as he nodded at the shoe in her hand.

She bristled at the realization he was mocking her. Patronizing her. She dealt with that type of "humor" while building her career in Boston. She battled it and won.

She'd be damned if he thought he could get away with it.

~ * ~

Logan MacDermot appraised the woman and her sudden change in demeanor. She went from adorably embarrassed to prickly and cold. Straightening her back, she raised her chin as if to assert dominance and prepare to battle.

For what? He didn't know.

But it was clear she wasn't about to back down, even if she looked ridiculous, all full of mud with her one heeled foot slowly sinking into the ground.

Her light brown eyes turned to honey as the sun broke from a cloud and shined down on them. They were beautiful, even if they were tiny slits staring him down.

"For your information," she said in a steely tone, "this *is* my home."

Logan cocked his head in confusion. "I'm sorry?"

She huffed a breath. Her tight smile was meant to intimidate. "I'm Cordelia Winchester. This is my family's home."

He recalled the photos scattered around the main lobby of the inn. Mariam and Ron had many pictures of their family, with Mike and his sister, Lia, in various stages of their childhood. They often featured a lanky, freckle-faced girl with wild curls who was always up to something. Hiking, working with animals, steering the Christmas sleigh. Every picture showed her with the biggest smile.

He took in the woman in front of him with her straight brown hair, unblemished skin, and curves he could tell were hidden under her jacket. Not a smile or freckle in sight. This couldn't be the same person, could it? Yet, out of all the stories Mariam had shared with him, she'd never once mentioned another daughter, so it had to be.

She held her head high as if she were royalty, and he supposed in a town like this, she was.

Although, for one wavering moment, uncertainty flashed across her face, but in an instant, it was gone.

"Cordelia." He let the name roll over his tongue. "You mean Lia? Little Lia Winchester? The prodigal daughter has returned." He hoped his light teasing would get her to loosen up a bit.

She scowled at him. He rewarded it with a smile that only seemed to irritate her more. "It's Cordelia. And you are?"

"Logan MacDermot. I'm the superintendent. I make sure everything's in working order at the inn." They both turned to the roof's gaping hole. "Well, almost everything. That'll be fixed in no time though." He held out his hand and she eyed it like he was handing her a dead fish, refusing to take it.

Okay then.

"Mac's our superintendent."

He dropped his hand and stuffed it into his pocket. Clearly, he wouldn't be getting a warm welcome from this ice queen. Lia may have grown up in the South, but her Southern hospitality was long gone. "Mac *was* your superintendent. He retired four months ago and moved down to Tybee Island. Wanted to enjoy the island life for his retirement."

She crossed her arms. "Why wasn't I told about this?"

He shrugged. "From what I understand, you don't want much to do with the inn." At least that's what Mike said when Ron urged him to call her after the accident.

If his statement bothered her, she didn't appear ruffled by it. "Well, I'm here now."

"That you are."

Out Now!

What's next on your reading list?

Champagne Book Group promises to bring to readers fiction at its finest.

Discover your next
fine read!
http://www.champagnebooks.com/

We are delighted to invite you to receive exclusive rewards. Join our Facebook group for VIP savings, bonus content, early access to new ideas we've cooked up, learn about special events for our readers, and sneak peeks at our fabulous titles.

Join now.
https://www.facebook.com/groups/ChampagneBookClub/

Made in the USA
Monee, IL
09 October 2023